Protecting Shaylee

THE FAE GUARD SERIES BOOK 1

ELLE CHRISTENSEN

Sarah,
Find your wings!.

Elle

Protecting Shaylee

Copyright © 2015 Elle Christensen

All Editions

Cover Design: Julie Nichols - JMN Art

Editor: Jaquelyn Ayres

❦ Created with Vellum

For my forever love.
The most perfect man I could ever write would be exactly like you.

Imagination will often carry us to worlds that never were.
But without it, we go nowhere.
-Carl Sagan

Prologue

IT IS common among humans to see things not as they are, but as what their imaginations perceive them to be. Experiences are romanticized, and folklore is created. However, some of these tall tales are not as far-fetched as you might think. For, within a lie, there is always a kernel of truth. Among these legends are those of otherworldly creatures and people. But, the truth is often so wildly distorted that you may not recognize them for what they are. So...let me enlighten you.

There is a world beyond the human realm, one of the creatures whose nature is between humans and angels. In fact, they are said to be descended from fallen angels. They are a species who crave the sun. Without it, they will lose their pure magic and wither away. They can see beyond the human eye and hear beyond the human ear. They possess white-blonde hair and bright, blue, or green eyes that shine like jewels. Their natural bodies are light—though, not transparent—but with an astral glow. Yet, they are changeable, and when they venture into the human world, their skin loses some of its luster, taking on a matte sheen that blends them with the humans.

They are a people of magic. Magic that is protective in

nature. Magic used for the care of innocents, the healing of wounds, and to fight the evil forces that would threaten the vulnerable. Though they can confuse you with their words, they cannot lie. For, if they do, they will become a part of a darker world—an evil existence. Their glow will dim, their lustrous blond hair will bleed into black, and their eyes will become the shade of the mud that has colored their soul. They will endeavor to bring more light over to the dark.

Children that are a mix of these people and humans are targeted because they are easier to turn away from the light. They must spend their early years in the human world until they are marked at the age of twenty-one. Then, their mixed nature will be detectable, and the magic will flow through their veins, allowing them to enter both realms. They are virtually undetectable as a halfling until they are marked. Still, there are those who can seek the dormant magic. They are protected because knowledge of their true people is built upon the folklore of the humans. They cannot fully comprehend what they will become, or the importance of keeping the existence of these people a secret. They are more susceptible to being courted by the darkness. And, in the dark, they are as their ancestors are—one of the Fallen.

Of what creatures do I speak?

They are the Fae.

One

SHAYLEE

MY FATHER USED to tell me stories about faeries. He spoke the tales about the mythical creatures with such passion that I was convinced of the truth in his words. As I got older, I began to wonder whether he was simply spinning fantasies to entertain me. My friends said there were no such things as faeries or any other magical creature. Nevertheless, he made me re-tell him the stories I'd been taught. When my imagination got the best of me, and I embellished, he would gently correct me, telling me to only ever tell these tales exactly as I had learned them from him.

When I was fourteen, my father was murdered. He was attacked and left in an alley, near our home, on Manhattan's Upper West Side. Standing in the cemetery, I buried the stories along with him. My mother asked me about the tales from time to time, but I was too stubborn to let her coax them from my lips. What did it matter? I didn't believe in fairy tales anymore.

I HURRY down the side walk of Columbus Ave, pulling my coat closer around me to shield myself from the biting, late November wind. As I turn the corner onto West 68th St, a shiver runs down my spine that has nothing to do with the cold. I feel as though someone is watching me. I glance around, but only see other New Yorkers walking swiftly to their destinations. No one is paying me any attention. I shake my head at my obviously, overactive imagination. The feeling continues to niggle at me, but I ignore it, and continue on down the street. Something about this day has me overly anxious. I feel as though there is an electric current coursing through me and it makes me want to jump out of my skin. I give my head another little shake to clear it; I'm being absurd.

I finally reach the restored, five-story brownstone that I grew up in and bound up the stairs to the elegant, wood door. Through the beveled glass window, I can just see around the right corner into the formal living room.

Balloons. Damn!

"Mom!" I call out to her as I step inside, shaking off the cold and hanging my coat on the tree stand in the entry. She's never listened when I told her I didn't want a fuss made over my birthday, so why would she listen this year? I sigh and walk into the room. The front room is light and open, with a large bay window taking up the whole wall on the right side of the room, looking out onto the street. The wall across from the entrance holds an enormous fireplace. Two vintage, Hepplewhite chairs flank it on either side, matching the rest of the Victorian furniture. Across the large mirror, over the mantle, a sparkly sign boasts the words "Happy Birthday!" And, of course, those ridiculous balloons floating in the air, their thin strings tied to sconces scattered on the walls.

The left side of the room has a wide, open arch, leading into a beautiful dining room with wood-paneled walls and an elegant chandelier, shimmering in the sunlight. I wander into the room and groan when I see the long, oak table, set with china and crystal for eight people. Across from me, the small door, leading to the kitchen, swings open, and my mom bustles in with a tray of cookies and sweets, humming "Happy Birthday".

Violet Bryden is almost my complete opposite. I am tall and slender; close to five-foot-ten inches with long, straight, white-blonde hair. She is a petite woman (a good six inches shorter than me), with chocolate-brown hair that is always twisted into an elegant chignon. Her Irish heritage shows in her pale skin and the smattering of freckles strewn about her face. She has warm brown eyes in contrast with the bright blue of mine; so like my father's. I am—in fact—his spitting image. I even inherited his unusual, white skin. Rather than tanning in the sunlight, we almost look as though we are luminous. There was no shortage of albino jokes from my friends growing up. See, even though my mother's skin is pale, there is a pinkish hue, giving her a rosy, healthy glow.

She stops when she sees me, and her face brightens with an excited smile. "Shaylee!" She exclaims, "Happy Birthday, honey!" She sets down the tray and hurries around the table to envelope me in the warmth of her sunshine and the sweet smell of cinnamon. Mom always smells like she's been baking. I hug her back, and inhale the aroma that always reminds me of home.

Once I step back, I give her a stern look. "I thought I told you no party. Again..." I'm not really mad, and I'm sure she knows it. I just don't care for birthdays. Every year I feel as though I'm counting down to something that will change the course of my life and I happen to like it just the way it is!

Her cheeks actually take on a little tinge of red, and I giggle at her slightly guilty face. It lasts for only a moment before a twinkle appears in her eyes and she goes back to beaming at me. She knows that if I was truly upset, I would tell her. I don't keep things from my mom. In fact, I don't say anything I don't believe. It just isn't in my nature to be dishonest. So, I either say what's on my mind, or keep my mouth firmly shut.

"How could you think we wouldn't celebrate your twenty-first birthday?" She reaches up and puts a hand on either side of my face. "I can't believe you're so grown up. I've been excited—and dreading this day—for years." Her eyes mist a little, and her smile turns almost wistful.

I laugh and take her hands down from my face, giving them a light squeeze. "You act like turning twenty-one is a huge, pivotal moment for me. I assure you, Mom, being able to legally drink doesn't have that big on an impact on my life. She just smiles at me and returns to the tray, taking it out to the front room, where she sets it on an elegant, mahogany, coffee table.

"Eight place settings, Mom?" My irritation creeps into my tone. She just winks at me and then returns to the kitchen. I sigh in defeat and follow her in there to help with the preparations for a party I can't escape.

We busy ourselves in the kitchen, and I fill her in on how I'm liking my classes at NYU and my job at a children's shelter in Hell's Kitchen. I'm halfway through my senior year and yet, I haven't settled on a major. I want to do something that will help protect children, but I can't seem to find the perfect avenue. Unlike most parents, my mother never pressures me to lay down a definitive plan for my future. She's always told me that I should enjoy being young because, all too soon, my life will cease to be within my own control. I figured she meant the demands I would face as an adult: boss, husband, children, etc. However, there were times when her response seemed cryptic, and I wondered if she meant something else.

Everything is finally ready, and we are sitting at the large island in the center of the kitchen, enjoying a cup of tea. I'm still curious about the amount of place settings at the table. I know she will have invited my three best friends and my father's sister, Rhoslyn. But, I have no clue who the last spot is for.

"Mom, don't avoid my question. Why eight?"

She sips her tea and beams at me. "Aden is coming."

I feel my jaw drop in shock. I haven't seen Aden in two years. Aden Foster was a sporadic presence in my life as I was growing up. He was a close friend of my father's, although he was at least twenty years younger. He'd stayed with us in the apartment on the fourth floor of our house, for a couple of days, two or three times a year. After my father died, he visited more frequently—almost every other month. He was always indulging me: slipping me candy behind my mother's back, playing board games with me, even taking me out for ice cream or to the zoo. He was my hero, second only to my father.

"Aden!" I run to the front door as fast as my six-year-old legs will take me. He turns from shaking my father's hand and swings me up into his arms before I barrel into his legs.

"What's up, Buttercup?"

I giggle at the nickname. "I'm not a buttercup! That's a flower."

"Nah, the flower is named after you, Buttercup." He kisses my cheek and then props me up on his shoulders, before bouncing down the hallway to the den across from the kitchen. On the way, he greets my mother warmly, bending down to give her a kiss. When he stands up, he pretends to stumble, and I begin to fall. I scream with excitement rather than fear; I know he'll catch me.

After I land in his arms, he puts me over his shoulder, like a sack of potatoes, and we continue on to the den to play with my toys.

I shake my head to dispel the happy memory. My mother is watching me with an eager look. I'm sure she's expecting me to be excited by the visit. After all, when I knew he was coming, I would always wait by the door, impatient for my Aden to arrive.

"What time did he say he'd be here, Mom?" I'm standing at the front window, anxiously searching the street. I hear my mother chuckle behind me.

"He said he'd be late, Shaylee—close to midnight. You should have gone to the dance with your friends." I don't respond to her comment. We've had this discussion many times over the last month. The sophomore formal was tonight and though I'd been asked by two boys, I'd opted to be home when Aden arrived. I'm sixteen; there will be more dances. I wasn't going to get into it again, besides, it was too late now. I know she's worried that I've developed a crush on Aden, and though I'd never admit it out loud, she's right. I know it's irrational; he has to be at least twenty years older than me. Though . . . as long as I've known him, he hasn't changed in appearance at all. He is still really hot. His muscular body gives him a rugged look that makes my friends and me all swoon. His is, quite simply, perfection. I sigh at my ridiculous thoughts. I know how silly my crush is and I'm determined to hide it before I make things awkward.

After another hour of sitting by the window, I see the white-blond hair of my favorite person, exiting a cab in front of my house. I jump up and run to the door. Flinging it open, I throw my arms around him as soon as his foot hits the top step. His laughter rings out and he swings me around.

"What's up, Buttercup?" He puts his arm around my shoulders and we walk into the house as I chatter on about what's been happening in my life.

My mom comes down the long staircase, on the left side of

the hallway, and leans up to give Aden a kiss on the cheek. From his six-foot-four height, he has to lean down for her to reach him. He puts his other arm around my mom's shoulders and gives her a squeeze.

"Hi, Violet. How are things?" He keeps his arms around us and starts down the hall to the kitchen. Aden can never resist Mom's cooking.

"Things are light. The darkness stays away." Mom always answers him with something ambiguous like that. It's weird, but Aden seems to get it, so, whatever.

When we reach the kitchen and he sees the fluffy angel food cake sitting on the counter, he smacks a kiss on the top of each of our heads. "Awe, you really do love me." He makes a beeline for the cupboard and grabs three plates.

The phone rings as we sit down to our dessert and Mom grabs the cordless from its cradle on the wall. "Brydan residence," she answers.

"Sure, just a second." She hands the phone to me. "It's Killian."

I grab the phone with a smile. Killian is one of my best friends, and one of the boys who'd asked me to the dance. We'd been considering the idea of becoming a couple and I think he was hoping the dance would be the perfect opportunity to take our relationship to the next level. He is almost three years older than me and, since it was his senior year, I felt bad for ruining one of his last dances. But, I encouraged him to take me out one night this week, so we could see where our relationship was going. I really like him and I want to give us a shot. If it helped rid me of my stupid Aden crush, even better.

I excuse myself and take the phone across the room to the den. "Hey, Killian! How was the dance?" I'd told him he could call me after, since I knew I'd be up late, waiting for Aden.

"I missed having you there, beautiful." No matter what our relationship, Killian is always free with the endearments when it comes to me. It makes me go warm inside and feel special.

"I know. I'm sorry I couldn't be there. Do you still want to go out this week?"

"Absolutely. How about I pick you up on Tuesday night and we'll catch a movie?"

I hop up from the couch and do a little happy dance. When I turn towards the kitchen, I see Aden frowning at me and whispering to my mom. She winks at me before turning to say something to Aden. She pats him on the cheek and then gets up to take care of the dishes.

After I finish my call, I walk over and give Aden a big hug. He seems a little less tense after whatever my mother said to him.

"Goodnight, Aden. I'm glad you're here."

He kisses the top of my head, then affectionately tugs on my pony tail. "Sweet dreams, Buttercup."

Aden had always protected me. Especially when Killian and I had a nasty breakup, near the end of my freshman year of college. We'd been a couple ever since our first date and, in the beginning, it was easy and so fun. We had so much in common and oddly, we even shared similar looks. His hair and skin were almost as light as mine. Though, as he aged, his features began to darken little by little. Genetics, I suppose.

Eventually, Killian had become controlling and overly possessive. I had begun to get uncomfortable, so I told him we needed to take a break. He got angry and I could feel the rage radiating from his body. He yelled that he wouldn't let me go, and I would be sorry if I went out with anybody else. I was seriously frightened. Aden was in town that weekend, and I sobbed in his arms until I'd fallen asleep. The next afternoon,

Killian called to apologize, and he kept his distance from me after that. He was always there, watching, but he never approached me. I was pretty sure Aden had had a talk with him, but neither of us ever brought it up.

During that first year of college, I was living in the dorm, and I didn't see Aden as much. I was all grown up and when I did see him, I was surprised to find myself noticing the sexy dimple in his left cheek when he smiled. I noticed how his shirts stretched across the muscles in his chest and the way his pants hung low on his narrow hips. I noticed his strong, chiseled jaw and sensuous mouth, and I wondered what it would be like if he kissed me (Don't judge. It's not like I did anything about those observations while Killian and I were still together.) I daydreamed about the white-blond hair he kept just a little shaggy, longing to find out what it felt like to run my fingers through it. But, I wasn't stupid. I knew he saw me as a kid sister, and I would never jeopardize our relationship. So, I shoved those feeling down deep, and locked them away.

Then, on my nineteenth birthday, we crossed that invisible line. The next day he left and never came back. He hadn't even said goodbye. I was torn to shreds. I'd lost my best friend, my hero, and . . . he broke my heart.

ADEN

I lay my bags down on the floor next to the bed and look around. The guest apartment on the Brydan's top floor looks the same as the last time I was here. I wish this were just another visit, like the ones I made when Shaylee was growing up. Memories of the little imp bring a smile to my lips.

Then, she had to go and grow up. I don't know the exact moment it happened, but one day I arrived, and she was no longer a child. She was just a few months shy of nineteen. She was a woman—a beautiful, and sexy-as-hell, woman. I began having trouble seeing her as my little "Buttercup". My body started reacting to her lavender scent, her luscious curves, and her mouth. That mouth was just begging to be explored with my tongue. What's worse, I could see the same desires growing in her eyes.

It was hard enough to fight my own desire, but when she looked at me with those passion-filled eyes, I wanted nothing more than to haul her into nearest bedroom, and learn what she tasted like—everywhere.

For her birthday, I'd given her season passes to the Bronx Zoo. When she opened the box and saw my little inside joke, she laughed so hard, tears were streaming down her face. That sound—the sound of her laughter—was what did me in.

I gave her a grin, and then stood, taking plates to the kitchen. I needed to clear my head, get control over my reaction to her. There was a large pantry off of the kitchen and I disappeared in there to put something away, and then stayed there for a moment, taking deep breaths and having a stern talk with my dick. Just as I was stepping out, I saw her waiting for me. She was leaning against the wall, next to the door, but moved in front of me as soon as I appeared. Her face was lit up with the most beautiful smile and any control I'd gained in her absence began to slither away.

"Thank you, Aden. That was the perfect gift." The way she said my name had visions of twisted sheets and naked bodies dancing in my head. She lifted up on her toes to place a kiss on my cheek and my feral instincts took over. I caught her mouth with my own, wrapped my arms around her waist, and dragged her back into the pantry. *Fuck, yes.* I kicked the door shut and shoved her up against the wall, devouring her mouth. She'd gasped in shock, when my lips met hers, and I took full advantage, plunging my tongue in and tasting the sweetness of her mouth. Damn, she was every bit as sweet as I knew she would be.

I was lost to her, to the passion raging between us. I grabbed her ass and hauled her body up to mine, grinding my cock against the heat of her pussy. She let out a little moan and I growled low in response.

"That is the sexiest fucking sound, baby," I said against her mouth. Her arms went around my neck, her hands running through my hair. My mouth traveled down her neck and I lifted her ass up a little higher, until her legs wrapped around my waist. With her back supported by the wall, I rocked against her a little harder. She moaned again and I became obsessed with the need to make her do it over and over again. I slid my hand up over her stomach to her breast and pinched her hardened nipple. Her gasp was sexy-as-hell, and when she started to suck on my neck, another thread of my control snapped.

I sealed my mouth over hers and my hand worked the buttons down the front of her blouse. When I'd done away with the last one, I pulled back just a little to look down. *Fuck!* Her tits were heaving with her labored breathing. They were spilling out of the barely-there, nude, lace bra. My eyes were burning into her flesh, and I knew she felt the heat when she arched her back, bringing those delicious tits to just the right height. With just the tiniest tug from my teeth, her breast was freed from its confinement, and I latched on to the pink bud. She cried out as I sucked it deeply into my mouth and then bit down lightly. Her hands were pulling at my hair and it fueled my need as I moved to give her other plump breast the same attention.

She began writhing and rocking her pelvis into mine. I wasn't sure I could last much longer without sinking my aching cock into her deep, wet heat. My mouth returned to hers and my hand continued to tease her nipples before moving slowly down to the button of her jeans. When I reached her belly button, I felt the dangling jewelry of a belly ring and pulled back to look at it. I stared for a moment. A tiny little Tinkerbell was winking at me. Later, I would recognize the irony in her choice, but at that moment, I was lost to everything but the feel of her body against mine.

"You like it?" her voice was breathy and so damn hot.

I looked into her green eyes, despite the passion darkening them, they somehow shined brighter. "It's fucking sexy, baby. Hot as hell."

A little smile played at her lips in response, and then she rocked into me again—hard. My head was spinning, only able to focus on one thing; I had to make her come. I needed to hear her scream my name. I unsnapped her jeans and dragged down the zipper before slipping my hand down to her slick folds. "Fuck, baby, you're so wet." She let out a little whimper and rocked against my hand. I wanted to turn that little whimper into a scream. I plunged a finger into her pussy and felt tight, tight suction. I'd never felt it so tight. *What the hell?* And then it hit me; *she was a virgin.* That's the moment when some of the fog cleared, and I realized who was in my arms and what the fuck I was doing to her.

Guilt assailed me. We shouldn't be doing this. But I needed to take something from this, something to keep with me. I couldn't leave her in this state, anyway. I'd give her what we both needed. I continued to work my finger in and out of her, while my thumb rubber circles on her clit. I licked and ate at her tits and when I could feel her pussy tightening even more, I put solid pressure on her swollen bud. Her body began to shudder and I muffled her screams with my tongue in her mouth. I worked her until the last of her shudders subsided. Then I hugged her close and filled myself with her scent.

I knew what I had to do, so I savored the moment: cementing her smell, her taste, the feel of her body; committing them all to memory. I also used the time to try and figure out what to tell her. I couldn't lie to her. But, I knew I couldn't tell my plans either. She'd try to stop me—to find excuses—but I knew what the right course of action was. When I pulled away and began to re-dress her, her eyes looked confused.

"We can't keep this up in here, baby." The passion began to clear from her eyes and she looked around, realizing where we were. A giggle escaped her mouth and she fought to keep from bursting into laughter. I couldn't find it in me to laugh with her and pretend I wasn't fighting the beast inside me that was screaming to make her mine.

When I had done up the last of her buttons, she stroked

her hand down the side of my face and I couldn't keep from leaning into her palm.

"We moved my bedroom down to the lower level a few months ago, and Mom is still up on the third floor. Why don't you come down after she goes to bed?" She placed a soft kiss on my lips and looked into my eyes for confirmation.

"Ok, baby. I'll come down later." It was the truth; I would go down and see her one last time before I left. I gave her one last lingering kiss, then opened the door and took a quick glance around. Seeing it empty, I let her pass me by and head toward the stairs that would take her down to the bottom floor. With one last smile thrown my way, she disappeared through the door and shut it behind her.

I waited until almost four in the morning, sure she would be asleep. I'd packed my bag earlier, so I grabbed it and quietly slipped down to her bedroom. She was lying on her stomach, her gorgeous light hair splayed across the pillows and down her back. Her pink lips were slightly parted and her breathing was deep and even. She'd left the card with eh zoo passes in the kitchen, so placed them on the nightstand next to her bed. I wanted her to know I'd been here, but I couldn't bring myself to say goodbye. I leaned down and kissed her softly before turning to leave. She was so beautiful, lying there, waiting for me.

She wasn't ready; I couldn't have her.

Yet.

SHAYLEE WAS my only assignment as a guard. I'd done it as a favor to her father. I spent most of my time training young fae who had decided to join the Mie'Lorvor, the Fae Guard. As the months passed, I began to doubt what I'd felt. I began to wonder if the passion had been in the moment and was all there was between us. I wondered if those possessive emotions were simply an effect of having protected her for so long. Perhaps my leaving had been the best thing for both of us in the long run.

For a year and a half, I went about business as usual, but I felt restless and empty. I decided to step away from my usual duties and spent six months working with the Ohtar faction of the Mie'Lorvor, whose job was to hunt the Ukkutae, the Fallen. Then, two weeks ago, I was called in to meet with the council once again and given a new, specific assignment.

Shaylee.

It went against every instinct I had not to argue with them. I'd convinced myself that Shaylee was a part of my past, someone to be fondly remembered and firmly put behind me. But, I knew as well as anyone, that it would do me no good. Once the council makes a decision, you don't have any other option but to obey. I was also pretty sure that their ulterior motive behind this choice was to make me realize and accept that Shaylee and I were fated. However, I wasn't ready to dwell on the dual purpose of this task.

Now here I am, forced to introduce Shaylee to her true nature and train her to survive the dangers that are, as of yet, unknown to her. I stood at the window and watched her arrive, then stayed in my room like a coward, not anxious to face her wrath.

I expected to hear her yell or possibly even stomp up the stairs to hand me my ass for the way I left. When that never happened, and the time for dinner drew near, I wondered if Violet had told her I was there or kept it a surprise. Sighing deeply, I decided to get it over with.

When I reach the bottom of the stairs, I see that I'm the first to arrive. I can hear the tinkling of laughter in the kitchen, and I follow the sound. When I hear my name, I stop and listen. Violet has just told Shaylee that I am coming to her birthday dinner, so I wait to gauge her reaction to the news. Instead of yelling, there is a long silence. Then, I hear her soft voice asking *why*.

Damn, her voice is sexy. It's smooth and rich and it flows with my blood straight down to my cock. *Seriously? This is so not the time to get a hard-on.*

I don't wait for her mother to answer but instead, go strolling in as if I'd never left. "To see you on your birthday, Buttercup," I answer. My breath catches suddenly at the vision before me.

Somehow, Shaylee has become even more beautiful. Her eyes are a deeper shade of blue, her skin is creamy and smooth, her breasts are fuller, her hips a little rounder. But what truly steals my attention is her mouth. I am clearly just as obsessed with it as I was before. That mouth was made to do dirty things, and I have no shortage of images concerning the activities it should be put to use for. I quickly look away, trying to get my cock to calm the hell down.

Walking swiftly over, I lay a kiss on Violet's cheek, then move to Shaylee and do the same. I ruffle her hair like I did when she was a child and her eyes swing up to meet mine. I give her a lopsided grin before quipping, "What's up, Buttercup?" To my surprise, there is no anger in her gaze. Instead, I see a flash of sadness, but she shutters her emotions so quickly, that I question if I saw it at all.

"Aden," she states my name in greeting with a small smile and then turns back to her mother. "What time will everyone be here?"

I am shocked by her docile response. Shaylee had always been filled with fire, a passion that bled into every facet of her life. Her reactions were never small. I suppose I could attribute it to maturity, but I have a feeling that it's something else, something that doused her spark. I hope the Shaylee I knew is still in there and isn't lost forever.

Three

SHAYLEE

HE IS STILL SO DAMN sexy. I keep my eyes on my mother, looking at her expectantly, ignoring the mixture of obnoxious fluttering in my stomach and the need to stomp on his foot. Yes, like a child throwing a tantrum.

Say hello to Buttercup, jackass.

My mother begins to chatter about the plans for the party, but my attention is fixed on the overwhelming presence beside me. Aden shifts, standing slightly behind me, and the warmth of his body seeps into my back. A shiver of desire runs through me before I can stifle it; my body heating up between my legs. *Damn it!* There went my hope that I'd gotten over my attraction to him.

I scoot a little forward on my seat and sit up straight, trying to distance myself. I hear a low chuckle behind me and then the heat moves closer. *What the hell?* After a moment, I feel a minuscule tug on my head and realize that Aden is playing with the ends of my long hair. Another maddening shiver courses though my body and when I hear another soft snicker, I realize that he's not oblivious to the reactions he's eliciting from me. The jerk is doing it on purpose!

19

My blood starts to boil, and not because I'm turned on. Well . . . that too. What is he doing? I'm so confused that my head is spinning. When I feel his finger trace down my spine, I jump up from my seat, desperate to get away. My mother looks at me in surprise, and but her attention is diverted when the doorbell rings.

I stifle a sigh of relief. *Saved by the bell.* Don't think I don't know what a cliché that is. Doesn't make it less true.

I practically run from the kitchen, down the hall, to get to the door, avoiding any and all contact with Aden. I reach the door and open it to see my aunt Rhoslyn, standing on the porch. Her back is to me, and she seems to be scanning the street but at the sound of the door, she turns to me and pulls me in for a tight hug.

"Happy Birthday, beautiful!" I sink into my aunt's embrace and inhale the scent of peppermint. Aunt Rhoslyn is my father's sister and we have always had a special bond. She moved in for a while after my father died and we grew incredibly close. I missed her terribly when she met her husband and moved out. However, they are only a few blocks away and their house was my "home away from home" growing up.

It's easy to see that we are related. Like me, she is tall and willowy, with straight blond hair, hanging to just below her shoulders. She always wears her hair pulled back away from her face, accentuating the one big difference in our looks—her gorgeous green eyes. If not for the eye color, she and my father could have been twins. From what I'd been told, their mother had green eyes, and their father blue. I couldn't verify that, one way or the other, since I'd never met my grandparents. Apparently, they live in a very remote area of Scotland that is hard to travel to and from. My father always promised that we would visit when I was older, but once he was gone, we never spoke about it again.

I give her a quick peck on the cheek, then usher her inside

as we chat about my job and school. I take her coat and hang it on the stand before leading her into the front room. Aden is standing at the large bay window, staring at the street, his face pensive. As we enter the room, he turns and makes his way over to greet my aunt with a soft kiss on her cheek.

To my surprise, she grasps onto his hands and looks at him intently. "It should be you." Aden inclines his head in acknowledgement of her words, but does not reply. My eyes bounces between the two, wondering what the heck I missed.

"What should be him?" I ask, my voice full of confusion.

Aden winks at me, but ignores my question and returns to his station at the window. I look to my aunt with a raised brow, expecting answers, but she just shakes her head and whispers, "In time. Beautiful. In time." At this point, I'm getting a little annoyed at all the cryptic conversation. I can't keep the irritation from coming out in a huff as I turn on my heel and return to the kitchen.

My mother sends me back out with a tray laden with tea cups and a steaming pot of English Breakfast—my favorite. My three best friends arrive and we sit down to chat for a while. Throughout the conversation, their eyes keep straying to Aden. *Not that I blame them.* Cassidy and Julie's expressions are of awe because, lets be honest, Aden is gorgeous. We met in college, so they have no clue as to who he is. Brenna, however, has been my best friend since we were five years old. She was the one I went to with my broken heart, crying over Aden for weeks. I built a wall around my heart, numbing myself in an attempt to assuage the pain from the hole he left in my life. She remembers what that did to me, and I can see the questions and worry in her eyes.

All I can do is shrug. I have no idea why he has shown up here. Aden doesn't lie—*ever*. So, there is some truth to wanting to see me on my birthday. I can feel the stirrings of of hope inside me. *Really, Shaylee? Because hoping worked out so well for you the last time? And the time before that? And...do you see where I'm going here?* I mentally give myself a good, hard slap back to reality and immediately squash those feelings down.

Mom comes out front the kitchen and announces that dinner is ready so we all shuffle into the dining room. She points out our seating arrangements and I inwardly cringe when I see that she put me next to Aden. Being in close proximity to his sexy body is so not what I need right now. I start for the kitchen, to help bring out the food, and give Brenna a meaningful glance. "Brenna, you want to give me a hand?" I ask. She scurries over, and we make our way to the pantry to avoid my mom walking in on our conversation. At the last minute, I realize how stupid it was to choose this room. The memories wash over me and suddenly, I grow wet and I can feel my pulse between my legs as desire swirls in my bloodstream. *Ugh! Get a grip on your raging hormones, you hussy!*

Brenna eyes my suddenly heated cheeks and gives me a knowing look before she rolls her eyes. "What's he doing here, Shaylee?" her voice is laced with irritation. I'm not surprised. She's still pretty pissed at the way Aden left me.

"I have no freaking clue. He said he wanted to see me on my birthday."

Brenna looks skeptical. "That's it? That can't be all."

I shake my head. "Aden doesn't lie, Brenna," I state emphatically. "That is clearly part of his reason for being here." I run my fingers through my hair and blow out a frustrated breath. "Although, I can't imagine why he has suddenly decided that I am worth his time. There's obviously another reason"—my eyes narrow—"and I think my mother and aunt know what it is."

Brenna sighs deeply. "Well, if your mom invited him, there isn't much you can do about it." She grabs my hand and squeezed it. "Just please promise me that you won't let him back into your heart. I can't stand to see you broken like that again. Promise me, Shaylee."

As much as I hate to admit it, I know I can't make that promise. The truth is, Aden has never left my heart, but I am determined not to let him break the shell I've built around it. "I don't think he's here to woo me, Brenna." I let sarcasm ooze from my words. "He clearly didn't want to be with me two years ago; I don't see why anything would have changed. He's not one to make the same mistake twice." I inwardly wince at the vocal acknowledgment that he views what happened between us as a mistake.

Brenna nods, seeming to accept my words, and we return to the kitchen, grabbing some random things to make it appear as though we'd stepped out for a reason other than our little powwow. When I reach my seat, Aden stands and pulls out my chair. I give him a small smile of thanks, and once I'm seated, I tell the girl smitten girl sighing inside of me, to shut the fuck up.

The conversation during dinner revolves around our plans for Christmas break. A lot of the girls in our circle have decided to go in together on a house in upstate New York, and ski the holidays away. I would never desert my family for Christmas, but I intend to join them a few days later for New Year's. I studiously avoid sending any looks Aden's way. But, for most of the meal, I can feel his burning gaze burning on me. My mom stands up to get my cake, and I jump up to help, grateful for an excuse to get away from Aden for few moments and regroup. Unfortunately, Mom is adamant that the birthday girl have her cake brought to her, and she scolds me back into my seat.

Aden leans back in his seat and casually drapes his arm across the back of my chair. He is deep in conversation with my aunt, who is sitting at the end of the table to his right. I begin to scoot forward in my seat, to avoid any accidental contact with him, when I'm stopped short. Aden's hand is lightly gripping my hair and he tugs softly to keep me from moving. I turn to glare at him, but the effect is ruined because it's directed at the back of his head since he is still talking to my Aunt Rhoslyn. Mashing my lips together with displeasure, I face forward again, my body tight with frustration. Then, his hand wanders down to my neck and starts kneading the tight muscles there. I can feel myself melting into his touch; the warmth from his fingers starting to spread. It sizzles under my skin and when it reaches, my now damp, underwear, I squirm uncomfortably in my seat. The whole situation is incredibly bizarre and I'm suddenly exhausted from the effort to keep my distance and protect myself, while attempting to figure out what the hell is going on!

We finish dessert, open gifts, and *finally*, the night comes to a close. I hug each of my friends and send them on their way, before turning to say goodbye to Aunt Rhoslyn. I expect her to be in the entry, putting on her coat, but instead, I find her sitting in the den with Mom and Aden. Aunt Rhoslyn and my mom are seated next to each other on the couch below a big picture window that overlooks one of the few big back-yards in the city. Aden is sprawled on the love seat across from them. As I enter the room, all three look up at me and their conversation comes to a sudden halt. They are staring at me like they are expecting me to sprout wings or something.

When did I enter the damn Twilight zone?

"Have a seat, sweetie," Mom speaks up first and as I glance around at each of their faces, their solemn expressions make me wary. I walk toward a recliner but stop when I notice it's piled with presents. The other is in the same condition and realize I have no other choice but to sit next to Aden. *Just peachy.* I make my way over there and perch on the edge, leaning away from him, with my elbow on the arm rest.

I look at my mother expectantly, but she just nods toward

Aden and gives him her full attention. I switch my focus to him an eyebrow raised in question. He smirks at me for a moment before his face smooths and turns serious.

"Shaylee, I haven't had time to prepare for this, so I'm sorry if I don't handle it in the best way. I wasn't given this assignment, until the last minute." He runs a frustrated hand through his hair. "Normally, we'd have more time to ease you into this information, but for some reason, you've attracted attention to yourself and we need to get you somewhere safe."

Attention? What the hell? "I don't understand."

"The thing is..." He looks toward my mother for a moment and when she doesn't jump in, he sighs and turns back to me. "There are things that you don't know and..." he trails off once again.

"Aden, just spit it out, would you?" I snap. "You're giving me a freaking headache." This time, he's the one who raises a brow.

"Alright, I'll just say it." He takes a deep breath and blows it out with a whoosh. "You're only half human, Shaylee."

Say what??

My mind is spinning at his words—they make absolutely no sense.

"You're also half faery."

I stare at him for a moment as rage begins to fill me. Before I can think better of it, I pull my hand back and send it flying.

Four

ADEN

DAMN IT!

Caught off guard, my head rears back slightly at the force
of the blow and the sound of the slap reverberates in the silent
room. I'm speechless with shock but I also can't help admiring
her strength. She packs a hell of a punch. Shaylee has jumped
to her feet and is staring me down with fire in her eyes. I
understand confusion at the situation, but I am taken aback
by the level of fury and disgust on her beautiful face. I glance
to her mother and aunt, but they are frozen, staring at Shaylee
with wide eyes and dropped jaws.

"Are you mocking me, Aden? I don't know what kind of
game you're playing, but I won't put up with it. I won't let
you disrespect my Dad by turning his beliefs and stories into a
joke," her voice is calm, monotone. "I want you to leave."

"Shaylee," Violet says softly. The look on her face is one of
understanding, and I feel relief that somebody knows what the
hell is going on. At the sound of her voice, Shaylee whirls
towards around. When she sees the look on Violet's face, her
anger begins to fade and is replaced by a bone-deep sadness.

"You knew?" her voice is confused and coated in despair.

"I don't understand, Mom. Why would you let him ridicule Dad?" Suddenly, it becomes clear where I went wrong. Shaylee had grown up with her dad telling her stories of the Fae. Stories she believed, until Orin died, and she became convinced that they were concocted in his imagination . . . told for her amusement. She didn't realize that Orin had been preparing her. He told her the stories so that the knowledge would be ingrained in her and, hopefully, when she was told the truth after her marking, she would find it easier to believe . . . to transition.

I don't wait for Violet to intercede. I decide to take back control of the situation. She needs to trust me. She needs to have faith in the things I tell her and not rely on believing it because of her mother's conviction. If she doesn't completely trust me, then I won't be able to convince her of one other truth. One I know she isn't ready to hear, so I'll keep it to myself, for now.

"Shaylee, have I ever lied to you?" I ask calmly.

She turns back to me, and I can see her thinking. I know her mind has wandered to her birthday, when I agreed to meet her in her room. I stress my point. "Have I ever *lied* to you?"

"No." Her eyes narrow in annoyance, but she admits to the truth.

"I would never tarnish your father's memory, baby." She stiffens at the nickname, but I don't give a shit. She'll get used to it.

"I loved him like a father, too." Her shoulders slump as her anger completely deflates, leaving her with only sadness. I pat the couch next to me, "Please sit, and let me explain." I can hear the urgency in my own voice. I need to make her understand. I need her to trust me. From the moment I saw her again, I knew the council had been correct. We were fated. *You shouldn't be surprised, dumbass.* I knew it when I left, but for some reason, I talked myself out of it once I'd put distance between us. Now I feel the pull, the need to be near her, to touch her. I hadn't been able to keep my hands off of her all night, and—I inwardly grinned—I particularly enjoyed her reaction. She is still attracted to me, even though she doesn't want to be. *And that's just too damn bad.*

She seems to consider my words for a moment, and then decides to let me speak my piece and sits on the far side of the couch. I fight the instinct to haul her over next to me, knowing she needs time to process it all. Once it appears that she is calm and open to listening, Violet and Rhoslyn quietly move to the kitchen.

"I need you to hear me out before you flip and hit me again, alright?" I see a slight lifting of one corner of her mouth, and want to breathe a small sigh that she has calmed enough to listen.

"The things your father told you were true." I put up my hand in a stop gesture when she opens her mouth to speak. I can see the mutinous expression creeping into her eyes. "You promised you'd listen." She harrumphs, but doesn't speak.

"Your dad was trying to prepare you for today. The day when you would find out who and what you truly are. If you'd heard the stories, especially from him, he hoped it would be easier for you to accept it." I can't keep the sorrow from my voice, "Of course, he intended to be here for this." I sidestep my emotion and continue on before she decides to stop listening.

"We keep our realm a secret from the humans to preserve our way of life." I look at her pointedly, "Humans are too volatile, too unpredictable. To be blunt, they cannot be trusted." I repeat my last words, emphasizing their importance. "They *cannot* be trusted." I don't wait for her to respond before continuing. "Your comprehension of the Fae world was limited, and it's too big of a risk to trust our secret to a child. So, we wait until you are marked to tell you the truth."

"While we are all protectors by nature and the Mie'Lorvor are our guards. We protect the Faeland, and those living in the human realm." I can see the word register with her, the meaning somewhat clear. "You're surprised that you know what it means, right?" She just nods. I'm not sure if I should be worried about her silence. Shaylee has issues sitting still for long periods of time, much less sitting and listening with patience. I'm wondering if there is an explosion on the horizon. But, I don't have the time to dwell on it. "When you turned twenty-one, you were marked. Basically, all of your Fae genetics, for lack of a better term, wake up. The language will come to you; you won't have to learn it. The magic will as well, but you'll have to learn how to use it." I stop and wait to see if she is following me. She is still calm, so I give her a chance to speak.

Her brow furrows for a moment. "Marked? What does that mean?" she asks.

"Mostly, it's just the term we use to describe what happens when you turn twenty-one. You're able to access your Fae magic and others are able to detect it." She raises an eyebrow at me and I have to stifle a laugh at her show of attitude. *There's my Shaylee.*

"We'll come back to *others*. For now, explain what you meant by 'mostly' a term."

"You do have a literal mark somewhere on your body." I can't help the wolfish grin that splits my face when I think of how fun it's going to be finding that mark. I shift a little in my seat trying to relieve some of the pressure from my, suddenly, very snug pants. Shaylee gives me an annoyed look, clearly aware of where my mind has wandered. I just wink at her.

"I don't have a mark, Aden. You'll just have to take my word for it, since you'll never have the opportunity to look for it." There is ice in her tone, but it doesn't faze me. I am well aware of my ability to make her melt.

"You'll only see it after today, baby. It wasn't there before. Look, we can get to that later. I have more to tell you," I inform. She sits back, gesturing for me to continue. "Since you are half human, you cannot enter Rien, the Fae Realm, until you are marked. For whatever reason, the magic simply won't work and it cloaks your family as well, keeping you off the radar, so to speak. That's why you grew up in the human realm. Your dad chose to stay with you and your mother. But, when you turned twenty-one, your parents intended to take you to Rien."

"My mother can go there but I can't?"

"Well, yes, until you were marked. Although, once she is there, she will not be able to leave. You have enough Fae blood that you are free to move in and out of the realms."

"So, Dad never went back after he met my mom?" Her face softens and I know she's thinking about how her dad had been hopelessly in love with her mother.

"He was going to take her there eventually. But, by not going back, even for a visit, he was able to age with her." I realize I've jumped ahead as soon as the words leave my mouth.

"He what?" Shaylee is looking at me intently, and then I see the realization on her face. "You've never aged. In all the years I've known you. I just thought you had really good genes." The wheels are spinning in her head. "You're not—you won't die?"

I nod slowly, watching for her reaction. To my surprise she seems to take it in stride. "If we spend enough time outside of our realm, our immortality diminishes." I gesture back to her aunt, "Some, like Rhosalyn, have made the choice to make the break permanent. Especially if they've found the one they are fated with here." I wince inwardly; I didn't want to bring up the issue of the fates yet. So, I rush on, hoping she won't dwell on that statement. "Shaylee, there are so many things that you will learn, but right now, we only have time for me to explain a few last things ,and then we need to go."

Shaylee scoots back on the couch, retreating from my words. "I'm not going anywhere, Aden. For crying out loud, I need time to process this all, to decide if I even believe you."

"Baby, we don't have time. You've been marked and I've got to get you to Rien where you'll be safe until you're properly trained." I grab her hand in mine and squeeze it lightly. When she tugs it back, I keep a firm hold on it. "Shaylee, don't think I won't drag your ass out of here to keep you safe."

She tugs a little harder and this time I let go. "Safe from what, Aden? Evil elves? Wicked witches? Black River werewolves? Give me a break. A few days isn't going to matter."

I roll my eyes at her sarcasm, but let it go. Today is not the day to get into the other species in the Fae realm. I debate whether to tell her what I've noticed all day. Someone is watching the house. I don't know how they found her so quickly; they must have known already and were waiting for her birthday. I only consider for a moment, I know she can handle it and hopefully, it'll get her moving so we can get the hell out of here. "You're already on their radar, baby. You're being watched."

She stiffens and I see awareness creeping into her eyes. She noticed. Good, her instincts are already sharpening. "You felt it today?" I ask.

"I had a funny feeling, but this is New York City, Aden. Some creep is always watching." Her excuse is feeble and she knows it. "Who is it?"

"Most likely, a Ukkutae." Once again, I see that the word's meaning is familiar to her.

"Evil?"

"Shaylee, if there is good in the world, there must be bad. There is always a balance. The Fae are bound by laws of honesty. I cannot lie and neither can you."

"How would you know?" She knows I'm right, but stubbornness is written all over her face.

An exasperated sigh escapes my lips. "I just do. Now will you shut it, so we can get going?"

Anger sweeps across her face and she jumps up from the couch, ready to stalk away. But I'm too quick for her. I grab her around the waist and pull her down onto my lap. Her expression turns defiant and she struggles to get back up. She's beautiful when she's angry and all the wiggling brings my dick to life. The moment she feels it, she stills. I lean down to her ear and whisper, "We'll talk about that later, too." I place a soft kiss on her neck and just stop myself from tracing the shell of her ear with my tongue. I feel the raw possession clawing at me. All I can think is—*mine.*

Five

SHAYLEE

ADEN'S BREATH on my neck has my heart racing. I want to sink into his embrace and run like a bat-out-of-hell at the same time. I settle for moving away from temptation. "Don't tell me to *'shut it'*, Aden." I shoot for venom in my voice and instead get mildly annoyed. Ugh! I hate what he does to me. "I'm not going to leave; you can let me up now." His arms tighten around me and he places another sweet kiss just below my ear. He buries his nose in my hair and breathes deep.

"I like you right here, babe." I just suppress the shiver. His voice is smooth and washes over me, causing heat to rise and the wetness to gather between my thighs. I pull away and he lets me go this time. I move to the other end of the couch and once I'm away from him, my mind clears of the lust-induced fog I'm always in around him. My brain leaps back into our conversation and I can feel the weight of all the information pushing on my shoulders and causing a tension headache to surface.

. . .

THE ODDEST PART about this all is that, after I calm down, I admit to myself that I already believe him. Somewhere in my heart, beyond the knowledge that he would never lie to me, I recognize that he is telling me the truth. The electric feeling I noticed earlier is probably the result of the magic that is now free of its restraints. I just don't *want* to believe him, so I'm being stubborn. *You're punishing him and you know it.* Okay, it's possible that I'm being overly difficult because I'm still pissed at him for ditching me the last two years.

It doesn't help that I'm completely confused by his attitude. It's like he wants to pick up where we left off and move forward. He's obviously still attracted to me, but I'm wary of his motives. Still, I feel a spark of hope that I can't tamp down. But, I don't have time to examine that right now.

"Exactly what is it that I'm supposed to be doing now?" I can see the restlessness in him and I decide he's told me enough for now. I have endless questions, but there is urgency in his eyes and tone. It irritates the hell out of me, but I trust him implicitly and if I'm in danger, I don't want it to threaten my mom.

"We'll go to Rien. You'll begin training. I'll teach you how to protect yourself and others by using your magic properly, as well as physical training." That stops me short and my lips turn up in a wicked smile. "Are you telling me that eventually, I'll be able to kick your ass?"

Aden rolls his eyes, "You can certainly try, baby." Warmth floods through me at the endearment. *Damn it!* I give him a sour look.

He gives me a roguish grin, "I'll certainly enjoy rolling around with you, on the ground, after I take you down." *Oh for shit's sake, does he have to keep saying things like that? Move on, Shaylee, back to what's important.*

I look around my home, the place I grew up, the place that holds all of my memories with my dad. And, what about my mom? I feel sadness at the thought of leaving the life I know, the people and places that I love. Aden reaches for my hand, as he did earlier, and this time, I don't fight him. He knows me well and despite my anger at him, I find comfort in his familiar touch. There was a time when he would have fallen into that category. Now, I just want him to leave my heart alone, no matter how much my body yearns for him.

"Baby, you won't be gone forever. I told you, you can travel in and out of both realms. You just need to learn to protect yourself from those who will attempt to turn you first." I open my mouth to ask, but he cuts me off. "We really don't have time to get into this, Shaylee. You need to say goodbye to your mother and aunt, so we can be on our way. Every minute we stay here is another minute you are in danger and I won't be able to breathe freely until you're safe."

I want to argue with him, but once again, I get that over-whelming feeling of trust and I know I'm going to follow his lead. "How long?" I ask.

He shrugs. "That depends on how quickly you learn. I've seen it take six months and I've seen it take several years."

Years? Tears burn the backs of my eyes but I blink them away with determination. It won't be years for me, I won't let it. I stand up and realize that I am still holding his hand. He smirks at me and I snatch my hand back as though it's been burned. Considering the heat that lingers from his skin, I would say that analogy isn't far off.

I walk to the kitchen, where my mom and Aunt Rhoslyn are sipping tea in silence. When I enter the room, they both look at me and I can see the tears they are trying to hide. My mom walks to me and pulls me in for a tight hug. "I've looked forward to and dreaded this day for so long," she says. "I want you to know who you are and embrace what your dad passed on to you. But, I'll miss you with every breath, sweetheart." I've never been away from my mom for more than a couple of weeks and I am cloaked in homesickness before I've even left.

"Everything was delivered from your dorm today. So, I packed a bag for you. You won't need much, but I knew what you wouldn't want to leave here without."

It occurs to me that my mother has been preparing for this day and I'm glad I didn't fight her too hard about my party. It was her send off. She was giving us both a sweet memory to tide us over. I hug her tightly and motion for my aunt to joins us. "I love you both so much." It's impossible to keep the tears from rolling down our cheeks as we say goodbye. Aden clears his throat from the doorway to get our attention.

"It'll be dark soon, Violet, we need to hit the road before the sun is completely down." My mom nods, and then gives me one last squeeze. She walks over and pulls Aden down to plant a kiss on his cheek.

"Take care of her, Aden. I trust you to be what she needs. They wouldn't have sent you back to her if you weren't." Aden gives a short nod, then looks at me and gives a chin left to indicate that it's time to go. But something my mother said stops me. *Sent you back to her.* He was sent *back* to me?

I want to get an answer to my question, but Aden has already left the room and my mother just gives me a soft smile and follows him out the door, my aunt quick on her heels. I decide to ask Aden about it later, but something about the statement continues to bother me.

I GLANCE at Aden from the passenger seat of the sleek BMW he rented for the drive. We'd left my house quickly and he'd hurried me down the block to a parking garage. Once we were out of the city, the tension began to slowly drain from his shoulders.

A thought suddenly occurs to me, "Aden, I left my cell phone at home."

"You won't need it, baby. It won't work in Rien," he answers distractedly. "We'll get you a new one when we get there."

Disappointment settles a little harder on my chest when I realize I will be completely cut off from my family. "Where are we going?" I ask. The scenery is becoming more open; residential areas and sweeping landscape. So far, we are headed upstate.

"Upstate." *Duh*. I'm about to make a snarky comment when he continues. "There are areas that are open, fields with plenty of sunshine during the day, and relatively low population. It will be easier to cross realms there. Now that we are out of the city, we'll find a hotel for the night and cross in the late morning."

"You said something about the sun earlier too. What's so important about sunshine?"

Aden chuckles before answering. "I can't believe you haven't noticed. Haven't you ever wondered why you feel weighted down and sluggish when you go days without direct sunshine?

I just shrug. "Everybody gets that way when it's gloomy for days."

I notice his hands tighten a little on the steering wheel. "Not everybody, some people revel in the darkness." Just as quickly as it came, the stress leaves him and he relaxes again. "I'm not talking about just feeling depression. You get physically sick when you're out of the sun for too long." He glances at me with his eyebrows raised. "I know your dad used to take you and your mom out of the city every weekend in October and November. Those months are notoriously dark; lots of rain, and even hurricanes."

I think about it and have to agree—I do react strongly to a lack of sunlight. "What's your point?"

"The Fae cannot survive without sun, baby. We would basically waste away. During those darker months, your dad made sure that you both were exposed to enough sun to get you through the week. We need the sun for our magic to be at its most powerful. I know it sounds cliché, but we are like solar panels. We soak up the vitamin D and it fuels us."

He takes his right hand off of the steering wheel and lightly grabs the long hair falling from my ponytail. He runs it though his fingers, and then brushes my cheek softly before returning his hand to its previous position. "Your hair, it is the lightest of golden blonde; like mine, your dad's, and your aunt's. The three of you have blue eyes that seem to shine in the light of day; they reflect like jewels. Your skin is so pale, it is almost without color, and yet there is a luminescence to it. Not quite a glow, but just an ethereal quality. We all share these traits, with the exception of some of us having green eyes." He glances at me again, his eyes caressing me from head to toe before refocusing on the road. "Though some faeries are more exquisite than others..." he trails off. I don't miss the way his eyes linger on my breasts, but I decide to let it go this time. *Because it has everything to do with the way your breasts got heavy and your nipples hardened at his look.* I seriously wish I could bitch slap my conscious sometimes—the twat.

I turn to stare at the scenery, trying to get my stupid hormones under control. Twenty-one years and they only cause problems when Aden is around. I'm staring out the window, ignoring him, when I remember my question from earlier. "What did my mom mean when she said *they* sent you to me?"

Aden shifts uncomfortably in his seat and, for a moment, I don't think he is going to answer me.

But then, he steals another glance at me through the

corner of his eye and sighs. "The Mie'Lorvor have many duties. One of the most important is to guard leath leanbh, children who are half human. While your magic is undetectable, that doesn't mean you can't be found. We protect from a distance, unless it becomes absolutely necessary to be in their life on a daily basis. In your case, your dad was former Guard. The council agreed that you didn't need me there as often as some, so I only checked in with him in person a few times a year. When he died, I upped my visits to you, but there wasn't a threat to keep me there permanently. Then—" I cut him off as his words clicked into place. Anger and devastation roiled in my stomach.

"You were assigned to me?" my question is practically a whisper.

"Yes but—"

"—You were never there just to see me, I was your job." I cut him off once again. I don't want to hear his explanation. Humiliation settles over my skin, a cold blanket that stifles my breathing. I was so stupid to think that he was my best friend. To think that he would come to visit—just to see me —a child. No wonder he went running after our heated session in the pantry. What was I, but another woman he was attracted to? One of the many, I'm sure. For shit's sake, he's gorgeous. He must have sensed that my naïve thoughts had turned to forever and took off before I embarrassed us both.

"So, you got the council to assign you elsewhere after we— after my birthday."

He doesn't attempt to respond this time, probably assuming I would cut him off again. *Smart choice, jackass.*

"Two years of nothing. You up and left with no explanation or goodbye. But then, why would you? You passed the baton and moved on, right?" He was gone, so—"Wait, why are *you* here, now? Why would they send *you* when you obviously didn't want to be assigned to me anymore?" This time I stop and give him chance to reply.

His knuckles are white from squeezing the steering wheel tight, and he throws me a sharp look. "Are you ready to let me speak now and listen to what I have to say?"

I scowl at him, but gesture for him to continue.

"I handled it all wrong, when I left." I don't hold back my sarcastic grunt of agreement and he gives me another withering glare.

"You were never *just* a job to me, Shaylee. You, your mom and dad, you're all family to me. But, I needed to go. You weren't ready for where our attraction was leading us." he hurries to continue, knowing I'm about to interrupt again, I'm sure.

"The council asked me to return for you and I had my own reasons for agreeing." He stops now and I wait for him to continue. After a minute, it appears that he has nothing more to say. He knows I will believe him and it takes some of the wind out of my sails. I'm still angry and hurt over the way he left, but I'm exhausted and so ready to be done with this conversation. I turn back to the scenery and begin to nod off.

ADEN

WHEN SHE FELL ASLEEP, some of the pressure eased from my hands and I lightened my grip on the steering wheel. I'd have this conversation with her, just not now. She is mine and she'll accept it, eventually. But, I need time for her to get over her indignation at the way I left. Sure, I'd handled it wrong. However, I came back, and she needs to get over it. I can't tell her about being fated until she's accepted the fact that I'm not going to let her go.

I see a small hotel ahead and pull off of the road into the softly lit parking lot. As soon as we left the city, I'd no longer felt the sensation of being stalked. I don't want Shaylee to know the darkness is practically nipping at her heels. I had to get us the hell out of dodge because I knew it was close. I'm convinced that somehow, a Fallen found out about her before she was marked and they are coming for her. My instincts are telling me that we are safe to stop here for the night. It's almost one in the morning and it's been a long day for both of us. The fatigue is catching up with me, and I'm ready to have my girl in my arms and get some sleep.

41

The hotel is built to look like a long, extended log cabin and when I enter the front office, I chuckle at the cheesy décor. They went a little overboard with the six point buck on the wall, his vacant, black eyes unnerving the guests. The desk is empty, so I ring the little, silver bell and wait for the attendant. A handsome, young man, in his early twenties, comes in through a door in the back and he checks me into a room with one queen bed. *I'm not even going to pretend that wasn't on purpose.*

With the key in hand, I jog back out to the car and pull it around back into the space for room number four. Shaylee still hasn't moved, so I get out and go around the car to her side. I gently lift her into my arms and carry her to the door. Heat surges through me when she snuggles up close, pressing her breasts into my chest. It's been too long since I've been with a woman, but even as I tell myself that's why my body's response to her is so strong, I know that's not the only reason. Nobody has ever turned me on like Shaylee. My dick is always half-cocked (pun not intended) and ready for action. I open the door to the room and walk to the bed. As I bend to lay her down, her arms tighten around me.

"Don't leave me, Aden," her voice is a whisper, and I'm not sure whether she is fully awake and aware of what she is saying. "I missed you so much."

I feel a pang in my chest, regretting the way that I hurt her. I'm determined to make it up to her, to make her forget, and to only see the future we are going to have together. "I'm not going anywhere, baby," I whisper back. She breathes a sigh of relief, and her grip on me lessens as she relaxes back into a deeper sleep. I leave her there for a moment to retrieve our bags, lock up the car, and finally, the hotel room door. At first, I grab her bag to find her a pair of pajamas, and then I think better of it and dig through my stuff to find her a t-shirt. The caveman inside me growls in satisfaction at the thought of her wearing my clothes. Being marked by my scent so that every male we come in contact with will have no doubt who she belongs to.

I strip down to my black boxer briefs and take the shirt over to the bed. I take off her shoes and socks, tossing them in the direction of our luggage, and then I unzip her jeans, slowly sliding them down her endless legs. The site of her sexy, little, black panties have my, already active, libido jumping into overdrive. I close my eyes for a moment and reach for some control. When I open my eyes, I keep them north of that lace-covered nirvana. I slip my arm under her shoulders and quietly encourage her to sit up.

"Come on, baby, sit up so I can get you dressed for bed." She half opens her eyes and looks at me blearily. Her lids slide shut again, but she puts a little effort into lifting up and raising her arms so that I can tug her shirt off. *What the fuck was I thinking?* Her beautifully round tits are once again encased in a barely-there lace bra. Black this time, to match her panties. I give silent thanks that she isn't awake enough to notice the tent in my underwear. I try to ignore the raging hard-on I've developed, knowing I won't be getting any relief tonight. My right hand travels up her stomach and over her delicious tit and up to her shoulder. *Okay, so I'm not above taking the opportunity to cop a feel when she isn't awake enough to slap me.*

As my eyes travel over her, I notice she's still got the Tinkerbell charm dangling in her perfect little belly button. I smile at the proof that she never really let go of the fairytales. She just didn't know how fitting it truly was for her to choose a fairy. Moving her slightly forward, so my hand, on her back, can unhook her skimpy excuse for a bra. I know I've tortured myself to the limit, so I pull my t-shirt down over her head and shoulders before slipping her bra off. Once it's gone, I pull her arms through the sleeves and lay her gently back down. She sighs and turns onto her stomach, sprawling out on the bed. My eyes travel down and that's when I notice that the back of her panties are missing. *A fucking thong.* I roll my eyes to the ceiling in frustration.

Grabbing her bra, I turn away to set if with her other clothes on a chair. As I put down the lace garment, a thought occurs to me. A woman doesn't wear sexy lingerie unless her intention is to let someone see it. Jealousy rears its head and rage burns in my chest just thinking about another man seeing what's mine. I didn't think to ask if she had a boyfriend. *Did you think she was just sitting around, pining for you?* Ok, so, maybe I did. I clench my fists, restraining the desperate need to shake her awake and demand to know who she is wearing this lacy shit for. It doesn't matter. She's *mine.*

After tossing it on the chair, I make my way to the other side of the bed and slide under the blankets. A queen size bed is tough for me to fit in alone, much less with another person. But, as I settle in, Shaylee rolls toward me. I lift my arm and she scoots up close, laying her head on chest and throwing an arm and a leg over me. Yep, I knew what I was doing when I didn't book a room with a king.

I wrap her up in my arms and let her heat relax me. The blue balls, I'm sure to have by morning, are completely worth having her in my arms. It takes a few minutes of thinking about ugly-ass Fallen, but eventually, I'm able to fall asleep.

～

I WAKE to the sound of a small moan and lift my head to make sure that Shaylee is all right. As my body shifts, I realize that she is pressed up to me, back to front. My morning wood is snug up against her ass, and somehow, in my sleep, my hand had wandered up the front of her shirt to hold her naked breast in my palm. I glance quickly down and see that her eyes are still closed, her mouth slightly parted like it was the last time I watched her sleep. But instead of deep and even, her breathing is shallow and slightly erratic. I can feel her faster-than-normal heart beat under my hand, and curiosity gets the better of me. I lightly squeeze the breast in my hand and the beat of her heart speeds up a little more. *She's fucking turned on.* She squirms a little and pushes her ass back into my cock. It takes everything in me not to rip away the string of her thong and thrust my cock deep into her pussy.

Instead, I lower my head and kiss the soft skin below her ear, squeezing her breast again, a little harder this time. She breathes out another little moan and whispers something. I lean down closer to her mouth and listen when I repeat the same actions.

She whispers again and I feel possession and deep satisfaction explodes throughout my body. It was *my* name that crossed her lips. The caveman in me roars and beats on his chest. I start placing hot, wet, open mouth kisses on her neck and my hand begins to slide south. When I reach her pussy, I run my finger over the material and feel that it's wet. I press a little harder and feel her pulsing on my fingers.

She shifts a little and I see her eyes begin to open, waking in a haze of lust. I lay another kiss on that sensitive little spot, below her ear, and slip my finger inside her panties. I slide it down and push it slowly inside of her. Her hips thrust up involuntarily and she turns her head to look at me. I don't give her time to clear her mind; I take her lips in a savage kiss. I push my tongue inside in the same rhythm as my finger is fucking her scorching heat. Without removing my mouth or my finger, I gently push her onto her back and cover her body with mine.

Tearing my mouth from hers, I bury my face in her neck, inhaling the lavender scent I didn't realize I missed. I can feel her pussy clenching, searching for relief, but I'm not ready to push her over the edge yet. I slowly remove my finger and smirk at the whimper of distress I hear. I nudge her legs apart with my knee and they fall willingly to either side. My lower body settles into the open v, my cock flush against her pussy. I kiss her deeply again, then pull back just a little and push her shirt up, removing it completely. Once it's off, I drop down again and let out a low groan when I feel our skin connect. *She feels so damn good.* My mouth returns to hers and this time, her tongue reaches out to explore my mouth as her back arches, rubbing her erect nipples against me. I growl in satisfaction and rub against her core, my mouth moving down her neck, eliciting a sweet little moan from her sexy mouth.

I'm so fucking hard, I can barely think straight. But in the far recesses of my mind, I know I can only let this go so far. The last thing I need is to give her one more reason to be pissed at me. I follow the rise and fall of her tits and decide, just a little more. Wrapping my lips around one hardened peak, I can feel her heart racing and her breath exhaling in uneven puffs. My tongue swirls lightly around before sucking her nipple deep into my mouth. She cries out and my hips jerk forward involuntarily, the friction causing my cock to tighten even further, so painfully hard that I know I won't be able to stay coherent much longer. I move to her other tit, once again pulling it deep while rocking into her a little faster.

"Baby, I'll never get enough of you." I whisper as I lift my head, intent on returning to her mouth. Her body suddenly stills. I glance up and see her face has hardened, her eyes swirling with a mixture of emotions, settling on anger.

"You had enough of me once before." She presses her hands against my chest and pushes, seemingly intent on getting up and away from this conversation. I grasp her hands and raise them above her head, holding her immobile, so she can't run away from me before we talk.

Her lips pinch in annoyance, but she doesn't struggle. She knows she won't be able to get up until I'm ready to let her. Her eyes are spitting fire and I'm momentarily distracted at how fucking sexy she is. I just want to—

My thoughts screech to a halt as a barrage of ice cold water suddenly drops from the air, soaking me from head to toe. The shock of it causes me to lose my breath. *Holy shit, that's freezing!* When my brain reboots, I jump off of the bed and stare at the ceiling wondering what the hell just happened! Shaylee is still lying on the bed, staring at me, her mouth forming a little "o" of surprise. It takes me a second to realize that she is completely dry. I feel my eyes narrow in suspicion. Did she—damn, I'm pretty sure she did.

"What were you thinking, Shaylee?" I ask curiously.

"I—I was thinking—um," She stutters. "I was thinking that you needed to cool off."

At her words, I burst out laughing. I laugh so hard that tears leak from the corners of my eyes. When I finally calm down, I notice Shaylee is glaring at me as she puts her t-shirt back on. I can't help but be disappointed to see her cover up. *Damn, she is gorgeous.* A shiver runs down my body, and only partly because I'm soaking wet.

"You want to let me in on the joke, Aden?" She's glowering at me and I realize that she thinks I was playing with her.

"Baby, I told you we have magic." I shake my head ruefully, but am still chuckling. "I haven't taught you how to use them yet, but they are there. You wanted me to cool off, so you doused me in freezing water." Honestly, it's not something I've seen before. When someone is newly marked, their magic makes small appearances, but usually in very small ways, like turning on a light bulb; simple things. For her to soak me, and keep herself completely dry...it's impressive. She's already using her ability to shield, albeit unknowingly.

Her face is filled with disbelief. "No way did I do that.

Stop messing with me, Aden." She stands up and puts her hands on her hips, scowling at me. "And, stop calling me *baby*."

"I swear; it wasn't me. You think I would do this to myself?" I meet her intense stare before adding, "And, no."

Seven

SHAYLEE

No way. No freaking way did I just conjure ice water from thin air and drop it on Aden. My mind is rejecting the thought, but the truth is fighting to overcome the disbelief. I don't want to admit that I felt a rush as the water fell, like a heated summer wind blew through my body. Just as I don't want to admit that if Aden hadn't spoken those words, I probably would have given in to the overwhelming desire for him —wait—words. My mind halts and then rewinds to something he just said.

"What do you mean 'no'?"

Aden closes the small gap between us. Keeping his eyes locked with mine, I see determination darkening his green gems to the color of fresh grass. I try not to notice how beautiful they are, holding tight to my anger and hurt, to keep from falling under his spell once again.

"Just what I said, *baby*." He emphasizes the endearment with a low, smooth tone and it washes over me, heating my skin and making my panties even damper. "I'm not going to play games with you, Shaylee—you're mine." His head lowers until his lips are at my ear. "And you know it."

Tingles work their way down my spine, settling between my legs in a dull throb. I want to respond with a snarky comment, to tell him he's wrong. But, I can't. The words won't come. Because he's right. I am his. He pulls back slightly and I see a smug grin on his ridiculously perfect face. My eyes narrow and I mirror his actions, bringing my lips to his ear and letting them brush against the shell as I speak.

"Maybe I am yours, Aden." I feel his smile widen as his cheek rubs against mine. I run a finger down the middle of his chest until it reaches the band of his boxers, molded to his impressive (*why deny it?*) erection. I slip the finger in and tug slightly, pulling him just a little bit closer. When I feel his breath hitch, I continue. "But, that doesn't mean you get to have me." I step back and bring my hand up to, condescendingly, pat his cheek. The smile has been effectively wiped from his face. I take advantage of his momentary astonishment and quickly step around him, entering the bathroom, firmly shutting the door, and clicking the lock. Perversely, I enjoy the fact that he is stuck, waiting for a nice warm shower after having been drenched in icy water.

And this round goes to Shaylee!

Once I grab a quick shower, I step out of the tub and wrap myself up in a scratchy, white towel, barely big enough to cover my chest and ass. As I stand here, dripping onto the rug, I contemplate my circumstances. Ok, so, I didn't think things through when I huffed into the bathroom—I forgot clothes. *Nice going, airhead.*

I don't want to step outside the bathroom in my, practically nonexistent, towel. And the obstinate twit in me doesn't want to ask him for help. The practical me rolls her eyes at my stubbornness, and her logic wins out. I call out to Aden and wait for his response but am met with silence. I call again and, when there is no response, I wonder if he has stepped out.

Maybe he went to get breakfast or some other errand. I sigh in relief, that I'll be able to get dressed before he returns, and open the door.

Damn it! I stumble on my feet, when I see Aden leaning against the wall across from the door, wearing a towel wrapped low around his hips. My body reacts and I pull the towel tighter around myself, not that it does any good. His arms are folded across his muscular chest, but his stance is relaxed as he lazily peruses me from head to toe and back up. A cocky grin breaks out on his face, "Forget something, baby?"

I glare at him and he just chuckles. *Jackass.* With an obnoxious (*ok, completely sexy*) wink, he unfolds his arms and reaches down to grab the handle of my small suitcase. He lifts it easily and holds it out to me. If I reach for it, I'll lose my grip on the towel. The arrogant look on his face tells me that he is completely aware of that fact. After a second of deliberation, I come to a decision. *Why the hell not? Maybe it'll torture him just a little.* I drop the towel and grab the suitcase before spinning around and storming back into the bathroom, kicking the door shut behind me. I can hear his laughter through the door. *Next round to Aden. Shit.*

Digging in my bag, I pull out an old pair of stonewashed jeans and a black t-shirt with the words, "*You're a great friend, but if the zombies chase us, I'm tripping you.*" I have a thing for funny shirts.

I braid my long hair, quickly finish getting ready, and then step out to let Aden shower and dress. He's standing at a small table, by the front window, munching on a doughnut, still in nothing but the towel. I stifle a groan. *Ugh, why does he have to be so freaking gorgeous?* I mentally bitch slap the panting whore inside me.

I clear my throat and work to keep my voice steady, "Um, the bathroom is free." He looks up and chuckles when he sees my top. Raising his eyes back to mine, they go warm, a genuine smile creasing his face. Gone is the smug bastard from earlier and I feel my irritation melting away at the reappearance of my Aden. The sweet, fun-loving Aden that melts my heart. *Don't pretend that the overconfident asshole doesn't cream your panties.*

I pad over to the table and set my bag by the door before plopping into a chair. Grabbing a doughnut, I watch Aden as he saunters over to his suitcase and grabs some clothes. His back is to me and I take the opportunity to study him a little as he heads to the bathroom. His back is defined with sinewy muscle and there is a small tattoo on the back of his neck that I never noticed before, but I'm too far away to really see what it is. My eyes drop lower to the most incredible ass I've ever seen. *Wow.*

The towel molds to the shape and with each step, it slips a little lower, revealing those sexy dimples at the base of his spine. I bet my tongue would fit just perfect in one of those little dips. I can just imagine how tight his ass is and how it would feel in my palms while he—*oh for crying out loud, Shaylee! Can't you think of anything but sex?* I just barely keep myself from banging my head down on the table in frustration.

My attention returns to my breakfast and I force my mind from the naked temptation on the other side of that flimsy door. So much has been thrown at me in the last sixteen hours; I haven't really had a chance to process it. It's seems surreal. Faeries, magic, fallen Fae, it's all been a part of my imagination. Now I have to accept that they are a part of my reality.

Closing my eyes, I remember my dad and listen intently to what he was always telling me. I can feel the truth in his words, but there is still a part of me that wants to wake up and have this all be a dream. I wanted my life to be simple and now it is more complicated than ever. But I know, if my father were here, he would have told me to hope for the future rather than lament the past. I open my eyes and look at the sliver of sunshine peeking through the ugly, floral curtains. *What is it with these hotels? Cheap equals ugly?*

The sunshine practically calls to me and I slide the curtain back to bask in the glow. The parking lot sits open in the sun but each of the three sides of the hotel sport an overhang that shades the walkway and doors. There aren't many cars, so I'm surprised when I notice movement in the shadows across the way. But, it was only for a second. I feel a rush of heat roll through me, just for a moment, so I scan the area again—there is nothing.

The bathroom door opens and Aden steps out clothed (a good thing, I suppose) and throws everything in his suitcase. He glances at me quickly as he checks around the room for anything we might have forgotten.

"You ready to go?" he asks distractedly. He doesn't wait for my answer, just grabs the keys to the car and throws both of our bags over his shoulder. "Let's go." When he reaches the door, he stops before opening it. His eyes close and I watch, mesmerized as his skin takes on a slight glow. I'm not talking about the sparkly vampire kind of light, or the aliens made of light that you read about in books. It's more like a radiance. The way skin looks when it's out in the open, soaking up the sun. But he's standing in the shadow of the door and yet, I see the brilliance of sunlight, even in that tiny glow.

He opens his eyes, and the light recedes. I find myself feeling the loss of it, as though I've been deprived of something that makes me whole. Aden grabs my hand and pulls me close.

"We have to hurry. When I open the door, step into the sunlight as quickly as possible and go right to the car. Got it?" His voice is strained. I just nod, confused at what's got him so stressed. Finally, he opens the door and moves quickly out of the shadows, into the bright light of the morning. The beams wash over me, the heat . . . a blanket of comfort, calming my racing mind and dissolving the tension in my body. Aden's posture has relaxed too, but he still rushes me into the car. After tossing the bags in the back seat, he climbs into the car and drives out of the lot onto the open road.

He glances in the rearview mirror a couple of times, before settling into the drive. After a few miles, he slides a look over at me. "Sorry. I didn't think they would catch up with us so fast. I wanted to get out of there quickly."

"There's that 'they' again." I make air quotations around the word and infuse my tone with light sarcasm. His lips twitch in amusement and he shakes his head slowly.

"Always the smart ass." His little smirk grows into a full blown grin and I'm struck once again by his features, the way they form a beautiful face, worthy of a marble statue at the Met. His jaw is square and strong, normally very chiseled, but the scruff he's sporting this morning softens the lines. I wonder how that scruff would feel on my bare skin. The images that thought provokes cause my body to heat and I feel my cheeks burn. Before he can notice the telltale blush, I school my features into a playful pout.

"But what a fine ass it is, don't you agree?" Aden starts laughing, and I feel relief that he didn't notice my momentary lapse of hormone control.

"Baby, there isn't a part of your body that I wouldn't like to worship. That sweet little ass of yours is just the place to start," his words stomp right down on my triumph, bringing all that delicious desire rushing to the surface again. He accompanies this statement with a glance at me, not bothering to hide the inferno raging behind his emerald eyes. My mouth dries out and my tongue sticks to the roof of it, preventing me from responding. I can practically feel the fire emanating from him licking at my skin.

Just as quickly as it came, the fire is gone when he turns his attention back to the road. The blaze inside me isn't receding as quickly, so I search my mind for a distraction. Oh. Right.

"So, I'm assuming this 'they' you referred to this morning is different than the ones who assigned you to me?"

Eight

ADEN

She is clearly trying to change the topic away from us, and at first, I consider not letting her. However, there are things that she needs to know before we get to our destination.

"Just to be clear, Shaylee. Don't think you're getting out of talking about us. But, for now, I've got other things to tell you that take precedence," I inform her. She squirms uncomfortably in her seat and I'm half tempted to pull the car over and help her relax. My cock is definitely in favor of that idea, but the head on my shoulders wins the argument with the head between my legs. She gives me a jerky nod, so I focus and start to tell her about the ones who are hunting her.

"I mentioned the Ukkutae before, remember?" I see the slight movement of her head in my peripheral vision, so I continue. "They are the ones who are after you." I rush on because she looks at me with narrowed eyes and opens her mouth. Most likely, in true Shaylee fashion, she is about to interrupt. If I didn't think she was so damn cute, I'd be annoyed. "Let me explain who they are, and then we'll get to why you're running from them." Her body shifts and she settles in her seat, facing me.

"I told you before, where there is good, there is evil. Think back to the stories your father told you. The Fae are descended from fallen angels. To make up for the wickedness of our ancestors, God gave us the opportunity to escape their punishment. We're created as protectors, our ability to manipulate the elements: air, water, earth, and fire, are used in defense, all though any magic can technically be used in the wrong way. But, as a people, we are good by nature. I don't mean good in the sense that we are all perfect; far from it." I stop for a moment, expecting her to insert a sarcastic comment. To my surprise, when I look her way, she is listening intently, an enthralled look on her face.

"However, we have a sort of..." I trail off, trying to figure out how to put it into words. "A sort of failsafe, I guess? Our honesty is innate, it keeps our souls pure." I give her a little time to absorb and ask, "Am I making sense?"

"I suppose so," she mutters, clearly a little bit lost in her own thoughts. "So, you're forced to act a certain way and do certain things? Am I going to lose the freedom to be me?"

"No," I'm quick to reassure her. "Just like any creature, we have the freedom to make our own choices." I give her an playful smile, "You'll still be able to be a capricious little imp, intent on pissing me off and kicking my ass" My words have the desired effect and she chuckles, the frown that was marring her beautiful face, easing away.

"However, the effects from our choices are more severe. You see, our souls were once pure like the angels. But, the fallen fell so far out of His grace, that the Fae are held to a higher standard." I hate to tell her the next part, make her aware of the truly wicked that prey on those with a white soul. While the human realm and darker parts of Rien possess those who are swayed into joining the Fallen, they are not the source of the evil, they are puppets. Shaylee is entering into a realm where the sources of true light and dark wage war.

"Shaylee, it only takes one discretion to push you out of the sun and into the shadows." Our conversation has caused the drive to go quickly, and we have arrived at our destination, so I pull over and park the car. It allows me to face her and let her see the truth and seriousness of what I'm telling her.

"I'm talking about a lie, baby. One little lie and you will tarnish your soul." I ruefully shrug my shoulders. "Its pure irony that we refer to them as little, *white* lies. A stupid way of making light of a serious grievance." I reach over and lightly grip her chin, "Do you understand what I'm telling you?" I wait for her affirmation before continuing. "I know you, baby, and you have no temptation to lie. You were born with a beautiful soul. It's important that you understand who stalks you and why." Her eyes widen a little and her head moves back in confusion. "The Ukkutae are those who have made the wrong choices. They have stepped out of the sun and thrive on the darkness. They've adapted and are able to use their magic, but it's shifted . . . tainted. They don't wither in the darkness the way that a pure soul would. They don't exactly thrive, either. But, they survive, preferring the cold of shadows to the warmth of light. They desire to bring as many Fae, to their way of existing, as possible. They also have a council, although they rule with more authority than ours, they are handpicked by Lucifer."

I wait while Shaylee absorbs what I've told her, the information sinking into an understanding. "Last night, you were concerned about getting away before dark." I just nod, knowing she'll work it out on her own. "And, this morning, in the shadows..." Her head jerks back in surprise and I see fear flicker in her eyes. Just as quickly as it appeared, it's gone, her eyes shuttering all emotion. "They were there, weren't they? I thought I saw something but I chalked it up to my imagination."

"You are easier to track than I thought you would be. I

have my suspicions as to why, but I want to hold off on specu-
lating until we meet with the council." I sigh in frustration,
knowing what's ahead. "Most likely, they'll send us right to
Fate."

"Ok. You want to share with the class why this bothers
you? Should I be afraid of—whoever that is?" Shaylee picks up
on the obvious reluctance in my tone.

I stay silent for a moment, loathe admitting my weakness.
However, I don't want her to be afraid when there is no need.
I gaze out the window, beyond her shoulder, keeping my eyes
averted. "Honestly, Fate, well, she—she kind of creeps me the
hell out." A quick glance to my right, I see Shaylee watching
me closely. Then she starts to giggle. To my utter mortifica-
tion, I feel my cheeks heat. *What the hell, Aden? When did you
turn into a little girl?* I bite my tongue and ignore the fact that
I'm fucking talking to myself.

Done with this conversation, I button my jacket, step out
of the car, and grab our bags. Shaylee follows suit, tugging her
coat closed against the cold, and looking around at our environment. We have pulled into a small turnout on an empty,
dirt road. The sun is bright and the vast, open fields of green,
surrounding us, reflect the rays cascading down. I soak in the
power from the heat, my eye wide open, staring directly at the
glowing orb. Our hearing and sight are stronger than a
human's in any situation. However, unlike humans with light
colored eyes, the vision of the Fae is amplified by the golden
hues and sunglasses would only hinder us.

I give myself over to my magic for a minute, searching for
the unnatural, cool rush that warns me when dark power is
near. But, I only feel the warmth of my pure magic. Oddly, I
feel it surrounding me, thicker than normal, with a stronger
heat that comforts me. When I open my eyes and turn to face
Shaylee, the heat begins to fade. She is staring at me curiously.

"Why do you do that?"

I raise an eyebrow in question as I walk around the car towards her. "Do what?"

"You sort of, um—" she stops, searching for words. "Glow isn't the right word. You just have a radiance about you sometimes. Like there is sunshine in your soul."

I laugh at her description and she wrinkles her pert little nose in exasperation. "That's just it, baby. There *is* sunshine in my soul. The sun is like air to us. We absorb it into our every cell. It keeps our magic pure and our souls clean."

"Why do you only look that way sometimes? You did it earlier this morning too."

"Anytime you use your magic, the radiance of the sun will shine through you." I grab her hand and hold it out into the sunlight. Her skin takes on a little glow and you just faintly see the outline of the bones in her fingers. "See how the sun lightens your skin, you can almost see through it."

She nods and I see a small smile playing at her lips. "We used to do this all the time when I was a kid. I liked to pretend I had x-ray vision." Her smile widens as she goes on. "Dad used to say that I shined from the inside out." The sweet smile that was gracing her face begins to fade, replaced by hollow look of grief.

Using her hand to pull her closer, I wrap her in my embrace. With one finger, I lift her chin and stare into the ocean blue of her eyes. "He was always teaching you, baby. Remember those lessons with the happiness of the moment. I know you miss him, but don't dwell on what was lost. He wouldn't want that. " I place a soft kiss on the tip of her nose and then my eyes drop to her pink lips. When her tongue darts out to wet them, I stifle a groan. Damn. The little things about her turn me on. I step away before she can notice the effect she is having on my rapidly, hardening dick. Something in her eyes tells me she already noticed, but now certainly isn't the time to be pursuing that avenue. Of course, my cock is in complete disagreement with that sentiment.

She throws a look at our joined hands, but doesn't pull away. *Progress.* I throw our bags over my other shoulder and begin leading her into the field.

"Aden, what are we doing here, anyway?"

"We're headed to Rien. It is always easier to cross in a deserted area with a lot of sun exposure. Especially since it's your first time, I don't know how smooth the transition will be for you." I jerked my thumb back behind us, indicating the car, "I've got a friend who will pick up the rental and take it back before heading home." Remembering why Ean is here has me chuckling. *What a pussy.* He's kind of hiding out in the human realm for a while." When Shaylee looks confused, I can't help but chuckle again. "I'll explain another time."

As we walk through the field, I think of home (Don't even think about bringing up The Wizard of Oz) and feel warmth begin to course through my veins. But an idea pops into my head and I stop, tugging Shaylee's hand to bring her to a halt as well.

"This morning, with the water. What were you feeling?"

She rolls her eyes, "That you needed—"

"No," I cut her off mid-sentence. *Such a smartass.* "What did you feel when the water began to fall." Her face becomes a little pensive as she considers my question.

"I felt a heat rush through me, almost like the humid air of summer."

My idea takes root and I decide to flow with it. "I want you to focus on how that felt as we transition into Rien, ok?"

Shaylee glances around. "Is there a portal here or something? Do I need to grab a boot?"

Her tone is laced with sarcasm and I echo it in my response. "Yeah, Shaylee. I'm taking you to Hogwarts. Did you bring your broom?"

Her eyes widen with feigned innocence. "Hey, Faeries are real, maybe Harry Potter is too." She looks at me in earnest, and if I didn't see the laughter in her eyes, I might have believed her naïveté.

I shake my head at her, but give her a wink. "Focus, baby. Remember what that sensation felt like, and think about crossing that barrier."

"Ok." She says hesitantly. I'm still holding her hand and I give it a light squeeze before beginning to walk again. When I see her body becoming more luminous, I let go of her hand and watch her steadily. With my next blink, she is no longer there. *Damn.* She shouldn't have been able to do that on her own.

Feeling the warmth flow, I focus on the power of crossing realms and then I am there, standing next to her. For the moment, I quietly observe her to see how she is handling the transition. She's looking around her with wide eyes full of interest, but there is no hint of fear in her expression. I'm not sure what I was expecting; for her to be overwhelmed and confused, I guess. I should have known better. Shaylee has always had inner strength. She was never one to fly off the handle and make assumptions. When she hauled off and hit me, I was utterly shocked that she'd let go of her tightly reigned emotions. Just imagining what it would be like to break down those barriers and see her completely let go, in bed, has my dick twitching.

I break out of my stupor, before I get any more of a hard on, and sigh in relief when I see that she hasn't noticed where my thoughts were heading.

"Baby, we need to get going."

She turns and looks at me in surprise, and I realize she has only just noticed that I'm there. "You left me." *Shit.*

Nine

SHAYLEE

ONE SECOND, I was walking though the field—I blinked—
and the next, I am here. I stumble backwards in shock and
almost fall on my ass. When Aden doesn't reach out to help
steady me, I turn to snap at him for being rude and realize that
he's not even here. *What the hell?* I'm alone. Again. I feel the
fingers of fear begin to grip me. Had he really left me to do this
on my own? Anger starts flushing out the fear, when I'm
suddenly distracted by my surroundings. I'm standing in a
parking lot, of all places. There are a few cars scattered
throughout the stalls, and across from me is a tall, white, stone
building, sitting, at least, eight stories high. On each floor, the
walls are about seventy percent windows. The sunlight reflects
off of them, giving the building a shimmering glow. There are,
what appear to be, athletic fields on the other three sides of the
building. Looking around me, it seems pretty normal. *Did I go
to the wrong place?*

Out of nowhere, I hear Aden's voice behind me. I whirl
around, startled to find him there.

"You left me." The moment the words leave my mouth, I
want to call them back. I don't want him to recognize that,

beneath my resentment of his departure two years ago, I'm vulnerable and wary that I'll be left alone again. I'm terrified that I'll let him back into my heart and he'll irreparably break it when he decides to move on again.

The smile drops from his face and is replaced with worry and regret. Or, maybe that's what I want to see.

"I was right behind you, baby. I just wanted to see if you could do it on your own."

I'm somewhat mollified by his words, and wanting to avoid getting into anything from the past, I latch on to the last part of his explanation.

"On my own?"

Aden peers at me, clearly trying to decide whether to let me skirt around the deeper issue. He scrubs his hand along his chin, bringing my attention to the scruff that has developed there. It's so damn sexy. I want to reach out and feel it, see if it's prickly or soft. What would that feel like, brushing along my naked skin? My cheeks heat a little at the thought. *Get your mind out of the gutter, girl.* I squirm a little, as butterflies converge in my stomach and try to listen to the logical voice in my head. *Off limits. Off limits. Off limits.* Maybe if I keep telling myself that, my body will get the memo.

And maybe the Cubs will win the World Series.

Stifling a sigh, I return my attention to the matter at hand: where the hell we are and what we are doing here. I wrap my arms around my middle, trying to contain my apprehension.

He crosses his arms, enhancing the rippling muscles in them and the solid expanse of his chest. I turn back to the landscape, avoiding any more distractions from his ridiculously sexy body.

"I've never seen someone so new to their magic be able to do the things you have done. Crossing realms on your own requires control over your power. Control you shouldn't possess yet." His tone doesn't give me any hint as to whether or not this is a good thing or not. "I'm not sure what to think about it, baby, other than the fact that it's not something to be concerned over. We need to understand the situation, but you don't need to be afraid of it."

I'm slightly comforted, but everything is so full of questions that I can't help feeling the stress weighing me down. "Where are we?"

"Rien."

"No shit, Sherlock," I snide. Aden's face breaks into a smile, his delicious dimple appearing, and I'm momentarily sidetracked by the beauty of his face. Why does he have to be so freaking hot? I reign in my thoughts and get back to my question. Gesturing to what's around us, I ask, "What is this place?"

"It's our training facility. Well, one of them."

"I don't understand. Everything looks so normal."

Aden seems to pick up on the hint of disappointment in my tone and looks at me curiously. "What were you expecting?"

"I don't know." I fight a blush when I realize that my expectations were along the lines of a Disney movie.

Don't try to pretend yours weren't either.

I don't know what to say. In cases like this, the truth is the hardest for a human to believe. If I told them what I was truly looking for, they'd laugh it off. But, Aden knows that the words that come out of my mouth are my reality. *Oh, screw it.*

"I, um, you know, majestic hills, waterfalls, some castles, maybe a unicorn or two." I look him straight in the eye, pretending I'm not feeling dumb for thinking I would find myself in fantastical fairytale. *Yes, I'm aware of the irony in that statement.*

To my surprise, Aden lets out a small chuckle, but he doesn't keel over in hysterical laughter and make me feel like a child. He just uncrosses his arms and tugs on my hand, beginning to walk toward the large building. I tug my hand to get it free, but he tightens his grip and winks at me. I let out a loud sigh of frustration. He just looks ahead of him with a grin. Something inside me warms at the sight of his confident smile. *Stupid dimple.* I quickly stomp it down. *Arrogant ass.*

"We are not so different from humans. We've adapted with the times like any other generation; modern styles of clothing, and the same technologies of the human realm. The difference is—we have magic. But, magic drains you and its better saved for when it's truly needed. So, things like using electricity, rather than magic, to light a room because it's effortless." His grin turns mischievous. "That doesn't mean I don't get lazy and use my magic to flip a light switch from time to time. But, you get the point. We'll talk about the unicorns later."

He throws the last sentence in so nonchalantly that I almost miss it. "Wait—we'll talk about—" I'm cut off because we've reached the large glass doors of the structure and he pulls me inside. We're in what I suppose is the lobby, of sorts, but it looks like a giant living room. The center of the room is sunken down about three steps and is lined by brown, leather couches and a couple of recliners. Even from the door, I can see that the leather is soft and comfortable. The décor is all muted tones: creams and rich shades of brown. The walls are covered with landscapes. I stifle a laugh when I see that the portraits all depict the kind of world I'd imagined we would step into. Sparkly sunshine, green hills, and mountains with waterfalls, peppered with creatures of fairy folklore. The back wall is entirely floor to ceiling window, only broken apart by a giant stone fireplace with a massive flat screen TV, mounted above it. The whole room is welcoming and peaceful.

Aden has stepped to my left where the room breaks off into an alcove that feeds into a long hallway. Nestled in the alcove is a desk, behind which sits a perky, young woman with shoulder-length, white-blonde hair, and beautiful green eyes.

Shocker. Aden lets go of my hand and strides over to her. She jumps up from her seat and runs around the desk to throw herself into his arms. She's petite and Aden easily lifts her up in a big bear hug. A low burn churns my stomach and my fists clench at my side. I stay back, not wanting to interrupt their moment, and tell myself that I don't want to get close enough to pull her off of my man by her hair. *No. Not my man! Ugh.*

When Aden finally puts her down, he whispers something in her ear and she turns curious, but friendly, eyes on me. He motions me forward and I start in their direction, watching as her smile widens the closer I get. I finally come to a stop in front of them, and stand awkwardly, not sure what to do now. A million questions run through my head, things I have given up the right to ask, but find myself desperate to know, none-the-less. Has he dated her? Slept with her? Is she the one he replaced me with?

My musings are interrupted when she grabs my hand and pulls me in for a hug. Surprised, I am thrown off balance and tumble into the embrace. She smells like cinnamon, and her arms are warm and comforting. I feel myself softening toward her, struggling to remember why I'd been upset.

"Shaylee, it's so great to finally meet you! Aden has talked about you so much over the years, I feel like I already know you." My eyes fly to Aden, gauging his reaction. His face is sporting a lazy grin, and he winks at me. His wink makes my toes curl. The pixie releases me and steps back, keeping my hands in hers. "I'm Laila, Aden's sister." The rest of my anxiety melts away, replaced by profound relief. *Sister. His freaking sister.*

"Alright, Laila, give her some breathing room." Aden ruffles her hair and Laila throws him a dirty look, but her eyes twinkle, full of love for her brother. He pulls my hands from hers, tucking me into his side, but before I can melt into him, I stiffen and try to step away. Once again, he tightens his hold and keeps me anchored. I'm so tired of fighting him; my body is aching from the tension. I give in and cuddle into his side, telling myself I'll pull away in a minute. *Maybe...*

I'm going to get her settled and show her around, we'll meet you at Mom and Dad's for dinner tonight."

Laila nods and pulls me in for another quick hug. "We'll have lunch one of these days and get to know each other. You're already a sister to me." Just like that, the tension is back and I hastily step away from him.

"Laila," Aden warns. Her eyes bounce back and forth between us, taking in the chasm I've created.

"I thought she was—"

"She is."

Laila's face clouds with confusion, but with a small shake of Aden's head, she lets go of whatever she was going to say. "I'll see you later, Shaylee." She gives me a bright smile and heads back to the desk.

Aden grabs my hand again and I let out an exasperated sigh. He squeezes my hand to let me know he heard me, and gives me another damn wink. He guides me slightly in front of him, and places his hand softly on the small of my back, showing me the way with slight pressure. An electric current flows from the spot where we are connected.

We head down a long hallway with more fantasy paintings hung on the right side, while the left is a wall of windows. The sun streams in and warms me, and I feel the rays building strength in me. We reach a break and the hallway splits, going in either direction to our left and right. Just before it turns, there is a set of wide, tall double doors on the right. They are carved wood with small symbols, scenes, and creatures. But, in the center, they each have a large set of wings. It's incredibly beautiful and I'm mesmerized by the intricacies of the art. My hand reaches out and I run my fingers softy over the carving, reverently tracing the wings. There is something about them that tugs at my curiosity, but the full thought eludes me. "These are incredible."

"Exquisite." I turn my head to agree and see that Aden's eyes are on me, not the door. His face is serious as he studies me, naked desire emanating from his eyes, deepening the color to a dark emerald. A flush washes over me and I feel the pink of my cheeks, reddening when he reaches out and runs a finger down the side of my face. Involuntarily, my eyes close and I revel in the sweet touch. When I open them again, the intensity of his gaze has waned, but it's replaced by a softness and a smile plays at the corners of his mouth.

I seem to be lost in a fog because I'm startled when he taps the end of my nose, opens one of the large doors and gives me a chin lift, encouraging me to enter the room. I drag my gaze away from his and walk ahead of him into a gigantic, open space. The ceiling is, at least, twenty feet high. Mats cover three quarters of the floor. The rest is hardwood. Mirrors line three sides of the other room, broken up by solid walls, about three feet across, with racks of weapons anchored on them. The other wall, directly across from the doors, is made of large windows. *I sense a pattern here.*

"What is this place?" I take in the sight with awe, keeping my arms hanging at my sides, but my fingers itching to explore. There is something about this room; it's charged with power.

Aden is leaning against the wall next to the door, his arms, once again, folded across his broad chest, watching me with a knowing smile. "This is the main training room. I'll teach you to use your magic here, to protect yourself physically and with your power."

Excitement fills me and I clasp my hands in front, fighting the instinct to bounce with anticipation. Am I going to learn to use all of those?" I ask, gesturing to the walls of weapons.

"I can give you a basic knowledge of all of them, but we'll

determine where your strengths lie and give you expert skill in those. To be honest, your most important skills will be your magic and fighting without any weapons."

I can't help it; I daydream, for a second, about kicking Aden's ass...his very *fine* ass. *Oh, for crying out loud, can't you keep your mind off of his body?* Apparently, I also need to work on my self-control. The images of fighting with him morph into pictures of us rolling around on the mats, sans clothes. *When did I become so obsessed with sex?* I shake off my thoughts before I give in to my hunger and attack him.

Aden steps off of the wall and returns his hand to my lower back. Reluctantly, I let him lead me from the fascinating chamber. "I'll show you your room and you can get unpacked."

Once we exit, we turn down the right hallway and walk until we reach, what looks like, another common area. Although, this one sports game tables and other things to keep people entertained. There are three people, two men and a woman, sitting on the plush couches, deep in discussion. The room sits off to the left of us, and straight ahead is a wide stair-case. Aden puts a little more pressure, hurrying me towards the stairs and I move a little faster, but continually sneak peeks at the group. Suddenly, one of the men look up and his stunning, blue eyes meet mine. A broad smile breaks out onto his face and he jumps up, swiftly moving in our direction. Aden halts and I hear a long suffering sigh behind me, his breath tickling the back of my neck, exposed under my ponytail. The man is tall and muscular, with wavy hair that naturally achieves that sexy, messy look. His eyes are a piercing blue with laugh lines creasing the side, and deep dimples appear with his infectious smile, softening the hard lines of his jaw. Holy cow, he is yummy. But honestly, he doesn't really compare to Aden. He reaches us in no time and grabs me up in a giant hug, twirling me around.

"I'm Brannon. I've been waiting a lifetime for you, beautiful!" Despite my cautious nature, I find myself laughing at his antics. When Brannon leans back and plants a kiss right on my mouth, Aden abruptly snatches me out of his arms, tucking me back into his side with a low growl. He's glaring fiercely at Brannon who has doubled over in raucous laughter.

"Shaylee, this is Brannon," he bites out. "My *former* best friend." Aden's words cause Brannon to laugh even harder.

The other two have caught up to him now and are watching the scene with indulgent smiles. I get the feeling that they are used to Brannon's boisterous personality. The woman stands slightly apart and rolls her eyes at him. The other man is smiling, his eyes on Aden, clearly enjoying his possessive attitude. Brannon finally catches his breath and his twinkling eyes land on Aden before he steps over and pulls him in for a back pounding, man-hug. Aden doesn't let go of me as he returns Brannon's embrace and hard pat between the shoulders.

"It's good to have you back, brother. I can see why you changed your mind."

My ears perk up at his comment. I look up at Aden and ask, "Changed your mind about what?"

Aden's eyes are shooting daggers at Brannon. "We'll talk about it later, baby." He abruptly changes the subject by introducing the other man and woman.

"This is Kendrix, he's Brannon's twin brother." Kendrix steps forward and leans in to kiss my cheek, giving me a mischievous waggle of his eyebrows when he notices Aden's grip on me tighten. He's acting like a complete cave man and I give him a death glare, which he returns, but loosens his grip. Kendrix is the spitting image of Brannon, but his countenance is calmer, more laid back.

"It's great to meet you, Shaylee. We've heard a lot about you." It seems an odd comment and I'm confused. They'd heard about me from Aden? I don't have time to dwell on it, as Aden introduces me to the woman who is still standing a bit off from our group.

"This is Hayleigh." He lets go of me to give her a swift hug and kiss on the cheek. I bury down the impulse to tug him back and away from the beautiful woman. She returns his embrace, a little awkwardly, and then gives me a warm smile.

"It's great to meet you Shaylee. I haven't been here long, but I've still heard a great deal about you and I hope we'll get to know each other better." Her voice is melodious and it only enhances her striking beauty. Despite the similar coloring of everyone, our features give us a distinct look that sets us all apart from each other. Hayleigh is tall, with a willowy body that is obviously lean with muscle. Her face is flawless, angular with a straight nose and plump lips. Her green eyes are the color of freshly mowed grass, fringed with heavy golden eyelashes and a slight up tilt at the corners, giving them a cat like quality. Her hair is long, just past her waist, and it's secured by black bands, spread intermittently, down the length. She looks like a warrior and I can't help feeling a little intimidated by her strength and beauty. But, once Aden is back at my side and my irrational thoughts are behind me, I decide I like her.

"I'd like that. It would be nice to connect with someone else who is fairly new around here."

Hayleigh nods in understanding, "We can talk tomorrow and set up some time to hang out. Of course, Laila will be there too, if I didn't tell her we were getting together, she'll flay me the next time we practice together." I laugh at her joke, the idea of Laila, besting Hayleigh cracking me up. However, she lifts her brows and I realize she's serious. *Okaaaay*. She gives a slight wave and leaves.

"We'll see you another time." Aden's voice is dismissive, obviously ready to get going.

"Oh definitely, we'll be at dinner tonight. Ean's going with you, as usual." Brannon winks at me, "Ean grew up with us. He's not as good looking as I am of course, but we're all tight anyway. "I'm sure he can't wait to meet you, either," he adds in a stage whisper. Brannon's got a Cheshire cat grin on his face, and I stifle a laugh at the way he likes to mess with Aden. "See you later, beautiful. I'll work on convincing you to run away with me then." He leans in, plainly going for another kiss, when an arm reaches around me and punches Brannon in the shoulder hard enough to throw him off his balance.

"Stop touching my woman and go handle your own, Brannon." Aden's voice is hard but it lacks venom. As annoyed as he is, he is well aware that Brannon is just trying to get a rise out of him, quite successfully. Brannon starts laughing again and I hear it trail after him as he walks down the hall. Kendrix and Aden exchange a chin lift and then he steers me toward the stairs again.

Ten

ADEN

My friends are such assholes. I know Brannon is just messing with me but, apparently, I have no limit when it comes to Shaylee. Next time I get him in the training room, I'm going to beat the shit out of him. And, if he kisses Shaylee one more time, I won't wait for sparring.

I guide Shaylee up the stairs and feel relief to finally have her to myself again. We reach the second level and I take her to apartment 2B, a small studio. When we go inside, she looks around in surprise.

"This is where I'm staying? I figured it would be more like a dorm room."

I chuckle at her assumption. "You're not a child, baby. You won't be treated like one. There are apartments in the facility for those who choose to live here, mostly for the convenience. However, a good amount of them live on their own. This facility is reserved for adults, but even in the facilities, where they train the children, they still live at home." I watch for her reaction when I say, "You really are hung up on the idea that you've come to Hogwarts, aren't you?" She rolls her eyes at me and turns to walk about the room, but not before I see the pretty blush on the apples of her cheeks.

She wanders around, getting to know her surroundings, giving me the opportunity to drink her in. She's so damn gorgeous. There is a part of me that still doesn't believe I finally have her here. I didn't even realize how much I missed her the last two years. It's killing me to know I have to go slow when all I want to do is drag her back to my bed and sink into her, lose myself in her essence. I discreetly adjust myself to take some of the pressure off of my cock, straining against my zipper. *Fuck*. I don't know how much time I can give her. She moves into the light from the window and the sunlight shines through her t-shirt, highlighting her perfect breasts and flat belly. I shift uncomfortably, my cock hard as a baseball bat. *Okay, so patience isn't going to work.* I decide on a new plan, a much more enjoyable method. I know she wants me and I'm going to use it to my advantage. I'm determined to have her give in by the end of the week. Five days—I've got five days. *Stop standing here and move your ass.*

"Shaylee," I call to her. She'd moved to the bed and was going through the luggage that I'd had brought to her apartment. She lifts her head, and I crook my finger at her. She stands, facing me, and plops her hands onto her hips in exasperation.

"Aden, you need to stop ordering me around like I'm still six years old."

I laugh at her comment, but my eyes become hooded as I slowly peruse her from head to toe. "Believe me, Shaylee, I'm very well aware that you aren't my little 'Buttercup' anymore. Now, get your ass over here."

She lets out a long, suffering sigh, but obeys me. When she's standing in front of me, she lifts her brow sassily. She's so damn cute. I snake my arm around her waist and pull her with me as I open the door and move to the door right across the hall.

"What are you doing Aden? Are you giving me a choice of apartments? Because I'm really fine with the other one, any apartment is a step up from my dorm room."

As I unlock the door, I can't help responding cryptically. "I'm definitely giving you a choice of which apartment you'd like to live in . . . for now." The last words are said under my breath and I'm not sure she caught them. I open the door wide and usher her inside.

This apartment is at least three times the size of her studio. When you walk in the door, there is an open kitchen to the left, stainless steel appliances, white cabinets, and black granite counter tops. A breakfast bar separates it from the large living room that takes up the rest of the space. The right and back walls are windows, washing the room in the dimming light of afternoon. The couch is black leather, bookended with deep, cherry wood end tables. It faces a low cabinet that holds a large flat screen. There are a couple of black leather lazy boy chairs as well. There are two good-sized bedrooms down the hall as well, each with their own bathroom. It's clearly a bachelor's apartment, and until today, that's what it was.

Shaylee takes it all in before looking back at me. "This is way too big for just me." Chuckling, I turn her back around and pull her back against me, my arms tight around her waist.

My words whisper in her ear, "It's not just for you, baby. You'll have a roommate." The movement of her cheek tells me that she's scrunched up her cute little nose. Loosening my hold on her, I bring her around to face me, but keep my hands firmly on her hips. "This is my apartment."

She narrows her eyes at me, her brows dipping in an irritation. "I'll stick with my own place."

Using my grip on her hips, I pull her flush against me, letting her feel what she's doing to me. The bulge in my pants is nestled right up against the heat of her—she is the perfect height for me, fitting my body seamlessly. I wait until she's locked in my stare. "You can stay in the other apartment." Emotion flashes in her eyes at my words and I almost grunt in satisfaction when I see the disappointment before she can hide it. She wants me to fight for her. *This is going to be easier than I thought.* I bite back my smile.

She tries to back away but I put pressure on her back and bring her even closer, leaning my lips to her ear. "You can stay there until the end of the week. Then, like it or not, you're moving in here with me. You have until Friday night to accept the fact that you're mine, baby. Because, by the end of the week, you'll be sleeping in my bed." I stop for a moment to let my words sink in, biting lightly down on her lobe and I swell even more, the teeth of my zipper digging into my aching cock. I want nothing more than to haul her back to my huge bed and fuck her until she isn't able to think about anything but me. But, I'll wait. "I suppose I should rephrase that. You won't be doing much sleeping."

Her sapphire eyes widen, dilate, and catch mine. "Are we clear?" Some of the haze clears and I see the defiance growing. *Time for reinforcement.* One of my hands slips up to the back of her neck and I urge her forward, crashing my mouth down onto hers.

She immediately sinks into me, going slack against my body, bringing her hands to my biceps and holding on tight. I use the hand at her neck to tug on her curls, giving me more access to deepen the kiss. The angle also opens her mouth slightly and I take the advantage, plunging my tongue into the warm recesses of her mouth. She tastes so fucking sweet. Her body trembles again and I slide both hands down her body, grabbing her ass hard and slamming her hips into mine, making sure she feels what she does to me. She gasps at the contact and I open my mouth wider over hers, plundering and tangling my tongue with hers. Grasping her ass, I lift her and wrap her legs around my waist, keeping the contact between our legs, pressing deep into her heat. Her arms crawl up around my neck and into my hair, yanking in desperation and I growl at the bolt of lust that each tug shoots straight down to my dick.

She weighs practically nothing, but my body is on fire and I need to find my balance. I opt for the couch and move in that direction with her still curled around me, her lips making their way down my neck. I finally reach the sofa and fall back onto it, the slight bounce bringing her impossibly closer to me. My hands begin to explore, burrowing under her shirt and traveling up her back, pausing only to quickly flick the clasp of her bra. I'm desperate to feel her, to fill my hands with those heavy globes, to lick those coral buds, make them hard, suck them deep into my mouth, and hear her whimper my name. When I reach her front, I whisper my fingers along the undersides of her tits and a shiver that courses through her, causing her to squirm in my lap, the friction of our jeans painful and I swear, I almost come right here, in my pants, like a fucking teenager.

I steel myself, grasping at what little control I have and circle her nipples with the pads of my fingers, swirling around them but never reaching the peaks. Finally, I get what I was aiming for, Shaylee moans in frustration and pushes her tits forward. I want her to ask for it, to want it as much as I do, so I continue to deny her the relief she seeks. "What do you want, baby?"

She thrusts her chest forward again and I give her nipples a little tweak before moving away from them once more. Her whimper of distress is louder this time. "Tell me, baby. What do you want?" Shaylee's head had dropped back, but now she lifts it and looks into my eyes, her blue ones dark and turbulent.

"I want you to stop toying with me and suck on my

fucking nipples." It takes absolutely everything in me not to come at that moment. Hearing dirty talk from my sweet Shaylee is the biggest fucking turn on and I know I won't hold out much longer. I whip her shirt and bra off and toss them, who the hell knows where, before latching onto one of her diamond hard peaks. Her head falls back again, grinding into me, and I have to lift her slightly away, so that I can maintain some control.

Her moan of distress is my undoing and I grasp her tight before flipping her so that she is lying on the couch underneath me. I move my mouth to the other breast, not to leave that nipple neglected. Her hands are all over me, exploring my back, while one makes its way to the snap of my jeans. I grab her hand, afraid I'll lose it before I can bury myself deep, deep inside her. Having sufficiently loved on her gorgeous tits, I return to her mouth, ripe and swollen from my kisses. Another flick unsnaps her pants and my fingers dive into her soaking wet pussy. Shaylee arches her back and cries out my name. It's the sexiest thing I've ever heard, but I know it won't compare to the sound of her screaming my name as I bring her to the ultimate explosion.

"Baby, you're so fucking sexy. I—"

Bam! Bam! Bam!

"What the fuck?" Someone is banging on my door.

"Yo! Aden! Move your ass, dude! We are running late and I don't need your mom busting my balls about it."

Fuck! Fuck! Fuck!

"I forgot about dinner with my family. Ean and I usually ride together because he lives here too." Shaylee has gone stiff as a board and the desire that was swirling in her deep blues, is quickly dissipating. Her expression is confused as she glances at the door, then she wiggles a little, indicating that she wants me to let her up.

I grit my teeth at the sensations sparked by her movement.

"Baby, don't move like that. I'm hanging by a thread here." She stills immediately, but throws a harried look at the door again. "It's locked, baby." Some of the tension leaves her body, but she's still taut as she pokes me in the shoulder. I take a deep breath and move to roll off of her when I feel a push of air and fall right off the couch onto my ass. When I look up, Shaylee is staring at me in surprise.

"Oops."

Damn, I've got to teach her how to control her impulses. She jumps up and rushes to gather her clothes, doing her best to avoid any eye contact with me.

"Aden! Move your ass, dude!"

"Keep your fucking panties on, Ean!" I yell back. After a couple of deep breathes, I'm able to stand without fearing that the zipper of my jeans will leave teeth marks on my dick. Shaylee is dressed and heading for the front door, but I grab her and whirl her around, bringing our faces nose to nose. "Don't, for one second, think that we won't be finishing what we started here." Before she can respond, I spin her back to the door and smack her ass, urging her forward. She tosses back a dirty look and I give her an innocent smile, then reach around her and open the door.

Shaylee gasps and stares.

I feel a growl rumbling in my throat and grab Shaylee, bringing her back to my front and wrapping her up in my arms. Ean is leaning against the wall next to Shaylee's door, flipping his keys in circles and looking incredibly bored. He looks like a GQ model. Women practically throw themselves at him. It's nauseating. I've never cared and I feel like a pussy for being jealous now, and yet, I still hug her a little tighter, reminding her who she belongs to.

When Ean hears the door open, he pushes off the wall and looks up.

"It's about fucking time—you must be Shaylee." His eyes

have landed on Shaylee and he gives her a head to toe once over. A slow, predatory smile creeps onto his face during his perusal. He steps forward, reaching out to shake her hand, but stops when I let out an involuntary snarl. Instead of backing away, like any normal man would, Ean's smile widens, all though he does drop his hand.

"It's nice to meet you, Ean." Shaylee's voice is friendly, but I don't hear any desire and some of the tension melts from my body, slackening my hold around her. I turn to shut—oof! Shaylee's elbow digs into my ribs and knocks the air out of me, forcing me to let her go completely. Ignoring me, she walks up to Ean and offers her hand in greeting.

Ean's smile is filled with glee, which is as shocking as Shaylee's elbow to the ribs. Ean doesn't show much emotion, he's always been somewhat reserved and quiet. After he lost a charge, he retreated so far into himself, that we were afraid we'd never reach him. He's returned somewhat, but he's never completely left the guilt behind and it drives him in his job to the brink of obsession. Looking at him now, I almost see the guy I grew up with, and I *almost* decide to let him get away with his plans to dick around with me. If it were anybody but Shaylee, I'd let him have his fun. But selfishly, I don't want Shaylee to see his good side. *I'm aware of what a bastard that makes me.*

Eleven

SHAYLEE

HOLY SHIT! This guy is hot, with a capital freaking H! His blue eyes are piercing, like the color of the ocean in the sun, surrounded by thick lashes that any girl would seriously envy. His hair is longer on top with a natural, messy look that softens the angular features of his face. He's leaner than Aden, but clearly still ripped with strength. When I first walked out the door, he had a dark expression on his face. Once he saw me, though, it transformed into a wide grin and I could've sworn his teeth sparkled like a toothpaste commercial. If I wasn't so hung up on Aden (*damn him*), I'd be drooling.

After giving Aden a well-deserved elbow to the ribs for his caveman tactics, I stepped over and shook Ean's hand. I wasn't surprised when there was no current between us. For some reason, Aden and I share a connection that is electric. After our little make out session, I really can't deny that I'm going to give in to him. But, not until after I've made him wait. I don't care how petty it is, he's going to have to chase me a little longer.

Ean slings an arm around me, ruffles my hair like a little

kid, and starts walking down the hall with me, still swinging his keys in circles on his finger.

"Ean," Aden snaps, "would you get your fucking hands off my woman?"

The hallway rings with the sound of Ean's laughter, as he removes his arm from around my shoulder. Aden huffs, but stays slightly behind us, letting Ean and I chat.

"So, Shaylee, what do you see in this oaf?" he inquires.

I chuckle at his question and shrug. "What can I say? Apparently, I have a thing for overly possessive and bossy guys. Don't worry; I'll kick his ass eventually." I can almost hear Aden's smug eye roll.

"I'd like to see that." Ean's smile turns sinister. "In fact, I'd be happy to teach you a few things to take him down," he offers. I laugh lightly, but raise my brow in question as to whether he's serious. He winks at me in affirmation. I just barely keep myself from rubbing my hands together in anticipation.

We head out to the parking lot and Ean leads us to a silver Audi A5 convertible. Aden reaches over Ean and snatches the keys from his hand. "I said you could drive it while I was gone, jackass." *This is Aden's car?* I'm not sure what I expected, but a car just seems so...normal. I definitely wasn't expecting an expensive and practically new one.

Ean hops in the back while Aden puts his hand lightly on my back and guides me around to the front passenger seat. Once I'm seated, he reaches in to pull my seatbelt across, but I smack his hand. "I'm not a child, Aden; I can buckle my own damn seatbelt," I hiss. He ignores my protests and clicks the lock into place.

"You don't have to remind me that you're a woman, baby. I've seen the proof," he purrs. *Arrogant ass.* I put my hands on his chest and shove, but he barely moves. He leans in again and places a quick kiss on my lips before standing up and slamming my door shut.

Once we are all in the car, he starts it and peals out of the parking lot. *Wow, this is a nice car.* Aden maneuvers it like an expert, and watching the muscles in his forearm ripple as he works the stick shift has me pressing my legs together a little tighter to relieve the sudden ache.

It takes about ten minutes to get past the fields and into civilization. The landscape reminds me of the more affluent suburbs upstate: nice houses, yards, and cars in the driveways. However, there is something—something that is different about the neighborhood. I watch more intently, looking for that illusive trait that I can't quite put my finger on. After a few minutes, I notice that the houses are all light colors and built with lots of windows. But, what really grabs my attention are the plants. The trees are a bright shade of green with flowers that resemble magnolias, but there are bright colors bursting from the leafy foliage. Some of the trees are sporting, what appears to be, a round hanging fruit. They are also brightly colored. The grass is a similar shade of green but it—it shimmers. I squeeze my eyes shut and reopen them. *Yep, it's still shimmering. Are you freaking kidding me?*

I gaze out at the expansive lawns and everywhere I look, the vegetation is sun kissed. *Wait—everywhere?* I can feel my jaw drop when I realize there are no shadows. No shade under the big trees, no darkness cloaking tight corners, not one spot that isn't lit up by the sun.

Aden slows down and turns onto a short drive, leading to a large wrought iron gate, set into a stone wall. As we reach the gate, I feel a gust of wind and it slowly swings open, allowing us to pass through it. There doesn't appear to be a guard shack, cameras, or an intercom.

"Did you open the gate?" I ask.

Aden smirks and nods. It's ridiculous that his cocky little

smirk causes fluttering in my stomach. He's too damn sexy for his own good.

"Used the force, did ya?" I sass. "What, no one to brainwash into thinking we aren't the faeries they're looking for?" Ean snorts with laughter from the backseat, but Aden just shakes his head in exasperation.

My attention is drawn to the sprawling house at the end of the drive. It looks similar to a log cabin (a freaking *huge*, log cabin), but the wood appears to be beach wood. Pale blue shutters adorn the windows, complementing the peach hue of the washed out bark. It's two levels, but the roof peaks in the center with a large, octagonal window, which I assume belongs in the attic. The front of the house has an open, wrap around porch with tan wicker furniture scattered about in little conversation nooks.

"This place is amazing," I say with awe. "Where are we?"

"My parent's house." Aden shuts off the car and steps out, unaware that I am, all of the sudden, glued to my seat. He opens my door and reaches down to help me out. When I don't move, he leans down, brows raised in a silent question.

"Meet your parents?" I audibly gulp. For crying out loud, like I haven't had enough sprung on me the last few days? Now, I've got to 'meet the parents'? *Seriously?* I fight the impulse to take my hair from its ponytail and check my makeup.

Aden squats down to be level with me. "I told you we were coming for dinner. What's going on, baby?"

"Aden, it's a little overwhelming, you know?" I lose the battle with my hands and start smoothing flyaway hair that has come loose. Aden's eyes follow my movements, and I snatch them back down when I see him fighting a grin.

"You're nervous to meet my family, Shaylee?" His grin spreads and his emerald eyes twinkle. "You're so fucking cute. They'll love you, baby." He grabs my hands, where they were clasped together in my lap, and tugs me from the car. Standing, he smoothly pulls me into his body and squeezes me, "You ready to admit you're mine?"

I scoff dramatically and lift my chin in the air haughtily. "Don't flatter yourself, Aden. I'd be nervous to meet anyone's family for the first time."

Aden smirks at me. "Whatever you want to tell yourself, baby. But, we both know you belong to me." He's right, but I refuse to give him the satisfaction of saying it out loud. The good news is, he's effectively turned my attention from worrying that his family won't approve of me.

He takes my hand again and holds it firmly, leaving me no ability to tug it away, and leads me toward the front door. Ean is walking on Aden's other side and I peek at him, noticing that his demeanor has drastically changed. His posture is rigid and his face has hardened, it's as though he has built a wall, shuttering his emotions. Before I can comment on it, the front door flies open and Laila comes bouncing down the stairs to greet us. She heads straight to me and envelopes me in a warm hug. Stepping back, she slips her arm through mine and takes me away from Aden. He lets out a long-suffering sigh, but doesn't stop her. As we turn back to face the house, she makes eye contact with Ean, her bright smile falters for just a moment, and his posture and expression become even more closed down and rigid. A chasm of awkward seems to linger between them before she pivots back to me, walking up the steps to the door.

Laila has calmed some of my nerves with her enthusiastic welcome and the tension in my muscles ease. We enter into a white entry way with stunning iridescent marble floors. To the left is an open room with thick, white carpet, just begging for me to squish my toes in, and earth toned furniture, lit softly by the sunshine streaming in through two walls of large picture windows. There are mementos and photographs elegantly displayed around the room, radiating the comfort of home. Nostalgia overtakes me for just a second and I feel a wave of homesickness. Aden's familiar arms wrap around my shoulders from behind and I can't help melting into the comfort of his embrace. It's unsettling that he can see through me so clearly.

I shake off the melancholy mood and follow Laila down a hallway, also littered with pictures. From the similar features, I immediately know that these chronicle the lives of this family. Aden removes one arm but his other whispers down to the small of my back, eliciting a shudder. At the end of the hallway, we enter a large kitchen, resplendent with all the luxuries you could want for baking and cooking. The left and right sides have long islands that divide the space into three rooms, a dining room on the right, and a family room on the left. The space is buzzing with activity. There must be over twenty people helping in the kitchen or lounging around and talking, while several children chase each other around, before collapsing in a laughing heap on the floor. It's a little overwhelming. What truly grasps my attention, though, is the similar ages of the crowd.

A woman, who very much resembles Laila, breaks away from the group and walks to Aden with her arms wide open. He lets me go to embrace her and leans down to kiss her cheek. I can see the similarities in their looks and age, so I assume that she is another sister.

Aden turns to me with a wide smile on his face, "Mom, this is Shaylee."

I'm pretty sure my jaw just came unhinged from dropping to the floor so quickly. I'm stunned speechless and I can only imagine how ridiculous I look. *His mom?*

His—uh—mother beams at me, grabbing my hands and giving them an affectionate squeeze. "I'm Elysia." She chuckles at, what I'm sure is, a dumbfounded expression on my face. "Hearing about it and seeing it are two very different things. I can imagine this is a lot to take in," she says, patting my shoulder sympathetically. I've managed to pick my jaw up off the ground, although I am still trying to wrap my head around what I'm seeing. I simply nod. She gives Aden a reproving look, "I'm so happy to finally meet and spend time with you, Shaylee. I'm just sorry my son didn't give you a little time to adjust before throwing you in the thick of it."

Kindness and love radiate from her and I find myself reminded of my mom, slowly ebbing away some of my tension and shock. Aden slips his hand around me and settles it on my waist. As much as I loathe admitting it, he chases away the rest of my fears.

"I do have a surprise for you, though." Elysia motions for us to follow her, and she moves to the family room. We walk behind her, through the aisle created when the group parts for us. A couple sits on a plump, cerulean love seat, looking anxiously in our direction. When I'm better able to observe them, I'm stopped suddenly in my tracks. *It can't be.* My eyes are glued to the man as he stands and takes a step toward me. I close my eyes tight and prepare to see something different when I open them, but the vision doesn't change. It's like I'm staring at my father.

The man peers at me with trepidation and takes a step closer. I'm rooted to my spot and as he nears, I see a small difference in his looks; his lips are thinner and his jaw a little more angular. I consider the woman next to him and see the lips, nose, and face shape of my father. It finally dawns on me, these people are clearly relatives. *My family.* Something in my expression must convey my conclusion, because the man hastens his approach.

"Are you related to my dad?" I question. I want so much to be right.

The woman's expression brightens at the clear longing in my voice. "We're your grandparents, Shaylee."

Once again, I am stunned into silence. But, I recover much quicker this time as joy floods my heart. There is a certain amount of awkwardness as I try to fit two people who look as though they are twenty-five into the box labeled "grandparents". It's quickly forgotten when my grandfather, pulls me into a warm hug. He smells like my dad, a woodsy smell like pine trees. I melt into the comfort he offers and fight back the tears that threaten. He releases me and I'm enveloped in the arms of his wife. While I still ache for my mother, the empty space is now partially filled with the familiar comfort of family. After a moment, she releases me and, taking my hand, draws me back to the couch.

I feel resistance and realize someone is holding me back by the belt loop on my jeans. Knowing who the offender is, I turn back to Aden and silently raise an annoyed eyebrow in question. He ignores my pointed look and quietly tells me that he is going to say hello to the rest of his family. Before I can respond, he grabs a front loop and gives it a light tug, pulling me just close enough to brush my lips with a lingering kiss before pivoting and heading toward the kitchen. I watch him walk away and it's then that I notice the stares of just about everyone, in the room, are on me, but they shift back to their conversations when they see I've noticed. The sly smiles however, stay firmly planted on their lips.

That freaking jackass! He practically branded me in front of all these people, *people I don't know!* I scowl at Aden's retreating back, and then roll my eyes in defeat. Whatever . . . I can't even focus on his antics right now. I make my way to the seat next to my dad's parents and am once again presented with knowing looks—or look. My grandfather is frowning fiercely in Aden's direction. His eyes soften when they return to me and he gestures for me to sit.

To my surprise, we fall into conversation easily. Their names are Cerylia and Durin, and I'm told to call them the Cery and Pop. I can't stifle a laugh at that, and he sheepishly tells me that he overheard it in the human realm and decided he liked it. We are often interrupted by others who stop by to be introduced to me, but I don't mind. It turns out that many of the visitors are my relatives and are there to welcome me home. I learn that my father was one of eight, and I have many cousins in the area. Cery and Pop lived in another city, several hours away, but have since moved here and I am excited to get to know them. It's going to take me awhile to get used to most of us looking the same age, with the exception of the children. I expect to find myself overwhelmed at some point, but it never comes. Instead, I feel relief that I am not alone; I am surrounded by family and those who will become great friends.

Despite the many things that are new and unusual, I discover that this world is amazingly similar to the one I was raised in. Everyone has jobs and hobbies, everyday goals that are commonplace in the world. But, a big difference is that there are no separations of class. Everyone is equal and share the same resources. Aden's parents have a large house to accommodate a large family, and while a family of two could choose a large house too, they often feel more comfortable in a smaller, cozier home. Living with complete honesty means little room for being vain or jealous, although it cannot eradicate it completely. This is not the city of Enoch, lifted up to Heaven for being perfect. The Fae must earn their place by keeping the purity of their soul intact until they are given the opportunity to replace their fallen ancestors in Heaven.

Eventually, we are called for dinner, a buffet having been set up along the counters in the kitchen. When our plates are full, I'm lead to a seat where I can continue to get to know people. Every once in a while, I see Aden checking up on me, when he sees that I am not being suffocated and am enjoying myself, a warm smile comes over his face, and he returns to visiting.

Long after the meal is done and put away, the exhaustion from the last couple of days starts to weigh me down. The sun is just beginning to set, though I feel as if it were late into the night, and I wonder at being tired so early in the evening. The crowds have dispersed, and it's just my grandparents left among a few members of Aden's family. He has an incredibly large family, with nine brothers and sisters. A yawn escapes me and I look at Cery and Pop apologetically.

"The last few days must be getting to me; I'm not usually tired so early in the evening," I explain.

Cery laughs, "You must be exhausted from it all, but it's also later than you think. It's almost midnight, Shaylee." I gape at her in astonishment, "Our nights are only about six hours long. You'll get used to it, but for now, we really should get going. I prefer not to be out at night."

"Even Rien has parts that have shadows, as well as where there are none during the day, such as here in Mivo (which I learned is the name of our city), we cannot avoid them when the sun goes down," she expounds upon her comment. She must've seen the confusion on my face.

I walk my grandparents to the front door. Aden follows, but hangs back, leaning against the door to the front room. They hold me close for a moment, before Cery pulls back slightly, "We're so happy you're here, Lirimaerea." *Lovely one.* My heart melts.

Pop is studying something beyond my shoulder intently, slight frown on his face, and after a glance back, I realize that he and Aden are having a stare down. Pop breaks the connection and looks back at me.

"We don't live far from the training center. You could come and live with us, if you'd like. There is plenty of room, so you would have your own space without feeling as though we are crowding you." Their offer is incredibly sweet, but as much as Aden pisses me off, I feel safest with him. I'm about to tell them this when I feel the heat of Aden's body behind me, and I'm yanked back against his chest. His hands fall heavily on my shoulders, holding me in place.

"She'll stay at the training center." His tone brokers no argument.

"For the love of—Aden, would you let me make my own damn decisions?" I shout.

His fingers tighten on my shoulders, a warning to keep my mouth shut. *Are you kidding me?* Pop's face seems to reflect the irritation that, I'm sure, is obvious on mine. He looks ready to challenge Aden, and I decide to let him hand Aden his ass. He opens his mouth but before he can get a word out, Aden mutters, "Saliysuli." *Forever.* I'm still trying to figure out how I can understand the words from his language. But, even if I knew why, it wouldn't clear up his cryptic message to my grandparents.

At the word, their eyes widen slightly, bouncing back and forth between Aden and me, like a spectator at a tennis match. Cery's face takes on a happy glow, and I am even more confused. She places her hand on Pop's arm, and a look of resignation crosses his features. He sighs and without meeting my gaze, leans in to kiss my cheek, "We'll see you soon, Liri-maerea." Then he turns, walking through the yard, but not before throwing a warning glance back at Aden. I feel Aden nod and find myself wondering what the hell that was all about. For the last few days, I've felt like all the world knows a secret that I'm not privy to, and somehow, I'm at the center of it. At the moment, my head is spinning with all that I've dealt with, and I am too drained to try and figure it all out.

Cery gives Aden's cheek a pat and then places a soft kiss on mine. "He's perfect for you," she whispers in my ear, then dashes off to the car. I watch her leave and give a little wave as they drive off. I feel a feather light kiss on the shell of my ear and Aden's arms slide down from my shoulders to hug me close. My tired body gives in to the comfort of his embrace until I remember his ridiculous caveman act and indignation replaces the fatigue.

I pinch the skin on his arms, deliberately yanking on his arm hair. To my satisfaction, he gives a little yelp and lets me go.

"What the fuck, Aden?" I snap. "This Neanderthal bull-shit isn't going to fly with me, so you can cut that crap out right now!" My voice has risen to a shriek and I know I look like a raving lunatic, but I've pretty much ceased to care. Then I look into his eyes and realize they have darkened to a deep green, the way they look when he's got dirty things on his mind. *He's turned on by this? Oh, that's right. Dirty mouth equals horny Aden.*

I know I'm not getting anywhere, so I stomp past him, into the house, and see his mom standing just behind him. Flames engulf my face, and I want to murder Aden repeatedly for making me embarrass myself in front of her. But, she is laughing, and then gives me a wink. "Don't let him get away with it, honey. Our men can get way too big for their britch-es," she whispers conspiratorially. I grin at her as she walks back to the kitchen, still chortling.

I give Aden the silent treatment on the way back to our apartments. I'm too damn weary to deal with anything else today. The sun has almost completely disappeared from the sky and the horizon is painted in brilliant shades of color, more than I've ever seen on any rainbow. The colors are muted by the night, but somehow, they still contain vibrancy in their pigment. It entrances me and I barely notice when Aden parks the car, until he holds my door open, reaching in to help me out. I grasp his hand and allow him to guide me from the car, then inside, through the building to the doors of our apartments.

Aden leans his back against the wall and grasps my waist, bringing me close until I'm standing within the V of his legs, cradled to his chest. I give in for the moment and snuggle into his heat. He kisses the top of my head, then my forehead, each of my eyes, my nose, and finally, brushes a sweet kiss across my lips. Tucking me back into his chest, he sets his chin on my head and exhales a sigh. "I'll try to rein it in." My eyes fly up to his and although I know the words coming from his mouth are sincere, I see it blatantly in his eyes and all my irritation recedes.

His eyes probe mine, and I see the desire lurking in their depths as well. "Despite your stubborn resistance to admitting it out loud, we both know you're mine. Body, heart, and soul, we belong together. You're also mine to protect, Shaylee, and I can't do that if I'm not there. I need you with me like I need air to breathe, baby."

My lungs are choked with emotion at his words. I want to let go and fall into him completely, but my wounds are still a little raw and I need time for them to heal. I lift my eyes and contemplate what I see in the green jade staring down at me.

"I'm not ready, Aden. I'll stay close and let you protect me. But, I'm not ready to open up my heart and soul to you. I don't think I can survive having it broken again." I place my finger on his lips to keep him from protesting. "Give me time."

He studies me, searching my face for something, and I know he wants to continue the discussion. My insides uncoil with relief when he brushes his nose against mine and releases me. "Go, baby. Get inside before I throw you over my shoulder and spend the night convincing you. I'll meet you in the training room around ten in the morning." He nods toward the door. I back away slowly, open my door, and duck inside. As I close it, I look out again and see Aden watching me longingly. "I'm serious, baby, shut that door right now or you'll be spending the night without any sleep." I shake my head in mock exasperation, but grin at him as I shut the door. I lean heavily back on it and my body slides languidly down to the floor. I hear a thump and the sound of fabric rustling. My lips curl up when I realize that Aden is sitting as I am, on the other side of my door.

Aden's voice is muffled when he groans, "You'd better lock the fucking door, Shaylee." A giggle escapes my mouth as I stand and flip the lock before I walk away.

Twelve

ADEN

My lungs are burning, my legs are screaming, and every inch of my body is dripping with sweat. But no matter how many miles I run, I can't wipe Shaylee from my mind. She consumes me, day and night. I've never wanted anything in the last seventy-six years like I want her. I don't just crave her body either, although I've had a permanent semi since the moment I saw her again. I want it all. I want her to give me her body, her heart, her perfect soul.

No matter how many miles I run, I can't get away from the fact that I've already given her all of those things. She fucking owns me, and I can't out run the reality of it. So, it's time for a game plan. I meant what I told her yesterday, she's got until Friday. If she thinks I'm going to give her space, she's out of her mind. I'm going to do everything I can to sweep her off her feet, and bring her to the brink of desire, so she is begging me to satisfy her need.

I hit the cool down button and take my speed down to a slow jog. Brannon hops onto the machine next to me and looks me up and down.

"You look frustrated." His voice is anything but sympathetic. A knowing look enters his eyes and I can see that he is fighting a smile. *Asshole.* "Shaylee must be living in the other apartment." I know he's being a prick on purpose, so I just grunt a response, refusing to take the bait. Brannon gives in to his laughter, but wisely turns to his treadmill without comment and begins his workout. I slow down to a walk, and then hop off the machine after five minutes. Grabbing a towel, I give in to my childish side and whip it right at Brannon's ass. He yelps (like a little girl) and stumbles, making me double over with laughter, before I give him a jaunty salute and make my way to the locker room and the showers.

At a quarter to ten, I head to the training room and get out the necessary items to begin Shaylee's training. Out of the window, I can see others training on the fields, and I'm grateful that this space is almost empty. Laila is coaching a sparring match between two teenage boys, at the other end of the room, and gives me a wave before focusing back on her students.

Laila chose to become an instructor after a decade or so in the Mie'Lorvor. She wanted the real world experience, but decided quickly that she preferred to "get to the good part", as she puts it. Most people underestimate her because of her size and short time in the field, but that just means they'll get their asses handed to them that much harder. She's one of the most powerful instructors at the facility and uses their ignorance to gain respect. Watching her take down an arrogant, know-it-all student is one of my favorite spectator sports. If I could sell tickets and popcorn, I'd make a fortune.

As I'm laying down footwork tape, I hear Laila call out a greeting. Setting the tape aside, I stand and turn toward the entrance, noticing that the boys have stopped practicing and are gawking at the door. I roll my eyes at their lack of focus and move my gaze to see what has their attention and stop dead in my tracks.

Oh, fuck no.

Shaylee is striding toward me, dressed in tight black running pants, molded to every muscle in her legs and showing off her spectacular ass. The straps of her purple top cross at the back of her neck, come down from behind and wrap around the front, just below her tits, before hooking in the back. The straps and support from the sports bra lift her generous tits up high and show off just enough cleavage to have every male mouth in the room filling with saliva. Way too much of her smooth, creamy skin is exposed. Before she reaches me, I hurry over, grab her arm, and lead her back out the door.

"Change. Now." I demand tightly, my jaw grinding. She was startled by my reaction a moment ago, but at my words, her eyes narrow and her lips pinch in defiance.

"No." She raises an eyebrow, waiting for my response, but when she folds her arms under her chest, I'm distracted by the plump flesh on display. The distraction just makes me that much more determined to get my way. Not to mention how difficult it would be to train her with a fucking hard on.

"Shaylee, don't push me." I warn. "Now get your ass upstairs and put on some clothes."

She inhales sharply and her blue eyes turn stormy, fury swirling in their depths. She can get as angry as she wants; I'm not going to budge a fucking inch. She must see the determination in my eyes because eventually she lets out a huff before spinning around and stomping down the hall.

"Hurry it up." I call. "And, leave the pout at the door, Buttercup." I hear a higher pitched shriek of frustration from around the corner and her clomping gets louder. That's when I notice ground trembling in time with each of her irritated little steps. Holy fuck, that girl needs to learn to control her power or every time she has a snit, we'll be staring down world destruction. I shake my head in exasperation and almost laugh at her childish attitude. *Almost.* I'm too busy trying to lose the damn tent in my shorts to think about anything else.

WHEN SHAYLEE RETURNS to the training room, she still has on the pants that fit like a second skin, which I'm not overly happy about. However, she'd put on a grey t-shirt with a Tinkerbell graphic on the front and, as she walks by me, I see that it says, "*I'm the happiness fairy. I just sprinkled happy dust on you. Now smile. This shits* expensive." My head flies back as I laugh so hard, my stomach begins to ache. I pass by her and give her a light swat on the ass, "That's more like it."

Shaylee halts and gets up in my face, "Did it occur to you that I didn't't pack my bags, Aden?" she hisses as her cheeks turn a little pink. "Most of my workout clothes are ridiculously skimpy."

This time, when I start laughing, I double over, barely able to stay on my feet. Her mother packed those clothes? Damn, Shaylee comes by her sassiness honestly. Shaking my head, I refrain from comment and just take her hand, leading her to the room with the cardio machines. At least, I'll be able to focus a little more with her new attire.

I start her off with a warm up on the treadmill and am pleasantly surprised to see that she's in good shape; her endurance is pretty strong. While she runs, I start off with the typical lectures on defensive techniques. It turns out, she has taken self-defense classes, which means, I don't have to start from the beginning and we can move faster. I also explain how we are going to train, spending the majority of our time on the physical aspects right now, but then, we'll incorporate her abilities more and more.

"You've got to pay a little more attention to your emotions, babe," I warn, remembering her little fit in the hallway. Defense is about awareness, knowing what options your opponent has and what you need to do to protect yourself. Your magic is a tool and inadvertently using your abilities without control could get us both hurt.

Hopping off the treadmill, she nods, "I'll try." Then she shrugs, "Just try not to piss me off."

Choosing to ignore her barb, we make our way back into the training room. For the next several hours, we concentrate on reviewing her knowledge of footwork and self-defense moves. I'm impressed with how fast she picks it up, and even more with her focus and determination to learn. She left the smartass in the other room and is genuinely open to what I'm teaching her. *Mostly.*

"Shaylee, keep your hands up," I chide for, at least, the twentieth time. Her eyes shoot daggers at me but she lifts her hands to her face once again. Sweat is dripping off her skin and I'm amazed that I'm able to keep my mind off of the way it molds her clothes to her every curve.

I've kept her in constant movement since the moment we began and I can see she is getting tired. But, I want to find her limits, to see just how hard I can push her. So far, my girl is already proving herself a force to be reckoned with. I've got her running footwork drills along tape lines, when her concentration is interrupted by the presence of someone behind me.

"Shaylee, concentrate! " I bark at her. She rolls her eyes and stops the drill to walk forward, smiling at whomever has arrived. I turn to glower at the person and see its Hayleigh. She's covered in sweat and mud; she must have been training out in the field. She nods a greeting at me, but turns to Shaylee with a full smile. Some of my irritation eases at the sight. I want Shaylee to be comfortable here and honestly, it's nice to see Hayleigh look a little less serious for a change. She transferred here from another city a couple of years ago and it was immediately clear that she was jaded by her past and looking for a fresh start. She's softened over the years, but she still wears a cynical shell that keeps her wary. Brannon was taken with her from the moment he met her, but damn, she is leading him on a not-so-merry chase.

Shaylee pulls her into a hug and she stiffens but to my complete astonishment, she doesn't pull away and after a moment, returns the embrace. I guess I shouldn't have been shocked; Shaylee has always had the ability to draw people to her.

Pulling back, Shaylee grabs Hayleigh's hands, "Please tell me you're here to save me from this torture," she pleads. Hayleigh laughs and I roll my eyes at her exaggerated description.

"Unfortunately, I just stopped by to see if you're free Friday night. Laila and I are vegging out with junk food and chick flicks." I open my mouth to tell her that Shaylee will be with me, but shut it just as quickly. I want her to find her rhythm here, so I'll give her the evening with the girls. I watch her face and see the tiny, but triumphant, smile when she steals a glance at me out of the corner of her eye. She thinks she's beat me at my game, and I let her, keeping my face carefully blank. *Yeah, we'll see who wins on Friday night.*

"Since you're not here to spring me, I'll take you up on it and demand that our night include boat loads of chocolate." They both giggle and Hayleigh agrees to her terms. She takes off for the showers and Shaylee turns to me with a beseeching pout on her face. "Let's take a break, Aden." She falls to her knees and then down on to her back, sprawling across the floor.

We've been at it for several hours. I was about to give her a break and get some food, but I decide to mess with her. Walking over to her, I put a foot on each side of her torso, lean down, and give her a stern face. "Suck it up, Buttercup. We've got work to do." Shaylee's eyes narrow at the patronizing nickname and before I know what's hit me, she brings up her left foot and pushes into the back of my opposite knee. Normally, I would be able to catch my balance, but just then, I feel a light push. I tip over to her right and she rolls left, just missing being crushed by my weight.

I twist in my fall and land on my ass, chagrined at being taken off guard by her. That's the second time she's used the air to give me a shove. The first time was an accident, but my instincts tell me that she's getting a feel for it and this time, it was quite deliberate. My brow furrows in irritation as I observe her clutching her stomach and shaking with laughter. *Damn.* My one saving grace for my pride is that none of my boys were here to see it.

THE NEXT FEW days are crammed with hand-to-hand combat training. Fae are protectors by nature, so physical and magical defense are mastered in a very short timeframe. The half Fae trainees should be at a disadvantage from the Fae who have grown up in Rien, having been training since they were teenagers. However, after their marking, the leath leanbh have a window of time where they are able to absorb all of the knowledge they've missed at an amazing rate.

Shaylee is excelling even faster than I expected and we'll be able to begin working on bringing her magic into the mix. For the most part, she's been able to control her abilities and we've avoided any major catastrophes. Though, it certainly wasn't without incident. Like the time I called her "Buttercup", knowing it would piss her off, since I was basically telling her to stop acting like a child. I've found that works well to make her mad enough to really focus. Except, if looks could kill, I'd be dead and buried. When the hole in the ground opened up beneath me, I just barely caused a stiff wind to blow back and keep me from falling. *Damn, that was hot. Artic shower tonight buddy.*

Her slip drills, bag and mitt work, and overall technique have become stellar. Her body, though already in great shape, has become leaner and stronger. Then every evening, after we finished up, she'd hightail it to her apartment and practically hide from me. Though, I know she is spending some time with Laila and Hayleigh and glad she is fitting in so seamlessly. Finding friends and, hopefully, making this home.

I'm not going to bullshit you; I fucking miss her. And, it doesn't help that I spend my days with my hands all over her while we train. It takes all of my effort not to let my restraint go, when we fall to the mats, and fuck her on the floor of the training room. But, I let her have some space, holding onto my patience with cold showers and the reminder that Friday gets closer every day.

I haven't let her get away from me completely, though. I left a bouquet of her favorite flower, bluebell roses, on her bed one night, knowing it would bring her a little comfort of home, since they don't grow in Rien. I put a box of animal crackers on her table to remind her of the zoo. My favorite moment was when I left a stuffed unicorn, prompting her to remind me of our first day here when she mentioned them and I told her we'd discuss it another time. She wasn't super happy about the fact that I was just messing with her and that we don't, in fact, have unicorns (where humans conjured up that piece of folklore is beyond me...). I swear, she almost looked disappointed.

To my relief, it's Friday. *You mean to your dick's relief. Ok, that too.* Shaylee has been sending me speculative glances all day, not surprising considering the heated looks I've been sending her way. I can't seem to stop devouring her gorgeous body and making a mental list of all the things I'm going to do to her tonight. It takes every thread of my control to concentrate on training her, but somehow, I get through the day.

Once we put away the equipment, she walks past me toward the exit, avoiding my gaze.

Nice try, babe.

My arm sneaks out and hooks her around the waist, pulling her up against me, her back to my front. I feather a kiss on the shell of her ear and smile into her hair when her breath hitches and I feel a shiver race through her. I knew the sexual tension this week hadn't been one-sided, but feeling the tension coiling her muscles, I realized that she is every bit as wound up as I am.

She is the perfect height to mold our bodies flawlessly together. But, I still have to lower my head to brush more soft kisses along the sides of her neck and nip at her earlobe. I inhale deeply, her lavender scent surrounds me, and her skin tastes like sun kissed strawberries, making my mouth water.

"I know you're aware of what day it is, baby." I'm practically purring. She turns her head to face mine, her eyes wide, trying valiantly for an innocent look. I almost smile, but manage to keep my smoldering expression, letting her feel the burn of how much I want her.

"I've got plans with the girls tonight." A twinkle appears in her eye. *This ought to be fun.* She's ready to be mine, I can see the acceptance lurking in the cobalt depths, but she's not quite done making me chase her.

"I haven't forgotten." My right hand slides back from her waist and slips down to give her ass a strong squeeze. "Just remember where you're sleeping tonight." With that, I give her another squeeze and let her go, spinning around and walking swiftly to the locker room door. I've got a plan. Reaching into my bag, I text Brannon and Kendrix, enlisting their help. They agree with some good natured grumbling, particularly about Ean getting out of it since he is off on assignment. Giving myself time to get cleaned up, we agree to meet in thirty minutes.

There is a very good chance that Shaylee will be pissed, but I'm confident in my tactics of persuasion. I might even decide to punish her for making me suffer all week. The thoughts running through my head have my cock perking up. *He's definitely liking where this is headed.*

Thirteen

SHAYLEE

I PRACTICALLY RUN out of the training room, booking it for my little studio and my standard post-training, cold shower. I don't know how I got through this week; I've been like a damn cat in heat. I have no freaking control over my body where that man is concerned. Luckily, the sessions were intense and I was able to put all of that excess energy into my training. But when I got home in the evening? Not so much.

My dreams weren't helping either. They were dirty and hot as shit! I had no idea I was that creative. I always woke up in the middle of the night panting, just on the edge, but never falling off of the cliff. Waking in the morning, feeling frustrated and unsatisfied, seriously ramped up my bitch-o-meter. On top of that, I woke feeling dark, as though I had been cocooned in the obscure blackness and I needed to peel the shadows off of me. There was something about that sensation that seemed vaguely familiar. But, in the morning, the sunshine washed it away and I didn't think much about it.

Arriving at my apartment, I stripped and stood under an ice cold shower until the heat raging through my every cell calmed down. My hair is almost completely straight and won't hold much curl, so I let it air dry, not caring much about the little bit of wave. I slip on a pair of black yoga pants, forgo a bra in favor of a thin camisole and an oversized t-shirt that slips off of one shoulder (not ALL eighties fashions are hideous). I have a thing about funny t-shirts and this one has a unicorn with the quote, "*Maybe, we don't believe in* you. "

Finding my stash of chocolate in the freezer, I lock my apartment and dash down to the elevator, punching twelve, heading to Laila's place. The door is open when I get there and Hayleigh waves from where she is already sprawled out on the floor, in front of a big, flat screen. Laila's apartment is laid out similar to Aden's, though it's only one bedroom. However, it's splashed with bright color everywhere. There are so many colors, it should look overwhelming and tacky, but Laila has an unbelievable eye, having mixed them all together just right so that the end result is cheery and comfortable.

I toss Hayleigh the bag of chocolate that I brought and swipe the bowl of Carmel Corn, before plopping onto the lemon-yellow sofa. Laila strolls into the kitchen and brings a pizza box and napkins over, then goes back for a bottle of wine, glasses, and a corkscrew. She opens the bottle, pours us each a glass, then takes a seat next to me on the couch. I'm about to ask what we are going to watch when I notice they are both staring at me expectantly.

I look back and forth at them for a minute before asking. "What?" Maybe, if I pretend I have no idea what they are talking about, they'll let it go. *Fat chance.*

Laila rolls her eyes, "Don't play dumb, Shaylee. If you didn't want us to pester you, you shouldn't have told us about Friday."

Yes, you should have known better. What were you thinking, idiot?

"Laila, do you really want me to talk to you about what your brother is most likely going to be doing tonight?" I quip.

Laila's face scrunches up in disgust and I feel just a little better having inflicted the discomfort. *Bitch-o-meter is nearing its limit.*

"Ok, so maybe you can leave out the details—"

"I want details!" Hayleigh interrupts, waving her hand in the air like a school child.

Laila gives her a dirty look before turning back to me, "I was just wondering what you've decided to do."

"I'd love to pretend that I'm not going to give in, but I think all three of know the reality, which is, that I'm crazy about your stupid brother," I offer. Laila claps her hands in excitement and I glower at her. Or at least, I try. But I can't hold on to the attitude and I feel my expression transform into a glowing smile. "I suppose it's time to put us both out of our misery."

"And the rest of us," Hayleigh mutters. I raise my eyebrow at her and she gives me a cheeky smile. "Come on, Shaylee. The sexual tension between you guys is palpable. We were all waiting for the day when you guys would snap. I don't know how you kept it up; it was exhausting just to watch." All three of us dissolve into laughter.

Laila reaches over and hugs me tight, "You're good for him, Shaylee. You're destined to be together forever and I'm thrilled that it's you."

"Destined? I don't know about that." I respond. She gives me an odd look and I can't help but feel like I'm missing something—*again*. But, I go on with the rest of my thought, "As for forever, only time will tell, I guess. The best I can do right now is give us a shot, while making sure I don't let him break my heart again."

Laila studies me for a moment more. "You and Aden need to have a serious talk. He has things he needs to tell you." She holds up her hand when I open my mouth to comment. "It's not my place, girl. You need to work it out with him. I'm only telling you so that you don't let him get away with avoiding it. So, just ask him about it."

I want to pester her for more details, but in the short time I've gotten to know Laila, I've learned that she is made of steel. She doesn't bend. I give her a jerky nod and swallow my desire to interrogate her.

There is a tense silence for a moment, before Hayleigh jumps up and grabs a DVD. "Oscar?" Laila and I set the tension aside and cheer in the affirmative. Having been on the guard for so many years, both Laila and Hayleigh are familiar with entertainment from the human realm, and it brings me a little bit of comfort to sink into a world that is more familiar to me for a few hours.

THE SUN IS FINALLY SETTING when we finish our second movie, which means it's going on one o'clock in the morning. And that in turn means, no more procrastinating. I hate that I'm so nervous, but it's a huge step to accept a relationship with Aden, to make myself so vulnerable and on top of that. Though he doesn't know, he's about to be my first. I was never into casual sex and my only, somewhat serious, relationship was with Killian. We'd gotten close a few times, but I'd never gotten comfortable enough with the idea to go all the way with him.

Laila, Hayleigh, and I trade hugs and then I take the long walk back to the elevator and my apartment. I reach my door and stand there for a moment, considering. Is he waiting for me to show up, expecting me to knock on the door and announce my arrival? Or maybe he fell asleep. I'm not sure which idea I'm rooting for. Finally, I chicken out and grasp the doorknob to my studio, inset the key and twist. The key doesn't move and the mechanisms don't click.

Stupid doors. I try it again, with the same results. *What the hell?*

My eyes wander over to Aden's door, narrowing as an idea forms in my head. *He wouldn't. What am I thinking? Of course he would. The bossy jackass.*

I march over to his door and raise my hand to knock, but change my mind and I try the doorknob. Unlocked. The door swings open and Aden looks up from where he is lounging on the sofa, in sweat pants and shirtless (he's so damn sexy), watching a sports channel. He's got a half smile lingering on his face, but I can see the wariness in his eyes.

"Hey, baby."

I'm instantly fuming at his nonchalant tone.

"Don't you 'hey, baby' me, you overbearing jerk!" I scold, marching over to him. "You locked me out of my apartment?"

Aden's damn dimple appears and I can see him trying to hold in a triumphant grin. "Baby, we talked about this. It's not your apartment anymore, so they changed the locks." He sits up on the couch, shaking his head at me in mock disappointment, as though I've simply forgotten.

I move closer and am standing right in front of him so that I can lean down and bring our faces level, "Don't patronize me, Aden. Did ever occur to you that had you asked me to move over here tonight, I might have agreed? Besides, how am I going to get all of my things with the locks changed?" A sheepish expression creeps onto his face for a few seconds, before he wipes it away and replaces it with a self-satisfied grin. Suddenly, it dawns on me. "You moved me in already, didn't you?"

Aden's hands shoot out, grabbing my hips, and with a strong tug, I fall forward and end up straddling his lap. I want to stay angry with him, but when he slides his hands down my arms, and lifts them so I'm circling his neck, warmth starts to blossom between my thighs. The muscles in his chest ripple with each movement, distracting me from whatever the hell we were discussing. He rests his hands loosely on my hips and leans forward to brush his nose against mine and the warmth starts to spread.

"I just figured I'd make things easier on you because now it's all done and you don't have to worry about moving. See?" He gives me a hopeful, boyish smile and I have to try and remember why I'm mad.

His hands grip my hips a little tighter, the boyish smile dissolving into a hungry look, turning his eyes a turbulent shade of emerald. Staring deep into my eyes, he watches me as he pulls me tighter against him, so that I can feel him hard and pulsing, pressing into me. "No more bullshit, Shaylee. Who do you belong to?"

I'm guarded about Aden breaking my heart again, but I'm so tired of carrying around the hurt and trying to deny the connection we have. In that moment, I decide to let the hurt go.

"Yours, Aden. I'm completely yours."

My admission seems to break open the floodgates and we come together with a fierce intensity, our mouths crushed against each other, our hands roaming everywhere. I can't seem to get close enough and I tug on his silky hair, encouraging him to deepen the kiss. Our tongues collide, rubbing and playing, thrusting in and out, desperate for each other.

Eventually, we have to pull away and catch our breath, but I'm still panting heavily as Aden moves from my lips and trails scorching kisses down my neck. My head falls back to give him better access and suddenly, I'm falling backward. My eyes fly open and I realize that Aden has lowered my torso, holding me firmly under my shoulders, so that he can continue to trail his mouth down until he reaches my breasts.

He looks up at me through his lashes and his eyes are dilated with his feverish arousal, the mossy green irises are just a sliver ringing the dark orbs. "You're so damn beautiful, baby." His words bring a rush of heat to my pussy, soaking my panties. He takes a hand from behind me and runs a finger along my collar bone, between my breasts, and tugs the fabric of my shirt down. The thin, cotton camisole I'm wearing underneath does nothing to hide the rigid points of my nipples. Under Aden's ravenous gaze, they tighten even further in diamond hard peaks. Slowly, he dips down and takes one into his mouth, sucking lightly. The sensation makes me squirm, and he growls from the friction of my pussy against his cock. He releases the nipple and then blows lightly on the wet fabric molded to my skin. *Holy shit.* My body wants to move but at my first shift, Aden pulls me up abruptly and wrapping my legs around his waist, stands and walks swiftly towards the back bedrooms.

My mouth is itching to taste him, so I lower it to his neck and run my tongue along the corded muscle before sucking. My back suddenly hits the wall and Aden slams his mouth down over mine. His tongue plunges into my mouth with the same rhythm as his cock rocking into my pussy. Every thrust has me whimpering, the sensations climbing, reaching for a pinnacle. Holding me tight against the wall with his hips, Aden breaks the kiss as his hands come up and roughly pull my shirts up over my head.

He returns to my mouth and when our heated skin meets, I moan, closing my eyes and savoring the feel.

Aden pulls back and when I open my eyes, he stares deeply into them, asking the question. He's giving me the power to say no and the gesture only fuels my need for him.

"I need to fuck you, baby. I need to bury myself inside of you . . . truly claim what's mine. But, I don't want you to give yourself to me because you're caught up in the passion. I want you to make the decision with no regrets. I'll wait, Shaylee. I'll wait until you're ready."

There is a barely leashed desire under his words and if he's half as desperate for me as I am for him, then those words gutted him. And in this moment, the wall I erected around my heart is obliterated; my love for him comes rushing in, surrounding me, and filling my soul with light.

I cup his face in my hands and place a gentle kiss on his lips, "I need you, Aden."

Hi forehead meets mine and his eyes shut tightly, his breath whooshing out. "Thank fuck."

I need to tell him. I know it won't bother him, but I'm nervous. I don't want to disappoint him with my inexperience. His hands slide under my ass and he continues down the hall until we reach the last door. Once inside, feelings of peace and comfort wash over me. He kicks it shut and strides over to the huge bed on the wall to the left of the door. The room is everything that is Aden: warm colors, and strong, bold lines. The bed is bigger than a king, making it comfortable for someone Aden's size. The platform bed is black/brown wood, carved with similar images as those on the doors to the training room. The headboard is smooth and empty with the exception of the word "Saliysuli" carved in script. A matching dresser adorns the far wall, with a beautiful writing desk set next to it. On the same wall as the entrance to the room is another door. Its wide open and I see a massive walk in closet that makes me drool almost as much as Aden.

The bed faces a wall of windows that looks over endless land, showing off the twinkle of each star at night, and I can only imagine the way they flood the room with sunshine during the day. Between the bed and windows is a cream sofa that looks soft and inviting, a place to snuggle and watch a sunrise.

This room was made for us. Not him, not me, but for us.

Aden reaches the bed and gently lowers me onto the mattress. Reverently, he begins to remove each piece of my clothing until I am completely bare for him. I've always been comfortable with my body, but beneath his gaze, I feel exquisite.

He stands back and begins to undress. I want to do it, but I am too enthralled by every bit of his body being revealed to me. When he pushes down his gray boxer briefs, his cock springs free—hard, long, and thick—jutting up against his stomach. My breath catches and my mouth waters at the sight. I experience a moment of apprehension wondering how the hell that thing is going to fit, but I'm distracted by his hand when if wraps around his length and pumps it twice. The silky looking skin stretches even tighter as his cock grows just a little bigger.

He prowls toward me and our eyes meet, consuming one another. Aden climbs onto the bed and oh, so slowly, lowers his body until he is covering me from head to toe. The moment our feverish skin connects, he shudders and lets out a guttural groan, burying his face in my neck. "Fuck, baby. You feel better than I could have ever imagined." I can only nod in agreement.

His pelvis settles over mine and he grinds his hips into me. I'm so wet, his cock slides through my heat, shooting unbelievable sensations from my pussy, making my toes curl. The feel of that hardness, at my entrance, reminds me that I need to tell him about my virginity.

"Aden?" He freezes at the hesitancy in my voice.

When he lifts his head, his eyes are full of worry and he's holding tightly to his control. "Are you all right, baby?" The caring in his tone just heightens the intimacy of the moment and I fall just a little harder.

"I, um—" I stutter, not quite sure how to say it. So, I just blurt it out. "I'm a virgin."

I watch anxiously for his reaction, the initial shock in his expression, making my heart skip. But, immense relief courses through me as his face transforms into a bright, beautiful smile. "You're a virgin?" I nod in affirmation.

"Baby, that's amazing. You were fucking made for me and knowing that there will only ever be me is like handing me the sun." There is a wonder in his voice that is so beautiful to me. It makes me feel loved and I pray that Laila was right and Aden is in love with me. Because, I've fallen too far; everything I am, everything I have . . . I'm his.

Aden draws my thoughts away when he gives me a deep but gentle kiss. "We'll go slowly, ok? This first time—I wish I could keep it from hurting." His eyes are soft and he traces my mouth with his finger, waiting for me.

"Aden, I'm ready. I—" I shut my mouth abruptly. *Shit.* I almost told him I loved him. I can't, not until I know he'll say it back. "Make love to me." He studies me for a moment more, and I know he noticed my halted response. But, he seems to set it aside for the moment and instead, he places a kiss at the corner of my lips, then moves down my neck to the valley between my breasts. The kisses become hot, open, and wet, until he comes to one of my rose-colored nipples and runs the tip of his tongue around it, avoiding the distended peak. My back arches, my body tremoring. He circles again but this time, he runs his tongue over the tip, and then sucks it into his mouth. The tight pull of suction sets off sparks in my pussy and my legs tangle restlessly against his.

He sucks and laves at both breasts until I feel like I'm going to splinter apart from the tight coiling in my belly. With one last pull, he lets my nipple go with a pop, and lifts up for a deep, bone-melting kiss. "You taste sweet, like strawberries. But, I'm betting that you taste more like honey and sugar in other places." He gives me a sexy little wink and returns to his exploration of my body, going lower and lower. When he reaches my belly button, he flicks my little charm with his finger and chuckles. "So fucking cute."

Each kiss takes him down, closer to my center, and I can feel each beat of my heart in the pulse between my legs. Finally, he kneels between them and admires the view. I want to squirm under his perusal, but I can see the naked appreciation and it bathes me in desire. Slowly, he drags a finger between the lips of my pussy and when he pulls it away, its slick with my arousal. Bringing his finger to his mouth, he sucks it clean, "Mmmm. Like I said, sugar." Another shiver courses through me. Aden smirks when he notices how his words affect me. "My girl has a dirty side. I noticed that before, the dirtier I talk —the hotter you get." I feel a flush on my skin, a telling blush that makes him chuckle. "I love it, baby. I think it's hot as fuck."

This time, the flush has nothing to do with embarrassment. "Aden." I'm begging, but I don't really understand what it is that I'm craving. He anchors one of my legs on each shoulder and then slides his hands under my ass, lifting me high. His eyes find a spot inside my left thigh and he places a tender kiss there. I'm confused at our position until he brings my pussy to his mouth and flattens his tongue before licking from bottom to top. He swirls it around my clit, careful to avoid it before returning, where he plunges it inside of me making me cry out. He repeats the process until I'm once again coiled so tight, I feel as though any moment I will shatter into a million pieces.

And I do. Aden brings his tongue back up and thrusts a finger inside me as he sucks my clit, his tongue fluttering over the sensitive nub. Aden's name rips from my throat on a scream as every cell of my being splinters and I fly away on the sensations, becoming shards of sunlight streaming down from the sky. As my body begins to descend, Aden's tongue calms my senses with long, languid strokes, lapping up every bit of my orgasm.

When I finally open my eyes, Aden is once again contemplating me with wonder. "Shaylee... Damn. That's the most beautiful sight I will ever see." I feel liquefied, boneless, but his words still cause heat to tingle at every nerve.

Aden takes my legs from his shoulders, laying them open wide on either side of him, and then glides up my body, keeping skin contact the entire way. He settles between my legs, his erection pressed snuggly into my core. We both moan when he tilts his pelvis into me.

"Are you on the pill, baby?" His words whisper along my ear, tight with need.

"No." I give a light shrug. "I didn't see any reason considering..." My words trail off, the rest of my answer implicit.

Aden groans in frustration, "Fuck!" I jump at the sharpness in his voice. "I'm sorry, baby." His hand runs along my hair, he kisses me softly and then meets my eyes with tenderness. "I'm not mad, I just—I want to feel you . . . with nothing between us." He stops for a moment and sighs. "It would also make this first time a little easier for you."

With another deep sigh, he reaches over to the nightstand and pulls a foil packet from the drawer, then abruptly tosses it on the table. He plants a hand on either side of my head and takes my mouth in a deep and hungry kiss, while shifting his lower body, rubbing his cock over me, making me wet and wanting. When he pulls back, we are both panting, our need climbing once again. "I'm going to go in bare, baby. I don't want to hurt you. But, I'll pull out, ok?" He's asking me to trust him, and I murmur my agreement without hesitation.

His eyes sweep over my face, landing on my lips and he pulls the bottom one into his mouth, sucking it gently. He releases it, only to drag me under with heavy, drugging kisses. Every scrape of his chest hair abrades my nipples and I feel the fire in my core igniting again. Aden's smooths a hand down my body, kneading a breast along the way, until he reaches my pussy. He slips a finger inside and thrusts it in a few times.

He emits a growl of satisfaction, "Do you feel how wet you are?" I can't form a response other than a whimper of need. He thrusts again and this time I cry out at the sensation. "Feeling how slick I make you, it's the biggest fucking turn on."

The things he says bring my insides to a boil and I'm desperate for relief. "Aden, I can't wait any longer."

It's like something inside of him snaps, and he ravages my mouth, pulling his finger away and replacing is with his cock. It probes at my entrance and I involuntarily lift my hips, aching to be filled. "It's going to hurt a little, baby." My muscles clench a little, prepping for pain, but Aden sends my mind spinning, kissing me with a ferocity, plunging his tongue in rhythmically. As his tongue invades my mouth, this time I feel a stinging pain shooting up from where our bodies are now joined. Aden stills, giving my body a chance to stretch around him, letting the pain recede.

As quick as it arrived, the pain begins to dissipate. A restlessness invades me and I lift my hips, feeling Aden slide in even deeper. Aden remains still, but when I shift again, I can't help the sounds of pleasure that release. This time, Aden's hips move with mine, meeting me with a deep thrust. His speed picks up and when he shifts his angle slightly, all of the sudden he hits that magical spot and every new plunge drags a scream from my throat.

"Yes! Yes!" My cries seem to electrify his movement and they become faster and harder, raising me up, once again climbing to the ledge.

"That's right, baby. I want to hear you scream my fucking name."

"Yes, Aden!"

"Fuck! Shaylee! Fuck! Oh FUCK!"

I can hear his loss of control and his words throw gasoline on the fire. I grab his ass (holy shit, its tight) and pull him deeper inside me, moaning and crying out his name as I rise higher and higher. The wind in the room picks up, swirling around us and I know it's a reaction to my turbulent emotions.

"Yes, baby! Take me fucking deeper. Fuck, Shaylee!"

His shouts create a heady sensation that tosses me right over into the abyss. It's the most beautiful place, where I feel surrounded by Aden, every part of me singing in pleasure, and all of me, *his*.

Aden pumps in hard, three more times, and on the last thrust, he calls my name as he pulls out abruptly and spills himself on my stomach. His head is thrown back in ecstasy as each spurt of cream releases until he stops pulsing and his muscles relax.

He is so beautiful and I want so badly to tell him that I love him. But, I'm still afraid, so I bury the impulse and instead, wrap my hands around his neck and bring his mouth down to mine.

Fourteen

ADEN

"THAT WAS AMAZING." Shaylee's whisper is filled with awe and I can feel the expansion in my chest, pride at knowing I satisfied my woman.

"*You're* amazing."

A beautiful shade of pink tinges her cheeks and the pressure in my chest morphs into something soft and warm. I climb off the bed and pad over to the bathroom, to get a warm, wet washcloth to clean her up. It took everything in me not to explode inside her, filling her with the evidence that she is completely mine. As I wipe down her belly, I marvel at the fact that I'm her only one. Her body will only ever be filled by me, stretched by me, loved by me. A picture flashes in my mind of this same belly, round and expanding. I expect the thought of getting Shaylee pregnant to freak me the fuck out, but instead, the idea takes root and I know that eventually, someday, I'm going to watch her grow with our baby. For now though, we are all each other needs.

. . .

I TOSS the rag into the hamper by the closet, and sit on the edge of the bed to plug my phone into the charger. My back is to Shaylee and I feel her fingers begin tracing along my neck.

"Aden, what's this?"

"My mark?" It dawns on me then that I forgot to explain about our mark. "I can't believe I forgot."

I glance back and see her furrowed brow, as she continues to trace the stained skin of my neck.

"Fairy wings?"

I laugh at the skepticism in her tone. "Seems cliché, huh?" She raises a single eyebrow, waiting for me to expound upon my question.

"Where do you think the folklore came from, babe? Haven't you wondered why you haven't seen anyone here with wings?"

Her eyebrow descends and a sheepish look crosses her features. She shrugs, "I guess it crossed my mind once or twice, but I haven't really thought about it." She gives me a lopsided grin, the embarrassment in her eyes growing. "I guess I thought—um," She stops and clears her throat, avoiding eye contact. Then she lets out a long sigh of acceptance. "I thought maybe I had to earn them."

I try. I really, really try to hold back my laughter but it explodes out in a howl of mirth. Shaylee's face turns bright red and her lips turn down into an annoyed pout. I get control of myself, and caress the side of her face, "You're so damn cute." Then I lean down to kiss her pout away. When I pull back, she gives me a little smile and I return it, before clarifying on the subject.

"You've experienced hurricanes in New York, right?" I ask.

"Sure"

"Walking with the wind in a hurricane forces you to move faster, pushing you into a run and practically lifting you off of your feet." I scoot back onto the bed, resting against the headboard and pull her to rest on my chest. "We often use wind that way, to gain some extra speed over the Fallen. They are more proficient with water because it doesn't need light to flourish, in fact, water is denser in the shadows without the light to evaporate it, and so the ability to manipulate the other elements accurately can be a huge leg up." I look down to see if she is following me and she nods, listening with rapt attention.

"You know how truth gets distorted. One human sees our mark, another sees our use of the wind and as the story is shared, it changes little by little, until—all of the sudden—Faeries are winged creatures who fly."

I glance at her face again and see her mouth open in a little O, as understanding fill hers eyes. She shuts her mouth after a moment and shakes her head ruefully. "I'm a little disappointed in humans. Their view of the world is so skewed," she states. I slant a look down at her. "Ok, so mine was too."

I snicker at her admission as I slide down back on the bed, tugging her with me so her back is snug against my front. I'm jarred back when she sits up suddenly. "Oh!" she exclaims. "I have a mark!" The second is stated in a matter of fact tone. She holds out her arms and studies them, turning them over, then moving on to her shoulders when her arms turn up bare. I tap lightly on her shoulder, chuckling and waiting patiently for her attention. She looks down examining her chest, but when I tap again, she lifts her head, cocking it to the side in silent question.

I smile mischievously and lean forward to run a finger up her leg from knee to hip, and lick my lips at the sight of her skin quivering under my touch. I trail back down a few inches and trace a circle in the inside of her thigh, and then tap it lightly, indicating she should take a closer look. Curiously, she bends down to see what I'm referring to. Right there, on the inner skin of her left thigh is a little set of wings, about the size of a half dollar.

I know that my mark is a mixture of muted shades of green, Shaylee's, however, is bright with a rainbow of color. The design on the wings is exquisite, just like her. I let her study it for a few minutes more, pull us both back down and onto our sides, molding Shaylee's back to my front. Reaching down with my top arm, I pull the sheet up over us, and then return my hand to rest on her stomach, just high enough that my thumb brushes against the underside of her tits. I want her all over again but I sternly tell my dick to stand down; Shaylee needs a little time to heal.

She wiggles in a little deeper into my embrace, finding a comfortable spot. I grit my teeth and hiss out a breath when her sexy little ass brushes my cock, and then settles tightly back against it. I run through bland images in my head, willing my hard on to go away, when I hear her breathing even out and know she is asleep. My arousal forgotten, contentment washes over me, and I quickly find myself drifting off.

I'M SURROUNDED by turbulent darkness and I'm trying desperately to claw my way into the light. The evil in the air is thick, almost choking me with its heavy presence. I can feel Shaylee in my arms and I hold on tight, afraid that if I let her go, the blackness will take her from me. But, even as I clutch onto her, I feel the pull separating us. The push of the wind, blowing us apart. Now, I can't feel her warmth, I reach out and grasp at nothing but air—

My body jackknifes up on the bed, my breath coming out in heavy pants as I look wildly around the room. There is nothing there, but even as the first streams of sunlight penetrate my windows, I swear I feel a lingering scent of evil in the air. Shaylee is resting on the other side of the bed, almost a foot away from me. As my racing heart calms down, I lie back down and pull her gently back against me. The touch of her skin, the feel of her in my arms, chases away any last vestiges of shadows and I slip back into sleep.

When I next wake, the sun is high in the sky, bathing my room with brightness and invigorating power. I stretch lazily, and then notice that Shaylee isn't in the bed next to me. For one second, I fear that she regrets last night and has taken off for her apartment, until I remember, smugly, that I changed the locks. Cocking my head, I listen and realize that I hear water running in the bathroom. The image of Shaylee wet and naked in the shower prompts a wicked grin and I hop out of bed and pad over to the slightly ajar, bathroom door. I open it fully and steam billows out, the heat washing over my already overheated skin. My morning wood is now hard as steel, and I move in the direction of the corner shower. The shower is an open design, it has no door. Instead, the privacy (I use that term loosely since the "wall" is made of frosted glass) comes from a tall wall that you have to walk around to reach the spacious area where there are three shower heads and a small built in seat. *The seat and all that empty wall space are certainly going to come in handy.*

I can see the silhouette of Shaylee' body, and all the blood rushes to my head. *Not that head, the other one.* Stealthily, I step inside and come up behind her, gripping her waist and bringing her body flush against mine. She gasps in shock, but it turns to a moan when I run my tongue along her neck and slide my hands up to cup her fucking gorgeous tits.

"Good morning, baby," I breathe, nipping at her earlobe. She lets out a strangled greeting, quivering from my hands squeezing and rolling her pink nipples. I can't keep the cocky grin off of my face, feeling how I affect her. "Let's see how we can turn this good morning into a spectacular one."

Shaylee turns to me and we get lost in one another,

coming together in an explosion of lust, playing and pleasuring until the water runs cold.

Satiated, we turn off the water and step out, wrapping ourselves in soft, large towels. We take turns drying each other off, and then I hightail it out of there before I give in to temptation and haul her back to bed for the rest of the day. It's Saturday, but we still have shit to do.

"I'm going to go make us some breakfast," I grumble, doing my best to ignore her heated looks. I kiss the tip of her nose, smack her naked ass on my way out the door, saying, "I'll meet you in the kitchen, baby. You don't need to wear training clothes; we've got some errands to run."

After pulling on some khaki cargo pants and a plain black t-shirt, I head to the kitchen and pull out all the fixings for omelets. I'm chopping up the vegetables, when my cell rings. Recognizing the number, I wipe my hands and answer the call.

I've been expecting this call, so I'm not surprised when I hear the pleasant voice of Calista on the line. She sits on the council and has called to set up a time to meet with Shaylee. Calista is a legend among the Mie'Lorvor, and she's cool as hell, so we shoot the shit for a few minutes, before agreeing to meet around noon. I've just hung up and turned back to breakfast when Shaylee saunters into the room.

Glancing at her, I immediately stop what I'm doing, completely distracted by her mile long legs, shown off by the short jean skirt she is wearing. I slowly drag my eyes from her feet, up those sexy legs, and land on her chest. I wouldn't have thought it was possible to divert my attention from those perfect tits, but I somehow notice that her yellow t-shirt has a colorful unicorn on it with the words, "*Always be yourself. Unless you can be a unicorn. Then always be a unicorn.*"

I burst out in uncontrollable laughter. She puts her hands on her hips and grins at me, making me laugh that much harder. "Where the hell do you get these shirts, baby?" I ask, still chortling as I go back to making breakfast. She strolls up to me and gives me a peck on the cheek before rounding the island and sitting on a stool, facing me.

"When I was a kid, eight or nine maybe, my dad got me a t-shirt that said, "*I run like a girl. Do try and keep up.*" I laughed so hard I had to book it to the bathroom before I peed my pants. From there, it became our thing. We always gave one to the other on our birthdays." The memory lights up her face and I'm mesmerized by the sight. I'm determined to be the one to put that look on her face in the future.

"After he died, it was a way to keep him close to me. Eventually, it kind of caught on and I get them from my friends and family as gifts, so I have quite the collection," she confesses with a giggle.

Taking advantage of her mood, I encourage her to continue talking to me and telling me stories. I finish up preparations and plate our breakfast, setting it out on the bar. We chit chat about light subjects while we eat, then clean up together, the whole time stealing kisses and subtle touches.

"Grab your stuff, baby. We've got to get going." I grab my keys from the bowl on the island and lift a jacket off the hook by the door. With our extended days and abundance of sun, the seasons in Rien are milder that the human realm, but it is December now and sometimes the wind can bring a chill.

Shaylee returns from the bedroom with yellow and black converse on her feet, a thick sweater, and her purse slung over a shoulder. How she pulls off being incredibly sexy and cute-as-hell at the same time is beyond me. But damn, that package is all mine.

"Where are we going?" she asks as she steps out into the hallway.

"We've got a meeting with the council at two, and then I've got a surprise for you after," I tell her absent-mindedly as I lock the door, then turn to leave, bumping right into her still form. I steady her with my hands on her waist, "Sorry, baby. You all right?"

Her head slowly moves from side to side and I tug on her hips, bring her around to face me. Her eyes are wide, the gears almost visibly working in her head, and her mouth is opening and closing like a fish. I raise my brow in question, but stay silent, waiting for her to tell me what's got her freaked out.

"Aden," She deadpans. "Could you maybe start giving me a little warning before you throw me to the lions?" Her voice is rising steadily as she speaks and her sapphire irises becoming turbulent, a storm of emotion brewing.

Before she can escalate into full blown panic, I take her face in my hands and lift so that she is focusing on me. "Chill out, baby. I promise, there is nothing to stress about. You're not meeting royalty, it's not a tribunal, or The Underground Kings. It's just a group of people who have the knowledge to help and guide us." Some of the tension seeps out of her muscles at my relaxed attitude. "Do you trust me?" When she nods without a moment's consideration, I take her mouth in a grateful kiss.

I lace our fingers together and we get on our way. We drive into the city, passing by the neighborhood where my parents live, into a bustling area, similar to Chicago. There are tall office buildings, streets of pedestrians (cleaner and wider than New York), and a river, although it runs along the border of the city, rather than through it. Shaylee is riveted to the scenery, everything catching her interest in a way that tells me she is once again surprised at the similarities of Rien to the human realm. I keep my mind focused on the drive and my amusement at Shaylee's reaction to everything, avoiding the knot in my gut, resulting from worry over what the council members might let slip to Shaylee. I still haven't told her about being fated, the timing just hasn't been right. Having some suspicions on how she'll react, I'm being a coward and avoiding the conversation. I need to know she has fallen for me completely before I tell her.

I park the car in an underground garage below a tall, glass building that sits right on the river. Exiting the car, I round the hood and open her door, helping her out. Needing to stay connected with her, I place my hand at the small of her back and gently guide her toward the elevator. We get inside and I hit the button for the thirtieth floor, before turning and backing her up into the wall. I grasp her hips and jerk her body into mine, crushing my mouth over hers in a soul stealing kiss. Shaylee sinks into me as our mouths devour each other, our tongues exploring the wet heat, and I hope that she doesn't feel my desperation.

As I told her, she has nothing to fear from the council, but I don't know what we are up against. While I know that we are meant to be together, I don't know exactly what is ahead of us. The feeling of being hunted has dissipated since being in the Fae realm, but it hasn't completely gone away. I'll do whatever it takes to protect her. I just hope the council can shed some knowledge on what we are up against.

When I hear the bell, indicating we've reached our destination, I pull back and admire the glazed look in her eyes. I love that I can take her to that place, make her lose herself in me and the desire between us. I kiss the tip of her nose and coo, "Are you still nervous?"

The haze is beginning to clear and she considers me for a moment, "Not so much," she muses, her voice laced with amusement. *So damn cute.*

We exit the elevator and I lead her through a set of glass double doors into a sleek lobby area. The walls are white, decorated with black and white photos of landscapes from all over Rien. Facing the doors is a tall gray desk with a young, male receptionist, sitting in front of a wall with the words "Fae Fer Li" in bold silver, block letters. *Life, Magic, Light.* The wall stops evenly with the edges of the desk and it practically glows from the sunshine streaming in the windows beyond it.

"Hey, Grady." I greet the young man with a smile and a handshake. He stands and returns it with enthusiasm, then turns to Shaylee and his whole face lights up. She reaches to shake his hand and instead, he grips it and kisses. Shaylee laughs and says hello with a twinkle in her eye.

I pin him with an annoyed gaze and when he sees it, he immediately drops her hand, but remains standing, smiling brightly at her. Grady is all of eighteen, and I can understand anyone being enamored with my girl, but that doesn't mean I have to be happy about it. I clear my throat loudly to get his attention and give him another pointed look. His face flushes bright red and I hear Shaylee suck in a breath. A glance in her direction shows that she is holding her breath in an attempt to keep from laughing, probably not wanting to further embarrass Grady.

"Where's Calista?" I ask evenly, stifling the urge to snap at him. I roll my eyes when I hear a giggle escape Shaylee's mouth.

"The north conference room," Grady answers, studiously avoiding looking at Shaylee. *Smart.*

I grab Shaylee's hand and drag her down to another set of glass doors. The offices take up the entire floor, so all of the exterior walls are made up of floor to ceiling windows, filling the open floor plan with radiance. The conference room holds a large, round, glass table with plush, black leather chairs. Currently, it's occupied by three women and two men, seated and making relaxed conversation. When we enter the room, they all turn to us with wide, welcoming smiles.

Calista is sitting closest to the door and she hops up taking the advantage to greet Shaylee first. "Hey, girl! Welcome!" She pulls Shaylee into a hug and then guides her to an empty seat at the table. For a moment, I worry that she will be overwhelmed by all of this, but I should have known better. Despite her attitude with me, Shaylee is very laid back and acclimates to unknown situations quickly. The way that she accepted the existence of this world so readily is proof of that. Instead of being wary, she follows Calista's lead, laughing at her gusto, returning her hug, and following her to the indicated chair.

The other four people wave from their seats and welcome her jovially. The relaxed air of the room seems to chase away any remaining nerves and Shaylee falls happily into conversation with them. I mosey over to the seat next to her and join her at the table. One by one, they each give me a nod, then dive right back into their discussion with Shaylee. I blow out an aggravated breath at being ignored, and then mentally whack the backside of my head for acting like a petulant child. Instead, I watch Shaylee bloom under their attention and admire her ability to captivate them. My heart fills with pride at the knowledge that this incredible woman is mine forever.

Calista brings the chit chat to a halt after several minutes. The council does not rank its members, but she has the biggest personality among the group and the rest often defer to her for mediation in group settings. It's funny as hell to see people expecting someone calm and poised (not that Calista doesn't possess those qualities, she just prefers to let her inner rebel roam free) and instead, they get a whirl wind of energy in the form of a tall, green-eyed, leather-clad woman with short, spikey hair, and three piercing on her face: nose, eyebrow, and lip.

She introduces the rest of the group: Flynn, Callum, Nissa, and Ailean. Each, in their turn, gives a little wave or a nod, and Shaylee graces them with a bright smile, lighting up the room. They've created a laid back atmosphere to put the people they meet with at ease. Their purpose isn't to rule, but rather to guide and, at times, handle dissension through mediation. And while their primary focus is the Fae Guard, they also have a hand in the daily lives of all the Fae.

"Shaylee, we like to meet with all of the leath leanbh at some point after they have arrived in Rien," Flynn speaks up. "This new reality can be a lot to process, so we want to help make the transition as smooth as possible."

"We are here to guide and help, sort of like a life coach," Nissa adds.

"More like fucking high school guidance counselors," Calista mutters. She looks directly at Shaylee, "The brutal honesty of the Fae is not always a good thing. You'd be amazed how petty people can be. I mean really," She huffs in exasperation, "What is so hard about the concept of 'if you can't say something nice, don't say anything at all?'"

Ailean lets out a small snort and Calista glares at her. "Pulease, Calista. You have no patience and no damn filter." In a stunning act of maturity, Calista sticks her tongue out at Ailean.

"I have no patience for people without any common sense," she says, sniffing in indignation.

"Touché." Ailean reaches out and they meet in a fist bump. As much as Ailean loves to tease Calista, her digs are all in fun. The other council members tend to make Calista deal with the petty disputes because her no-nonsense attitude puts people in their place. She isn't exactly happy about that role, but she understands it.

Shaylee's eyes are bouncing back and forth between the two women with amusement, seemingly sensing the lack of hostility in the exchange.

"However, under the circumstances," Flynn continued, ignoring Ailean and Calista, "we thought meeting with you now would help us all get a grip on what's going on." He looks at her expectantly, and seems satisfied when she nods, so he continues, "We still aren't sure how, but the knowledge that you are Fae got into the wrong hands before you were marked. It's not like this is impossible, but it's definitely very rare. The Ukkutae seem to have been hunting you and from the chatter among the fate readers, they are still determined to have you."

"Fate readers?" Shaylee asks.

"Her minions," I comment sarcastically.

Flynn gives me a reproachful look, but the tiniest of smiles is playing at the corners of his mouth, ruining the effect. "They help Fate see. Like many other things of this realm, the human portrayal of Fate is completely skewed," he explains. "She isn't a fortune teller or an all seeing eye. Besides that, the future is never set in stone, and it changes every time a person makes a different decision. Imagine it changing one hundred different times for one hundred different people, every second." Flynn shudders, "Just thinking about all of that activity in one mind makes me want to have a nervous breakdown."

"For the most part," Nissa pipes up, "Fate focuses on conceptual ideas for the future. She stays around the edges and gives you information to help shape your decisions but not direct them. The other difference between reality and the human idea of Fate is that she doesn't talk in riddles. She's not going to give you mumbo jumbo to decipher. She'll lay it all out for you."

"She's definitely not one to beat around the bush," I grumble. "About as subtle as a fucking sledge hammer."

"*Any*way," Nissa says, drawing out the vowel and giving me a dirty look. "The fate readers help her to identify the half human children and work with us to assign them a guard. They help with smaller issues and just relieve some of the pressure off of her, give her the ability to have some down time."

I can't help muttering a little more under my breath. In my opinion, Fate's form of crazy is best served far, far away from me and my...well, just far away.

Nissa ignores me and moves on. "Anyway, Aden mentioned that you accessed your magic very quickly after you were marked. You crossed the realms on your own?"

Shaylee's eyes slide toward mine, for a second, then away again with a little huff. *Ok, so she's not completely over it. I'll just have to work extra hard to make her forget about it.* Ideas of how to accomplish this start filtering through my mind and I shift in my chair, trying to find a more comfortable position. It's a hard job (the fourteen-year-old in me snickers) but somebody's got to do it. *And it sure as fuck better be me.*

"So, it's unusual that I've been able to get a grasp on my abilities in such a short time?" Shaylee's face becomes slightly wary at her question. She clearly doesn't know if this is a positive or negative development. Her hand is resting on her thigh, so I reach over and fold it into mine, giving it a reassuring squeeze and she returns the gesture.

Nissa cocks her head to the side in thought, "No, but it's not overly surprising that your magic is more powerful, considering your relationship with Aden." I stiffen at her words. *Damn it!* The last thing I need is for them to spring our fated status on her before I have a chance to explain.

I meet Calista's piercing green eyes and give a minuscule shake of my head. Her brows shoot up into her hair, when she realizes that I haven't told Shaylee. Then, she gives me an over-dramatic eye roll and a jerky nod, her irritated expression visibly saying, *you owe me.* "I understand that you've been progressing at an incredible pace." she abruptly changes the subject. I'd mentioned it to Shaylee, so she murmurs an agreement, but with a slight shrug, indicating that she is only slightly informed on the situation.

"Aden exhibited some of the same tendencies as you when he was young. Excelling rapidly, accessing his magic before he knew how to control it." Calista gives me an evil little smile.

Aw Fuck.

"My favorite was when he accidentally set his sister's clothes on fire, and then instead of dousing her with water, he pelted her with hail." Shaylee giggles and I give Calista a warning look. She ignores me. "Or the time in high school, when he was trying to break up with a girl and she was crying all over him. I guess she was clinging to him like a vine and he thought perhaps she'd like to know what it felt like to be bound in the plant."

Shaylee is outright laughing now, holding her stomach and trying to catch her breath. "He didn't!" she gasps.

"Oh, he did. Ivy sprouted from the ground and wrapped itself all around her. But, she'd been leaning up against the side of the school and the ivy just kept growing until she was lifted up and tied to the wall. Damn, did he ever catch hell for that." Calista's face is smothered in delight at, what I'm sure is, a mutinous scowl on my face.

"Or the time that—"

"Alright," I interrupt. "Story time is over."

Shaylee and Calista obviously find my reaction hilarious because they fall over into renewed peals of laughter. Turning to Flynn, I make an effort to move on.

"Have you come to any conclusions as to why her abilities seem to be so enhanced?" I inquire. From an earlier conversation with Calista, I learned that apparently, the strength that we gain in our magic from being together is also more powerful than normal.

Flynn shakes his head, watching Shaylee thoughtfully, before meeting my gaze. "I don't think there is a logical explanation for us to find." He suddenly gives me a sympathetic grimace. "You need to go see Fate."

Damn. Damn. Double damn.

I'm unable to keep the cringe off of my face.

"Oh, for fuck's sake, Aden." Calista barks, "You knew how this was going to end, so wipe that pout off of your face.

You look like a pussy." She stands up, walks swiftly over to me and slaps me soundly on the back of my head, gives Shaylee a fist bump, and prances over to the fucking door. Just before she's out of the room, she turns, "Let's have coffee, Shaylee. We'll have story time." Then, with a cunning smile and a wink, she's gone.

I can feel Shaylee shaking beside me and I look over to see her holding a hand over her mouth, silently laughing so hard that tears are leaking from the corners of her eyes. I try to give her a look of reproach but fail miserably when I start chuckling too. Calista knows exactly how to push my buttons, but I love her like a sister and I'm not above conceding that she took the victory point in this round.

Fifteen

SHAYLEE

WE SAY goodbye to the other council members, and I'm still giggling when Aden walks with me out to the car. Calista is awesome. Anyone who can give Aden shit like that, and get away with it, is a star in my book. I had built the council up in my mind, so I was incredibly nervous when we walked into the building but to my relief, Calista and the others quickly made me feel comfortable. Unfortunately, I walked out feeling like I had as many questions as when I walked in.

Once I'm seated and buckled, Aden gets in and starts the car. "Are we going to meet with Fate? Was that your surprise?" It seems odd that he would choose that, considering his clear aversion to the woman.

Aden's face twists with what appears to be...yes, he's pouting. I bite back a chuckle at how ridiculous and, ok, adorable, he is. "No, Grady will get in touch with her and let me know." It won't be for a while anyway. We need to focus on training you and not on what will come after that."

"Ok, so where are we going?" I notice that he isn't heading back toward the training facility, but this is my first time down town, so I have no idea what he is planning.

Aden just smiles at me, his face a little smug. "If I tell you, it wouldn't be a surprise."

I give him an irritated scowl and face forward again. "That's what people always say. But, hasn't the surprise train already left the station by that point? I mean, it's only a 'surprise,' if I don't know about it in the first place. So, now I'm expecting it and just because I don't know what it is, doesn't mean it's a surprise. It's just...another secret you're keeping from me." When I see the hurt flash across his face, I know I took it too far and immediately feel guilty. I know it wasn't his choice to keep me in the dark my whole life, but I have to admit that the wound it still a little raw. I need to let it go, and I shouldn't have used it against him.

"That was uncalled for, Aden. I'm really sorry." I turn back to him, reach over and lace our fingers together, giving his hand a tight squeeze. He returns the gesture and gives me a smile that doesn't reach his eyes. "I promise, I'll make it up to you." I coo in a deliberately seductive voice.

He instantly perks up, looking at me from the corner of his eye. "Make it up to me how?" He asks innocently.

"It's a surprise," I scoff, infusing my voice with indignation. The effect is ruined when I can't keep the grin off my face.

"Smart ass."

"You know it." Giving him a wink, I watch the scenery passing by, trying to figure out where he is taking me. To my (yes, I'm going to say it) surprise, he pulls into the parking lot of a small restaurant and parks the car. He comes around to my side and helps me out, a wide smile on his face, his dimple peeking out to make my panties wet. *Damn dimple.*

"Lunch?" I'm a little disappointed. After all the surprise talk, I guess I expected something more grandiose.

"Baby, would you shut it and let me do my thing, please?"

"Aden, if you tell me to shut it one more time, I'm—"

Suddenly, I find myself in a crushing hug, Aden's lips effectively ruining my tirade. As I melt into him, I realize I don't care what I was saying anyway. My heart is pounding and my panties dampen with need as he kisses me hungrily. He presses me up against the car and I start to think, maybe we should just head back home.

"Shaylee!" I hear my name called out and jump away from Aden. Well, I attempt to put some space between us, but Aden keeps a tight hold on me and even though we aren't in a lip lock anymore, I'm still plastered up against his body.

Craning my neck to see over Aden's shoulder, I blanch when I see my grandparents waving and walking towards us. Heat infuses my face as the blood rushes back with a vengeance when I realize they most likely, saw us making out. I try a little harder to get out of Aden's embrace, but he holds tight and buries his face in my neck, shaking with laughter. *I just want to die.*

"Aden, do you think you could stop mauling my granddaughter for a few minutes so that I can give her a hug?" Pop asks, his eyes twinkling and smothering his laughter with a cough. Aden gives me a squeeze then steps back with an unrepentant grin, allowing me to step into Pop's open arms. He hugs just like my dad and I sigh in a moment of contentment, feeling a little closer to him.

Cerys hugs me tight as well, then loops one arm through mine, and uses the other to smack Aden in the chest, "Can't you control yourself?" She shakes her head in mock disappointment, but I can see she's fighting a grin. "You're like a hormone ridden teenager." Without waiting for an answer, she pulls me around and starts toward the entrance to the restaurant, leaving Aden and Pops laughing behind us.

We spend several hours with Cerys and Pops, and I'm in heaven getting to know them, but mostly hearing all the stories they have to tell me about my dad. Between the easy conversation and Aden's arm across the back of my chair, softly kneading my muscles, I find myself truly relaxing for the first time since my birthday.

Eventually, we call it a night and, with promises for future visits, we part. On the way home, my mind is absorbed in all the things we talked about tonight, and a thought occurs to me.

"Aden, was my dad killed by one of the Fallen?"

Aden sighs, "Yes." His fingers tighten on the steering wheel and my stomach twists in fear.

"I don't understand. You told me that whatever was suppressing my magic, extended to my father so that he couldn't be detected either."

"It does, baby. Well, in his case, it cloaks it rather than suppresses it. That's one of the reasons we are at a loss. We aren't sure how they found out about you and your dad." He blows out a frustrated breath, "For that matter, we don't know how they were able to best him. Your dad was one of the best on the Mie'Lorvor we had before he met your mom and took a leave of absence."

"So, if they knew my dad was Fae, they had to know about me." I observe.

"That's the logical conclusion, yes. But, I never detected their presence around you while I was there." His tone turns wary when he alludes to his unexpected departure from my life. He doesn't seem sure whether to expect a fight, and honestly, until this moment, I couldn't have told you what I would do. But, the past is behind me and I want to look to my future with Aden. I'm trying to get beyond my fear that he will find an excuse to leave me again. Right now, he has no intention of ever going, but what if, someday down the line, he gets bored of me, or meets someone else? The thoughts cause pain to knife through my chest, so I quickly shake them away and focus on our conversation.

"Were you replaced? We didn't have anyone who was consistently around, like you were."

Aden shakes his head and scratches his chin, a thoughtful expression on his face. "Not really . . . I mean, they sent Guard members to check on you from time to time, but without any indication that you were in danger or had been detected, they came and went before you ever noticed them. They would have reported any indication otherwise, and it wasn't until the day I got back that it became obvious that you were being watched."

Confusion fills my mind and I want to pepper him with more questions. But the relaxation I felt earlier has dissipated with our discussion and I can tell that Aden doesn't really have the answers I am looking for. He must sense my troubled thoughts, because he reaches over and takes my hand, bringing it to his mouth, sweetly kissing it. I settle back into my seat and we spend the rest of the ride in silence.

I FLOP down onto the mat, a sweaty mess and try to calm my rapidly beating heart. We'd done a wide range of activities from training on the clinch, grappling, work on the heavy and speed bag, while throwing some Maui Tai into the mix. Last, we mixed magic in with it all, and now, I am exhausted, like bone-deep tired.

For the last week, Aden pushed me harder every time it seemed that I had mastered something. I was excelling fast, and he wanted to keep the momentum and get me trained as quickly as possible. The only positive was that, after we were done, he would run me a hot bath and then use his magical hands to work out the knots and kinks all over my body. In fact, he made it his mission not to miss one spot and, by the time he finished, I was sated in more ways than one. I'd almost blurted out that I loved him a few times, but something was holding me back; fear, I guess.

Aden plops down next to me and I'm distracted from my musings. His magnificent body is covered in a sheen of sweat, but, to my great annoyance, he's not even a little winded. However, my annoyance is over shadowed by the sight of his muscles, particularly that delicious v dipping into his pants, a v that I very much enjoy running my tongue along.

Get your mind out of his pants, Shaylee.

Right. Concentrate on something else, come up with a topic of conversation.

"I'm going to set you up with Laila for some sparring time next week," he speaks up.

I turn my head to peer at him. "Laila?"

"Yeah, she'll work with you outside first, and then, when you've got a handle on everything, she'll bring you back inside to feel what it's like to truly fight with limitations. Basically, we don't want you to accidentally demolish the building." His voice is laced with amusement, but I'm stuck on the fact that he is pushing me off onto Laila.

"Why aren't you going to continue training me?" Has he tired of me already? Panic begins to course through my veins and I am faced with the realization that he is the reason I'm so grounded and accepting of this new reality. I'm afraid that, without him, I would lose the battle with my nerves and lose my freaking mind.

"I'll keep training you; I just won't be sparring with you." His tone is matter of fact, oblivious to the cautious fear seeping into mine.

"Is that normal?" Maybe this is what everybody does; maybe he isn't trying to distance himself from me. "To split the training between two teachers?"

Aden shrugs, "Well, no. But I think it's best for you. I won't be able to push you like she will." I want to keep my mouth shut, to play it cool, and not let on that I'm terrified he is going to disappear again.

Get a grip, would you? You're strong enough to handle whatever life throws at you.

My inner pep talk makes me feel a little better, but I lose the battle to remain silent.

"Why not? Why is it best for me?"

Aden finally turns his head, his green eyes surveying me, probably trying to see beyond the forced subtlety in my questions.

"I don't want to hurt you, baby."

"Excuse me?" Indignation heightens my volume, but I instantly lower my voice when I realize it. "You think I couldn't take you on?" My question clearly amuses the hell out of Aden because he starts laughing, the sound coming from deep in his belly.

Without answering my question, Aden jumps up and reaches a hand out to help me up. I don't like the disadvantage my current position puts me in, so I grip his hand and let him pull me up. He drops a quick kiss on my nose, then lifts his chin to the locker room door, and gives my arm a little tug, indicating that he wants to continue this discussion in private.

We enter the wide room that reminds me of the club house at a baseball stadium. It is a wide rectangle, each wall lined with tall, and somewhat wide, wooden lockers, though each sports a full length door, so they are more like closest. Benches sit a few feet back from them, following the same pattern around the room. But, a big difference with this space, is that the center has two little "conversation nooks". Each has two comfy couches, facing each other, and they are flanked by overstuffed, reading chairs, and creating a sort of semi-circle in either side. There are also three full size bathrooms at each end of the room, for students and trainers who don't live at the facility.

The room is empty, but Aden continues walking, pulling me into one of the bathrooms and shutting the door behind us. It's a decent sized space, but Aden crowds me up against the countertop, just to the right of the door, his face level with mine.

"Baby, I have no doubt that eventually, you'll be able to hold your own with me. But even then, I won't spar with you."

Now, I'm just so perplexed. I frown, "I don't understand. Have you done this with any of your other students?"

Aden's eyes roam my face, pausing on my mouth, and his tongue darts out to wet his lips. I just barely catch the groan that wants to escape, my eyes riveted to his mouth. It's ridiculous how hot he can make me with the slightest action. I just want to fuse us together and sink into his kiss.

He lifts his eyes and stares deeply into mine, the emerald darkening to a mossy green. "No."

I'm so caught up in the lust sparking in me, that for a millisecond, I'm not sure what he is saying no to. No, he won't kiss me? I inwardly snort at the thought. *Yeah right.*

Then, I remember the question. "Why haven't you done this with anyone else?"

Aden grabs my hip and lifts me onto the counter, settling himself in the v between my thighs. Our faces are perfectly aligned now and his eyes bore into mine.

"Because I wasn't in love with any of them."

I gasp in shock, my mind completely lost to anything but those words. *He loves me?* Relief pours through me and I feel freer, like I've shed a heavy coat and can bask in the beautiful breeze.

I'm about to get sappy. Are you ready?

The breeze is his love.

I warned you.

My thoughts clear and Aden is still watching me intently. I

don't see any fear or uncertainty in his eyes, and I realize he's confident that I return his feelings.

What the hell, let's just lay it all out there.

I place a hand on each of his cheeks and kiss the tip of his nose, each eyelid, and finally I place a sweet kiss on his mouth.

"I love you too."

Sixteen

ADEN

HER WORDS SNAP the tenuous hold I have on my control and with a hand at the back of her neck and another on her lower back, I pull her forward and slam my mouth down onto hers. Plunging my tongue in, a deep growl rumbles from me when she sucks it deeper and I grab her legs guiding them around my hips. She gives a soft mewl of desire as I press forward into her heat. Our bodies are already warm and slightly sweaty from our workout, but the temperature of her pussy is ten times hotter and it burns my cock in the sexiest way.

My mouth moves down, kissing and licking along her chin, neck, ear, and on down to her collarbone, where I stop to suck on the salty skin. I can still taste the sweet strawberries and, the mixture of salty and sweet, sets my cock in stone. One hand wanders down to her breast, squeezing it and plucking at the nipple, while the other grabs a fist full of her hair and gently yanks her head back to give me better access. Shaylee cries out and her legs clench, clasping my cock even tighter to her core. The sound rips through me and I can't think of anything but plunging my dick into that velvet heat, feeling her walls clench around me in a rough, hard orgasm.

I pull her legs down and grip her hips, setting her on the ground and slip off her shirt before spinning her around to face the mirror. Then, I peel her tight, Lycra shorts off of her perfect, endless legs. The sight of all that flushed, creamy skin has my need for her ready to explode. Her tits are encased in a tight sports bra but when I notice the front zipper, I decide who ever invented it is going to get personal thank you note. I slide it down and her tits spill free into my eager hands. I lift them up and squeeze them tight, rubbing my palms along her nipples, before using my fingers to twist and pull at the rosy peaks. Shaylee's head falls back onto my shoulder, her eyes closed, and her lips slightly parted letting out a little puff of air. I pinch her nipples a little harder to get her attention.

"Open your eyes, baby. I want you to watch what I do to you."

Her eyes struggle open and when I see the explosion of lust swirling around in them, I just can't wait any more. I bend her forward over the counter and pull her hip out and up, pushing my rock hard dick into her ass for just a moment. She moans and her eyes begin to droop again. I grab another chunk of her hair and tug it, not enough to hurt her, but enough to make it sting.

"Aden!" she cries out but shoves her ass back into my cock, letting me know that it was a cry of pleasure.

"Keep looking at me, baby. I don't want to have to tell you again," my voice is rough with hunger and I practically growl at her. She gives a tight nod of understanding and once again, I feel her ass pressing back. I swiftly pull the drawstring on my pants and let them drop, my cock springs free, and I gasp at the pain from the pants pulling on it as they fall.

I slide my hand along her hip, around to her stomach and down, grabbing ahold of her panties, ripping them off, and tossing them behind me. She moans loudly and I slip my hand down to her bare pussy. Fuck, I love that my girl is completely on display for me. My fingers plunge into her and are immediately coated with her wetness.

"You're so ready for me, baby, aren't you?" Her eyes are staring intently at her pussy, watching my fingers move in and out. "Do you want me to fuck you hard?" She doesn't seem to hear me, her attention still riveted to the action between her thighs. I yank again on her hair to get her attention and her gaze jumps up to meet mine, a whimper of need escaping.

My fingers come out and circle around her clit, passing over it every few rotations but never putting any pressure on it. Another tiny tug, "Answer me. Do you want me to fuck you hard, baby?"

She nods and it causes her hair to pull a little making her cry out again. The sounds she makes during sex are hot as fuck, and I know I'm about to lose my mind. "Out loud, baby. What do you want?"

"Inside." She pants.

"Inside what?" Her pupils are dilated so big that all I can see around the black orbs is a bright sliver of blue, making her eyes look as though they are glowing. She's so fucking beautiful.

"I want you inside me."

"You want what inside you." My filthy mouth turns her on to a rabid degree and I give it one more nudge before I can't take it anymore.

"Your cock. Inside. My pussy," she continues to pant, blowing out her words on each breath. She presses back into me roughly. "I want you to fuck me, Aden. Hard. I want to feel you tomorrow, sore and sated from your cock pounding and stretching my pussy."

Holyfuckholyfuckholyfuck!

I grasp my dick and line it up, then thrust inside her, and feel her clench at the invasion. She cries my name and it causes a frenzy in me. I begin hammering into her with every bit of my strength, holding her hips tight to keep her from being pushed into the counter. Our skin slaps together loudly, sliding the surface from the sweat already dampening our skin and mixing with the perspiration from our feverish pace.

"More, Aden!" Shaylee yells, desperation in her voice. "As deep as you can go, baby. Give me all of you."

Fuck, yeah.

When Shaylee starts talking dirty, I think my brain short circuits. I suddenly pull out and remotely hear her cry of distress, but I'm focused on what I'm doing. I flip her around and grab her ass, lifting her up so that her legs wrap tightly around me. I shift a step to the left and slam inside of her as her back hits the door. The new angle and the use of gravity deepen every plunge and I use the leverage to thrust harder.

"Aden! I'm almost—oh fuck! Yes!"

I won't last long and I can feel her tightening, clenching my cock in a vice grip with her pussy.

"I want to hear it, baby." I'm fighting to get the words out; my breathing is labored and uneven. "Let me hear what I do to you."

Reaching between us, I apply pressure directly onto her clit and watch her face as she flies into a euphoric oblivion, screaming my name. The clutch of her orgasm on my cock shoves me over the edge and I slam my hand against the door as I explode inside her, still thrusting deep until every single tremor has subsided.

I finally still and rest my forehead on hers, still buried deep inside and I can feel her pulsing around my cock. Nothing can compare to the ecstasy of bringing Shaylee to orgasm and then coming so very deep inside her. Well, maybe it comes second to the feelings I have when she tells me she loves me. I knew she wouldn't tell me first, so I was waiting for the right moment, a special moment to say it to her. But, I just couldn't wait anymore. I knew if I told her how I felt, she would open up to me. Finally.

Our breathing has slowed to normal levels and I place a lingering kiss on her sweet lips before stepping and pulling out, letting her slide down my body until she is standing. I don't even try to keep my eyes from roaming all over her exquisite body. As much as she turns me on (and that's a whole fuck of a lot), my heart swells with love for her as I take in her beauty inside and out. I wrap her in my arms and hug her tightly to me. "I love you, baby. For eternity."

Shaylee lifts her head and beams at me, "I love you too, Aden. Forever."

The freedom to tell Shaylee that I love her anytime I want puts a bounce in my step. *You don't think I know that this makes me sound like a girl? I do, so shut the fuck up.*

WE SPENT most of Saturday and today, in bed fucking or just cuddling and watching movies. We've gone through an entire pack of condoms over these two days. I had to run to the store for more. And, as I stand in the checkout line, I just now realize that I hadn't used protection Friday night. I know Shaylee will be pissed as hell if I get her pregnant. I'm not really ready, either. I want to have some time together, just the two of us. But a small part of me, the asshole who makes stupid decisions and gets my ass handed to me when I listen to him, is whispering that if Shaylee were to get pregnant, she would be tied to me completely. A picture of her, lying on our bed, cuddled up against me, with both of our hands, resting on her round belly, flitts through my mind. My breath catches at the image, and a feeling of utter contentment settles over me as I imagine Shaylee with our babies.

Babies? As in multiple?

Yeah, wow. Babies.

I need to get my head on straight. Now isn't the time to be thinking these things, there will be time enough for that in the future. I push the thought out of my head and take the condoms home.

SHAYLEE WAS sore as hell the next day and I couldn't help walking around with a smug smile, knowing my girl felt me inside her every time she moved. Over the next few weeks, each day was better than the last. I can't believe she is finally mine, forever. I knew I wanted her, but fuck, I had no idea how much I would crave her. Not just her body, but her love.

When Christmas came, it was the best one of my lifetime. Shaylee missed her mom and aunt terribly, but we spent Christmas Eve with my family, her grandparents, and extended family. The party was full of fun and laughter and it helped take her mind away from her homesickness. Christmas Day, we had a lazy morning, (well, there was some vigorous activity) and moseyed our way to the living room to exchange gifts. I gave Shaylee a pair of one carat diamond earrings. It wasn't the diamond I truly wanted to give her, but I wasn't sure she was ready. Besides, I decided to talk to her mom the next time I am in the human realm; not only to ask her permission, but also to find out what would be the perfect ring for Shaylee.

She gave me a book of fairy tales that had been her father's. When I opened it, I realized he had written down all of the stories that he used to tell her. He'd made notes of where the humans had created folklore and the history behind the stories. While living in the human realm, Shaylee's father had taught history at NYU, and his students had adored him for his enthusiasm and unique outlook on all things relating to myths and legends. This book took his skill and applied it to the history of the Fae. It was absolutely amazing, and the fact that she would give up something that belonged to her father, made it absolutely priceless to me.

But, guilt continues to nag at me. I haven't been as diligent with the condoms as I should have been, but it was only once or twice. There is nothing like being gloved by her pussy with nothing between us and a couple of times, I gave in to that need, the need to be completely fused together as one. However, I still haven't told her about being fated. It gnaws at me. I can't lose her, I won't.

"Dude, how about you think with this head?" Brannon taps his finger against my temple. "And maybe focus on what you're supposed to be doing?" He gives me a wide smile, popping his dimples that for some reason, chicks seem to go crazy over.

"Sorry about that. It doesn't take much brain power to wipe the floor with you, so I let my mind wander."

Brannon flips me the bird (not that I can see it through his boxing gloves, I just know him that well) and laughs as he shuffles around a little, warming up his muscles. Shaylee is working with Laila today and while I would normally watch, Brannon wanted to get in a workout and I needed to burn off some of the guilt that had begun to get stronger with each passing day.

"I still haven't told her."

Brannon stops moving and contemplates my statement. "About being fated?" I nod.

His eyebrows slide up almost to his hairline, "You're cruising for a bruising, brother."

"It just never seemed like the right time," I explain. "I wanted to wait until she fell in love with me, but now I'm wondering if I should have just told her in the beginning and dealt with the fallout then."

Brannon shakes his head, a rare serious expression on his face. "I don't know what I would have done in your position, Aden. But it is what it is and you should tell her now. If you wait too long, or she finds out from somebody else, she could go off halfcocked and do something stupid."

He smiles widely at me once again, "Like fall into my waiting arms."

Serious moment over.

"You're right." I flip him the bird when he gives me a 'duh' look. Mine is more effective since I've removed my gloves. "I've got to head out for a few days and check on my other charges."

I cut him a dry look. "Can I trust you to watch over my girl?" I rethink the statement and add, "From afar?"

Brannon laughs raucously, and I can't help but smile. His damn laugh is infectious. "Yeah, brother. I'll keep her in line with an iron fist, and keep her away from my, or anyone else's iron rods."

"You realize you sound like you're twelve, right?" He just grins at me unrepentantly as he removes his gear.

We head to the locker room where Brannon's stuff is stored. He lives in a house out in a nearby suburb, so he hauls a bag back and forth. He begins to pull out his toiletries for a shower and throws me a questioning glance. "When do you go meet with Fate?" he asks the question with a deadpan expression, but I can see the mirth dancing in his eyes. Brannon and Fate get along really well, go figure, and find it absolutely hysterical that I'm so uncomfortable around her.

I narrow my eyes at him, warning him off of the direction he is likely to take this conversation. I'm not is the mood for him to fuck with me about my issues with Fate. "After I get back. I'll call Grady, when I cross, and tell him to let her know we'll be there a few days after that."

Brannon nods, and then slaps me on the back as he leaves to take a shower. "Good luck, dude. I'm sure you've noticed, being so whipped and all, but Shaylee's got a kick ass attitude and as much as I'd love to see her beat the shit out of you, solely for my own entertainment, I might shed a tear if she kills you." He shrugs, "Just saying." Then he disappears into the bathroom, narrowly missing the wind I sent to knock him on his ass. I can hear him chortling on the other side of the door.

I'd love to give as good as I get with him, but some of Brannon's humor is masking his own girl problems and heartache. His normal personality is big, fun-loving, and care-free, and he does a stellar job of only letting people see that side of him. However, Ean and I have been friends with Brannon and Kendrix all our lives. As his twin, Kendrix knows him better than anyone, but it didn't take too much observation for Ean and me to see the pain he hides. I love Hayleigh, but I hope she comes to her senses soon and sees that Brannon is the surest bet she'll ever find. Because if she irreparably breaks his heart, we'll cut her out of our lives without a second thought.

I RETURN TO MY APARTMENT, determined to finally lay everything out for Shaylee. Not hold anything back and try to work through what I'm sure will be a huge fucking fight before I have to leave.

After a quick shower, I dress in a pair of pajama pants, forgoing the shirt. *I'm not completely stupid; I'll take any advantage I can get.*

I get busy in the kitchen and start making dinner in hopes of impressing her. I also grab a couple of bottles of wine because I figure loosening her up a little wouldn't hurt, either.

Miles Davis is playing softly from the stereo and dinner is

just about ready when I hear the lock on the door turn. Shaylee comes in, smiling brightly and looking like my own personal wet dream, with her skin glistening with sweat and her clothes plastered to her luscious body.

Down boy.

She drops her stuff and takes in the soft music and lighting, the dinner waiting to be served, and my naked chest, her mouth slightly parted in a cute little o. Her eyes get a little glazed as she takes in my appearance from head to toe.

Mission accomplished on that front. I silently thank my abs for their support.

I walk around the island, stop in front of her, and give her a lingering kiss. "Hey, baby, why don't you go grab a shower. I'll put your stuff away and get dinner finished up."

The bright smile she walked in with, lights up her face again, and her eyes are soft as they look into mine. "Thanks," her voice is soft and sweet, but her eyes get a naughty little gleam. "Too bad you have to get dinner ready. Now, I'll just have to wash every inch of my body, all by myself."

A groan slips out before I can stop it and her bright smile turns instantly seductive. *Shit. Focus, asshole. Don't you have any control? You don't want dinner to be ruined; stick to the plan.* "I don't want to ruin dinner, so I'll take a rain check, ok?"

Disappointment flashes behind the sea of blue in her eyes.

I lightly kiss her nose and whisper, "I love you." Just like that, the disappointment is gone and replaced by a calculating glitter. "I love you too. Ok, rain check." She sighs and I can hear the fake acceptance in her tone. She's up to something. Before I get sucked into whatever she has planned in that mischievous little brain of hers, I practically run back into the kitchen and grab the garlic bread and salmon from the warmer in the oven. I keep my gaze on the food and fight the instinct to watch her ass and hips sway as she walks back to our bedroom.

Ten minutes later (yeah, she the perfect fucking woman... and my mind is officially screwed now that I'm picturing how I'd like to fuck her tonight.), I hear the bedroom door open and Shaylee's soft footsteps coming down the hall. I grab two wine glasses and the bottle and move over to the dining table sitting in an alcove, next to the kitchen, on the other side of the hallway entrance. I feel her presence behind me, stopped in the doorway, and after setting the bottle down, I turn to tell her to have a seat.

Holy fucking hell. I'm suddenly grateful for my carpeting because the wine glass slips right out of my hands and onto the floor, where my jaw has conveniently fallen as well. Neither break. Despite everything else falling down, my cock has come up with a vengeance and I'm immediately in pain at how hard I am.

Shaylee is posed in the door with her arms spread out, one on each wall. My gaze starts at her stiletto clad feet. Black, sky high, fucking stilettos. As my eyes climb her black stocking-covered legs, *oh fuck*, thigh high covered legs, over the garters holding them up, taking in the sheer black teddy clinging to her body. The top wraps around her neck and each side comes down over one of her mouthwatering tits and tucking into some kind of belt. It leaves her middle bare, as well as either side, and I can see the roundness of her tits peeking out from both sides. My eyes continue back down, stopping at her barely-covered pussy.

Is that? I squint and look a little closer, then glance up at her face for confirmation. She gives me a sexy wink as a nod. Crotch-less panties. My knees go a little weak and for a moment, I think I'm going to crash to the ground in a red haze of lust. I manage to stay upright, until she cocks her hip sassily, placing her hand on it.

"Are you coming?" She turns around and that's when I have to reach out for a chair to steady myself. My dick is so fucking hard, I'm seeing spots. There is no back. Just two pieces of ribbon, one across her lower back, and the other dropping from there and disappearing into her round little ass. I stare, mesmerized by that ass as she sashays back to where she came from. "Judging from your face right now, I'm sure we'll both be," she calls over her shoulder.

What was the plan again? Fuck her. No, dinner and then fuck her. No, there was something else. Oh right—fuck her.

Without another thought, I follow my cock, which is anxiously chasing the pussy walking down the hall.

"I'll be back in a few days, baby." I wrap Shaylee up in my arms and kiss her soundly. Damn, I'm going to miss her.

She returns my kiss with fervor, then pulls away and pats my butt. "No worries. Just be safe and I'll see you when you get back."

I feel my face droop into a pout at her easy acceptance. *I am so fucking whipped.* I sigh at my ridiculous behavior, but give into the attitude anyway. "Won't you miss me?"

Shaylee grins at me, her eyes dancing with laughter. Yeah, if I were in anybody else's shoes, I'd be laughing at me too.

"Of course, I'll miss you." She pecks me on the lips and then steps away, motioning toward the door. "The faster you get out of here, the faster you get back and get welcomed home the way you were sent off."

I groan deeply and pull her in for another crushing kiss. Just thinking about last night has me hard and practically desperate. I'd fucked her with her heels and teddy still on, through the magic little hole in the lingerie. Then I'd stripped her and fucked her naked. Then I eaten her pussy until she was screaming my name so loud I thought the neighbors might come banging on the door, before she rode me hard and I ended up shouting the rafters down too. I was pretty much in a fucking coma after that, and yet, I'd managed to work up the energy to fuck her against the wall in the shower. Then I'd woken up with her warm, wet mouth wrapped around my cock as she sucked me until I was coming down her throat.

We never did talk. Well...I suppose that depends on your definition of *talk*. There were all kinds of dirty things being said, moaned, and screamed. The guilt is building up in me and I used found excuse after excuse to avoid talking to her about it.

But, that wasn't the only guilt eating at me. I hadn't used a damn condom the first time last night. Shaylee doesn't notice much when she is that riled up and when she didn't point out my slip up in the bathroom Friday...I figured it wasn't worth pointing out. But, then I *forgot* again last night. Yeah, I'm stretching it with the word forgot. It may have flitted through my mind briefly, but then I was coming and it shot right out.

I pull away abruptly and plant a kiss on her forehead before taking off, yelling over my shoulder that I love her and for her to be good. I just barely hear her snort and mutter "Yeah, ok." before I shut the door.

Seventeen

SHAYLEE

I MISSED Aden more than I expected to, especially when his trip took a week, instead of a few days. I worked with Laila during the day, keeping my mind occupied. I spent an evening with my grandparents and another, having a girl's night with Laila and Hayleigh. But, when the time with them was done, I went back to our apartment and lied down in our big, cold bed, wrapping myself around his pillow, breathing in his scent. I'd finally gotten a cell phone and I looked longingly at it, wishing I could reach Aden on it. Instead, I'd pull out my e-reader and wait for my eyes to grow heavy.

I've lost the light. I feel as though I'll never find it again, like it's beyond my grasp. The darkness is pressing on me, smothering me, and I'm struggling to breathe. I open my mouth wide, trying to gasp for oxygen and flail my arms in an attempt to dislodge the source of evil suffocating me. My heart is pounding so hard, struggling for every beat. Is this it, then? Will I be swallowed by the darkness?

My limbs begin to feel so heavy and I stop fighting the inevitable. At least I'm wrapped in Aden's scent; I can take a little part of him with me as I succumb to the oblivion I'm hovering over. I think I hear whispers, soft phrases floating into my delirium. "You let him touch you." Who? "You should have been mine." I don't understand! "He can't have you." Who are you? My mind is screaming, railing at the darkness, determined to know why it wants me.

Finally, I resort to begging through my gasps of what little air I can catch. The tears aren't helping, they are clogging my throat and the blackness is edging into my consciousness. I try to ask why, to beg for my life, to find the light once again.

Suddenly, the thick darkness becomes a little less heavy. Each attempt to breath results in a gush of air filling my lungs. I feel a cool brush of something down my cheek, almost like a caress, wiping at the tears that are falling from my eyes.

I heave a huge gasp as I sit up in the bed, clawing at my shirt, pulling away anything that could impede oxygen from getting to my lungs. The tears that had obviously started in my dreams have morphed into gigantic sobs that shudder through my body. How could a dream be so real? I look down and see Aden's pillow resting on my lap. I pick it up, ready to hold it close to me for comfort, but a feeling of terror washes over me and I hurl it across the room.

Jumping out of the bed, I stumble to the bathroom and reach for the light switch just inside the door. Before I find it, I freeze. My brain is ordering me to turn on the light, but I feel a pull in the shadows and the fear of illuminating what's there grips me tight. Ripping my senses away, I rush into the bathroom, slam the door behind me and turn on the light.

When I turn to the mirror, I'm shocked at how haggard I look. My skin, though flushed with fear, has a blue pallor to it. My eyes are pale and lackluster, with only horror to see in their depths. Though my sobs have subsided, the tears continue to pour silently and I wrap my arms around me, backing away from the person in the mirror. No longer able to look at myself, I turn and lean against the wall, still feeling dizzy and out of breath. I shuffle forward, turn on the shower and as I'm waiting for the water to heat up, my eyes drift to the door. I pad over to it and silently turn the lock. A small bit of relief trickles through me and I hurry to get undressed and step under the heated water, hoping it will wash away the rest of my anxiety.

After some time in the shower, my breathing has mostly returned to normal, though I still feel a slight burn with every breath. My muscles have started to relax and exhaustion is quickly overcoming me. When I feel like I can no longer stand, I step out of the shower and wrap myself in a big towel, before collapsing on the floor, my back resting against the tub. I stare at the door and wonder if there is any light yet, since I have no idea what time it is. I've never been afraid of the dark. But now, the thought of leaving the bathroom before the sun is up terrifies me and it keeps me sitting on the floor, staring at the crack in the door, until my eyes get heavy and I slide into a heap and fall into a fitful sleep.

"SHAYLEE!" Laila yells from across the room. "Remember to keep your magic wrapped tight around you. Only let the element you are using extend out from you. But, keep it on a leash; don't let it control you."

We've been working all day on purposely separating my abilities for each element. I've used specific ones before, but it was an accident. When I've made the effort to bring my magic into a fight during training, I always seem to call on them all. I'm also trying to rein it in so that I don't do things like blow the walls down when all I need is a small burst of wind.

Brannon has been working with me so that Laila can coach from the sidelines. Every time, I lose control of my magic, he calls me "Buttercup" (Aden is so going to pay for that) and I'm about ready to go for the groin. I know he's teasing, but I'm tired and cranky from my lack of sleep and the residual fear from my nightmare.

Brannon steps closer and reaches out his hand, a glow forms until a small ball of fire (that's right, a freaking ball of fire. I'm really starting to think I've stepped into an X-Men movie. Something to do with exothermic process...blah blah blah. It's still a ball of fire.) is hovering just above.

"You don't need much to extinguish this, Buttercup."

Aden is a dead man.

I narrow my eyes at him in annoyance, just revisiting the urge to stick my tongue out at him. He gives an unapologetic, lopsided smile and I've forgiven him already. Ugh. How does he do that?

Looking at the small fire, I think about collecting water molecules and using air to drop the temperature without creating a large gust of wind. I can feel the heat begin to spread, the warmth of the sun giving me energy. Just as I start to push the cold water toward Brannon's hand, the warmth of my magic intensifies and the pulse gives a boost to both the water and the air, causing me to practically shove a large amount of the icy liquid (at this point, some of it is icicles) at Brannon and I'm suddenly terrified that I'm going to flay him with the shards of frozen water. The force of the pulse knocks me backwards, just as Brannon topples over the other way.

I scramble to my knees and my breath whooshes out of me in relief when I see the air sizzling with humidity all around Brannon. Laila had used the air around him to combust with fire and it quickly melted and evaporated the water. Brannon is staring at me in stunned silence, but Laila's attention is now focused on the door to the training room. His eyes dart in that direction and a look of understanding dawns on his face. His dimples dig deep when he grins at me and starts laughing uproariously.

Okaaaaaay. I think he might have a screw loose in that head of his.

"Hey, baby." The sound of Aden's voice whips my head around and I jump up with a scream of delight, before running over and throwing myself into his open arms. Our lips crash together and he grabs my ass, lifting me higher to align our bodies. I wrap my legs around his waist and plaster myself against him, the warmth left over from my magic growing into a burn.

I pull my lips away and just hold him tight, whispering, "I missed you so much, Aden."

His eyes sparkle at my words and he rubs his nose softly over mine. "Yeah?"

I don't even try to keep the big, goofy smile off of my face when I answer, "Yeah."

"Oh get a room, would ya?" Brannon jeers.

"We have one." Aden's amused eyes never leave mine as he responds,

"USE IT!"

"Shut your trap, Brannon," Laila interjects. "Aden, you can have Shaylee later. We aren't done for the day."

Aden smirks, still not looking away, "Oh, I'm going to have you. Every single way I can think of, in every room of our house, over and over again," he growls in a lower tone only I can hear.

I'm pretty sure I just had a mini orgasm.

He completely ignores Laila and keeping a firm hold on my ass, turns and leaves with me still wrapped around him like a spider monkey.

Another sleepless night.

≈

I'VE BEEN DRAGGING TODAY, but I can't bring myself to be sorry about it. Laila finally called a halt to training, giving me an irritated scowl, to which I responded with a properly contrite smile.

"Hey," I chirp. *Man, I'm in a great mood*. "You want to get a late lunch? Aden has to meet with Callum to talk about some issues he had with one of the kids he guards."

"Are you going to remain this chipper or act like a normal person?" she drawls, sarcasm behind each word. I just laugh at her attitude and give her a big hug. "Damn, my brother must be a god in bed," Laila mutters. "No," She holds her hand up for silence. "DO NOT respond to that comment."

I break out into hysterics, and then clap my hand over my mouth to keep my noisy actions from disturbing the others in the training room.

Laila rolls her eyes and turns to walk away. "Get the keys to Aden's beamer and we'll go to Bridget's Café," she throws the statement over her shoulder as she walks out the door.

I tell Aden to borrow Ean's car and grab his keys. When he protests, I very thoroughly convince him to see things my way. Besides, Ean is out on assignment anyway.

Laila and I grab a booth at Bridget's, a ridiculously cute little diner about ten minutes away from the training facility. The first time we walked in, I found it incredibly funny that I was standing in a 50's style restaurant. It just seemed...so human. But, I suppose their history isn't that different from ours.

The red vinyl booths sparkle in the sun, shining in from the window we are seated up against and the warmth feels delicious. The waitress (yes, she's wearing a poodle skirt and saddle shoes. I told you...) takes our order and we settle into conversation.

"Laila," I suddenly remember something I wanted to ask her about. "What was up with the power yesterday? I had complete control and then it felt like a new heat wave was practically pulsing right through me."

Laila's phone beeps and she shrugs as she pulls it out. The message puts a deep frown on her face. "I'm assuming it was Aden. When you're fated, your magic is strongest when you're together. Aden walked in unexpectedly and since you've not really been away from each other since you got here, I'm assuming it was just the shock of feeling your power enhanced like that. I mean, the longer you're apart, the stronger the feeling of reconnection is," she answers absent-mindedly, still staring down at her phone, unaware of the effect her comments are having. "When Aden found out you were fated, he changed his mind, and let the council reassign him to you. I'm surprised that Aden didn't mention the boost in strength to you when he explained about being fated."

She finally looks up as she finishes and her eyes grow wide at the site of me. I feel all the blood draining from my face and I can only imagine the devastated look on my paler than normal skin. My stomach has started churning and I wrap my arms around my middle—grateful I haven't eaten anything yet.

"Shaylee..." she trails off, clearly not sure what to say. "He hasn't told you, has he?" She rubs her temples and lets out a grunt of frustration.

I shake my head in answer to her question.

She sighs. "It's not like it sounds. Being fated isn't like the idea humans have created of being 'mated.' They've once again, taken a simple idea and blown it all out of proportion."

She stops for a second and gives me a sheepish look, "No offense."

"So, how is it different?" I croak; my mouth has gone completely dry.

"You're not two halves of a whole who can't survive without the other, nor are you doomed to walk the earth alone if you don't find 'the one' you're meant to be with. Being fated is more like a meeting of compatible souls. You are fated to one person, however everyone has their own choices to make and it can, like any other decision, change the course of fate."

Laila is watching me closely, but I have no reaction to her words. I'm trying to comprehend the fact that Aden wasn't going to come back to me. Until he found out that I could make his magic stronger.

My emotions must come through my eyes though—she must be able to see the pain from the way my head is suddenly pounding, because she opens her mouth and pauses like she's trying to find the right words to say. "I swear it's different, Shaylee." She finds them. "Being fated doesn't mean you *have* to be together." She pauses and this time her hands move to rub the back of her neck. "I've only known it to happen once or twice, but sometimes fated couples don't fall in love. Their souls mesh, and they become the very best of friends, but they never seem to find that spark. The problem there is that no significant other wants to be with someone whose soul is claimed by another. These couples go to Fate and have the connection broken. There are some instances where one person simply chooses not to be with the other. If it were truly the case, that we each only had one soul mate, then some of us would be really screwed if our other half decided not to be with us."

Laila's phone beeps again and without looking at the message, she puts in on silent and throws it in her bag with a look of disgust. "Sometimes, those people are just too bull-headed to accept that what they need is right in front of them and if they'd stop being such stubborn fucking asshole, they might just find some happiness. But no, instead, they cling to their ridiculous ideas and push away the best thing that will ever happen to them." The anger has built up in her voice and I'm taken aback by it. *What is she talking about, exactly?*

She must notice the look of confusion on my face because the waves her hand around as if dispelling her last comment. "A discussion for another day."

The waitress steps up with a tray and Laila waits for her to place our meals down and leave before she continues. "Anyway, for the person being rejected, Fate would have to be a real bitch to let them suffer like that. Don't get me wrong, she has a short fuse to her bitch switch, but in both of those cases, and in a lot of others, Fate will step in and help you to find another soulmate. Although, she's more helpful at certain times than others." The last sentence in dripping with sarcasm. "Sorry, digressing again." Laila shakes her head, getting her mind back into focus, then places her elbows on the table and leans forward, staring at me keenly. "Anyway, my point is that Aden could have made the choice not to be with you. It wasn't an all or nothing situation."

There is a spark of rationality in the back of my brain that knows she is right, but it's over shadowed by bigger emotions of hurt and anger. The churning in my stomach has expanded into full blown nausea and when my eyes drift down to the turkey sandwich on my plate, my hand flies up to cover my mouth and I bolt to the nearest bathroom. I make it there just in time to lose what little I've eaten today, then plant my ass down on the floor, bringing my knees up to my chest and lowering my head to rest in the crevice between them.

"Shaylee?" Laila's voice is filled with concern. "Are you alright?"

"I'm fine, Laila, just give me a minute, please," my voice is muffled, my face still planted on my knees.

"Ok." She sounds uncertain, but her footsteps fade as she returns to the door. "I'll be right outside."

My mind is a whirl of thoughts. Aden isn't capable of lying to me, so his declaration that he had come to see me for my birthday was not a falsehood, but it was still a manipulation of the truth. And, while I knew that he loved me, it hurt to know that he had only come for me because our destinies were tied together. I had hoped that he had been as lost without me as I had been without him. I was terrified that my love for him was stronger and that his reasons for loving me weak, meaning that it might not take much effort for them to slowly disappear over time.

A tight knot continues to coil in my belly, but the nausea had subsided. I stand up, rinse my mouth, splash some cool water on my face, and step to the bathroom door. I open it, but I hesitate to fully walk out when I hear Laila on the phone a few feet down the hall.

"Well, you should have told her, jackass! I didn't figure you for being such a coward, Aden, so it didn't occur to me that she didn't know!"

I obviously can't hear the other side of the conversation, but my mind is racing to imagine what he was saying.

"You better fix this, Aden. Not only will Fate and the council be pissed at you, but I'm going to kick your ass from one side of Rien to the other if I lose her friendship because you were too stupid to be upfront with her."

I can't help the small smile on my face knowing that Laila will always be my friend. I miss Brenna almost as much as my mother and aunt, but my time with Hayleigh and Laila have helped me settle into my life here.

Laila snorts in derision before responding to whatever Aden has said. "Yeah, good luck with that one, Aden. Shaylee isn't a pushover and I don't think your powers of seduction are going to help you. I'll see you tomorrow when you're limping from the kick to your balls *I'm sure* is coming your way." She snaps the phone shut without waiting for a response and mutters something unintelligible.

She turns to walk back my way but stops when she sees me waiting there at the door. "Hi. Sorry about that. Please don't be mad at me for warning him." She comes forward apprehensively.

"It's fine, Laila. Just because he knows to watch out for my ball shot, doesn't mean he'll be able to avoid it."

Laila's face washes with relief at my humor. As soon as she reaches me, she slings an arm through mine and we walk together out to the car. She stops me with a hand on my biceps as I go to walk around to the driver's side.

"He really didn't have to come back for you, Shaylee. My brother is an idiot, but he's been in love with you since the moment he no longer looked at you like a child. He loved to tell stories about you as a child. Then one day, he didn't say much at all anymore. But, I think each of us took a turn dragging it out of him because by the time you arrived, I felt like I already knew you." She grasps me a little tighter and her voice persistent. "He'd made the choice to be with you before he knew you were fated. It just hadn't truly registered in his mind. I swear it."

I sigh, "But, we'll never truly know that, will we Laila?" The hurt in my heart becomes sharp and knifes through me. Laila's face falls and she steps back, her shoulders slumped in defeat. "I love your brother. And, I'll love him forever, but I don't want to wait around and see if his love for me is born of this connection between or souls, or if it is a result of the connection between our hearts. He broke my heart, Laila. I don't think I'd survive it a second time."

Laila nods and without a word, gets into the car. On ride

home, I contemplate what I said, but I realize, I've sunk too deep. I know I'll forgive Aden because I love him too much to let him go, until he leaves me. That doesn't mean I'm not going to let him have it, though. I perk up a little at the thoughts of what I can do to make Aden suffer just a little bit. The little devil in me cackles.

Eighteen

ADEN

Damn it all too fucking hell.

I run my hands through my hair for the twentieth time, gripping the roots and tugging so that the little pinpricks of pain take my focus off of the confrontation I know is about to happen.

That's what you get for being a pussy.

I ignore the inner taunting in my mind as I pace back and forth in the living room, keeping my eyes trained on the door. I never meant to keep this from her for so long, and now, by not telling her, I'm sure she thinks that I held it back so I would not to have to confess that I wanted her simply because we were fated.

My thoughts are interrupted when the door to the apartment slams open, bouncing of the wall. Shaylee marches in, fury blazing in her beautiful eyes. The blue is so penetrating that I feel myself reacting—*seriously? Get a fucking grip, dude.*

Just as I open my mouth to speak...

"I don't know why you didn't tell me about being fated, Aden," Shaylee cuts me off. "I don't know why you felt that I wouldn't be rational enough to consider the facts and trust that it only makes our love stronger. But, by not telling me, by omitting it, you've come perilously close to lying." Her hands are gripping her hips and her voice is low, her tone deadly. *Ok, that's better than hysterics, right?* Mad is better than hurt. *I think?*

Her words hit me a little hard and I flinch. "Baby, that's not what happened, I—"

"—Whatever, Aden. You weren't going to come for me until you found out. You didn't have an uncontrollable need to be with me, you weren't consumed by your love for me, no —you were doing what was best for you. And isn't that always your MO? To do what's best for *you*?"

I know she's hurt and angry, but her words piss me off and I can't help jumping to correct her ludicrous assumption. "Shaylee, this convoluted reasoning you've conjured up couldn't be further from the truth." Apparently, my stupidity knows no bounds, because as soon as the words leave my mouth, I know they were the wrong thing to say.

"Convoluted?" she questions. At the look in her eyes, I take a step back, a little worried that she might open a grave under me, this time on purpose.

"Look, I shouldn't have used that word. I just meant that you're seeing the situation wrong."

Shaylee scrutinizes me and for a moment, I think I see her becoming willing to finally listen to me, but then she stomps past me, headed for our bedroom. I don't let her get far. I grab her arm and whirl her around, pinning her to my chest with my arms banded tightly around her.

"You can be as mad as you want, baby. But don't be so petulant that you won't even listen to what I have to say," I demand. She scowls at me, but gives me a short, jerky nod of acceptance, then squirms a little trying to get out of my hold.

"No, I think I'll keep you right here, so you can't run off without hearing my side of things." Besides, all her wiggling rubs our bodies in all the right places and I can't help feeling a little smug when I see the desire in her eyes as well. She rolls her eyes at me but stops pushing against my arms, since she knows she won't be able to break my hold.

"You're right; I hadn't intended to come back to you." Hurt flashes stronger on her face, before she schools her features into a flat expression. "I let myself believe that I'd imagined the connection between us—that it was just physical and it wouldn't be right to give in to that when there was someone out there that you were fated with. When the council reassigned me to you, I realized what I'd overlooked before— it's me. You were always meant to be mine."

Shaylee's eyes soften just the smallest amount and she looks down to hide it, but I can tell that she is listening intently. "Since the day my little Buttercup disappeared and a beautiful, grown up woman appeared, I've been addicted to you. To be fated with you just gave me permission to accept what I was feeling for you. To allow myself to give in to what I knew deep down—that I was—that I am, completely in love with you."

To my relief, I can see that my words are having at least some effect on her. However, hurt is still swimming in the blue depths of her eyes. "Why didn't you tell me?"

"Honestly, I was afraid of how you would react and I wanted you to fall in love with me first, so that you couldn't just walk away. I admit, I wasn't giving you enough credit. I wasn't thinking about the Shaylee I really know, the one who would listen and consider the situation before reacting to it." I lower my forehead to hers and close my eyes, sighing. "I don't know what the hell I was doing, baby. I was just terrified that, for some reason, I would lose you. I meant to tell you so many times, but we've been so happy and content, I couldn't bring myself to disturb it with the unknown."

I drop a soft kiss on her lips and despite the fact the she doesn't respond, I feel hope that she didn't turn away from it. "Can you try and step back, look at this as if I'd told you right from the beginning?"

Her head drops and she lays her cheek on my chest, just over my heart. After a deep breath she sighs. "I can't forget, but I know I'll forgive you. I'm just not ready right now, Aden. I need some time to process all of this. Every time I start to think I've got a grip on this new life, something else drops in my lap and takes me back. Two steps forward and one step back." She pushes against me a little and, this time, I let her go. Her eyes are tired with dark circles ringing them—she's exhausted.

I kept her up for most of the night, but she looks as though she hasn't slept in days. I put my hands around her neck and use my thumbs to lift her chin so that I can study her face. "Baby, are you alright? You look like you're about to fall off of your feet."

Shaylee shrugs, her hands fluttering around before returning to hang at her sides. "I'm just tired. I didn't sleep well while you were gone."

I carefully suppress any smugness from my voice but I can't help asking, "You missed me?" I slept like shit without her.

As I watch her, she seems to droop, like the world is pulling her down. "Yes, but mostly I just had terrible night-mares and when I woke, I couldn't go back to sleep. Look, I'm going to go take a hot back and lie down for a while. I need to be alone," she adds quickly. Evidently, she knew I was about to ask if she wanted company.

Now, it's me drooping. She'd said she would forgive me, but I can't help feeling defeated, knowing she is hurting and wondering how long it will be before she lets me in again. I reach for her and she allows me to place a soft kiss on her forehead. Then she turns and makes her way down the hall.

When the sun begins to descend, I crack open our bedroom door and walk in softly to avoid waking Shaylee, who is sleeping on her stomach, her head facing me. After our argument, I figured she would sleep in her pajamas and I'd prepared myself to sleep without her warm, naked body snuggled up next to mine. But, she looks as though she simply collapsed and passed out on the bed after her bath, not even bothering to remove her towel.

I pad over to her and remove the damp towel as carefully as I can, so as not to disturb her. Quickly, I strip out of my clothes and go to my side of the bed, slip under the covers and gently pull Shaylee into my arms, before drawing the covers over her as well. With her warmth seeping into mine, I sigh in contentment, and let myself succumb to sleep.

MY EYES FLY open at the awful sound emanating from behind the bathroom door. I sit up, noticing that Shaylee's side of the bed is empty and I hurry to see if she's all right. She's lying, curled up on the floor, in front of the small room, housing one of the toilets, her forehead resting on the cool marble below her.

Kneeling down, I feel to see if she has a fever, but her skin is cool and a little clammy. I stand back up, grab a cloth and dampen it with slightly cool water. Returning to the floor next to her, I turn her face and wipe it tenderly before placing it on the back of her neck.

"Are you all right? Can I get you anything, baby?" I ask as I rub her back softly.

"No," her voice is subdued and weary, as though even that

one word took too much effort. After a moment, she sits up and carefully crawls into my lap, wrapping my arms around her and practically burrowing into me.

"Are you feeling better?" Her head bumps my chin when she nods. "Want to get back into bed?" Same response.

I anchor my arms under her and lift as I get back onto my feet. I sit her on the counter by the sink and keep her upright while I put toothpaste on her toothbrush and hand it to her. She lazily brushes her teeth and when she's done, I lift her back into my arms. Back in the bedroom, I softly lay her down, then climb into bed and cuddle up next to her, spooning with her back right up against my front. A glance back at the clock tells me it's just after 6am, so I snuggle her in a little deeper and go back to sleep for a couple of hours.

My alarm goes off at eight thirty and I groan, feeling as though my eyes are filled with sand and glued shut. After a few minutes, I manage to peel my eyelids back and turn my head to see how Shaylee is feeling. Once again, I find her side of the bed empty. I hope she isn't sick again. Frowning, I get up and grab a pair of pajama pants on my way to the bathroom. Finding it empty, I wander out to the kitchen and stop, entranced by the sight before me.

Shaylee is frying up bacon on the griddle, a bowl of eggs sitting next to it, ready to be scrambled. She's humming softly to herself and she looks fresh and much more rested than the night before. Her little nightie is riding up as she sways her hips, and my morning wood is instantly at full attention. I want to fill my hands with her luscious ass and kiss her until she's begging me to take her, but I don't know where we are at after yesterday, and I'd like to avoid pissing her off further. I tell woody to go back to his corner and relax and, for once, he listens. Mostly.

'Good morning, baby." I step up to the bar and debate on whether to attempt a kiss. "Are you feeling better?" *Why not?* I lean over and to my relief, she lifts her face to meet my kiss.

"I feel great. Nothing like a good night's sleep." She sounds oddly cheerful and I'm a little confused. Last night happened, right?

"So," I coax tentatively, "Are we ok?" My hands grip the counter top a little tightly and I sit as I anxiously await her answer.

She continues to watch the bacon and has added the scrambled eggs, but she glances up with a small smile. "I don't want to fight with you, Aden." She sighs and turns around to grab two plates from a cupboard. Setting them down, she starts to fill them as she continues. "I was so hurt when I first found out, and then so angry, I didn't think I'd be able to handle wondering if your love was based on an idea that we belong together rather than knowing in your heart."

I want to interrupt, but I can see that she isn't finished and I don't want to press my luck, considering where I think this is going.

"But, I was thinking about all the times you've shown me what I mean to you over the last several weeks." She turns off the griddle and comes around the bar, setting both plates down. Then she moves to stand between my legs, my hands come to rest on her hips, and she loops her arms around my shoulders. "I trust you. I know you better than to think you would ever settle. We both know this is the real deal." She kisses my lips softly, "We both know we're it for each other." Another kiss, "And we both know this is forever."

This time, when she leans in for the kiss, I grab the back of her head and bring her mouth solidly against mine. My other hand flexes on her hip and tugs her closer, melding our bodies as I devour her lips.

"I love you, baby." I breathe against her lips. "Forever."

She pulls back and beams at me, "Forever. I'll love you forever."

Sweeping her up in to my arms I stalk toward the bedroom, breakfast forgotten. Shaylee laughs in delight and smacks my shoulder telling me she is famished. I ignore her and have my favorite breakfast until she's screaming my name. Then I go back for seconds. After all, breakfast is the most important meal of the day.

We finally get back to the kitchen and heat up the food, devouring it, not caring one bit that it's a little dry. Shaylee practically inhales hers before eating another large helping. As we clean up the kitchen together, I can't help teasing her.

"Worked up an appetite, huh?" I'm pretty sure that if I were wearing a shirt with buttons, they would be popping off from the satisfaction swelling my chest.

A sly smile creases her face and she winks at me. *Damn, she's sexy.* "You did. But, for some reason I am incredibly hungry today. It must be because I got sick twice yesterday."

I frown at her statement. "Twice?"

"Yes, the first time was at the restaurant."

Guilt slithers in and takes up residence, deflating my ego. It was my fault she'd gotten sick at the diner and probably the stress of our fight made her sick again this morning.

"I'm sorry." When her head snaps up and she stops loading the dishwasher. From the look on her face, it occurs to me that I never really apologized. "I should have said that first. I really am sorry, baby."

Her face dissolves into a bright smile and I can't help but admire how heartbreakingly beautiful she is.

"Thanks, Aden," she says brightly. "That means everything to me. It's forgiven and forgotten, ok?" My answering smile is so big, it almost hurts my face. I love her so fucking much, it overwhelms me sometimes.

"I guess we should get to our workout." I announce seriously. Her face falls and I stifle a snicker, doing my best to keep my face neutral.

She gives me a half smile and shrugs, "Ok." Then turns to head down the hall. I rush up to her and grabbing her waist, I throw her over my shoulder and continue on to the bedroom. She shrieks in surprise and I give her ass a swat, making her laugh. "I was thinking we should workout in the bedroom today."

~

AFTER OPENING the door and allowing Shaylee to enter, I grab her hand and lace our fingers together. I got a call from Grady yesterday, not that I answered it, seeing as how I was rather busy.

Really fucking busy. (Pun totally intended)

Fate was ready to meet with us. I groaned long and loud when I listened to the voicemail. I'd put it on speaker phone at my reaction, Shaylee flopped down on the bed, peals of laughter dancing through the room. Fate seriously brings out my childish side, because I stomped into the bathroom and pouted in the shower. *What?* Don't tell me you don't ever do it. We both know you're lying your ass off.

So here we are, ready to meet with her. Shaylee looks up at me with a raised eyebrow, silently asking if I'm all right.

I nod. *Just peachy.*

Fate lives in a large old Victorian house on the other side of the city. The outside is painted and decorated accurately to the time period in which it was built. The inside is another matter altogether. Each room reflects a different style, or in this case, different personalities. The front room is splashed with color, modern art, and really weird furniture scattered around in what I'm assuming is a specific arrangement.

We pass by a rec room, decorated like nineteen twenties

speakeasy, a retro fifties kitchen, a gallery of Grecian art, and on, and on. We finally reach the door that leads to her office and I raise my hand to knock. Before my knuckles meet the wood, a feminine voice calls out for us to enter. I roll my eyes. *Show-off.*

Opening the door, I usher Shaylee into the room and follow behind, before stopping in my tracks to take in what's before me. *Are you kidding me?*

The room that used to be a calm and professional office is now decorated like the inside of a tent in India. The floor is scattered with colorful sitting pillows, surrounding a low wooden table, holding a—*what the fuck?* In the center of the table is a fucking crystal ball. What is she up to?

Shaylee's jaw is practically unhinged as she gazes around the room, taking in the statues and other art, the fabric draped along the walls and ceiling, and the ridiculously large hookah pipe standing in a corner, by the door, on the opposite side of the room.

"Come, come, and have a seat Baccē." The words float from behind some of the scarves, obscuring a portion of the room along the left side. The voice is low and accented, and I really just want to know why the hell she is being so weird. Par for the course, I suppose, but this is a little overboard. "I am Ashareera vani, the oracle." Now I understand why she's hiding behind the fabric. Ashareera vani is the Hindu version of an Oracle, a person without body who relays messages from God.

Shaylee walks over to the table and sits on a cushion, staring at the crystal ball, as if to see if that's where the voice is coming from.

"Seriously? What the hell is going on, Fate?" I ask, not even attempting to hide my irritation.

Fate steps from behind the sheer curtain and throws me a dirty look. "Way to ruin it, Aden. I mean, come on, don't you know you're not supposed to pay attention to the man behind the curtain. Or woman, in this case," her voice has raised to a normal pitch, but I find myself gaping at her getup.

I've entered the fucking Cuckoo's Nest. I restrain myself from looking around for Nurse Rachet.

She's dressed in a billowing white robe, a puff god turban, and several strands of beads hang off the headdress, as well as around her neck. She looks completely ridiculous.

She snaps her fingers to bring my attention back to her face. "I was just about to practice my fortune telling skills with the crystal ball." She gives me a scowl, "But, you've ruined it now. Honestly," she huffs, "you're such a stick in the mud. If you didn't have such a juicy, fine ass, you'd be no fun at all. " Her look turns from reproachful to a leer in seconds, making me shift uncomfortably.

Waving her hand, her clothes turn into a short (I mean, short) wrap thing and a tight halter that shows off her flat stomach. Her blonde hair is messy waves around her shoulders and she has a diamond choker around her neck. On a lot of other women, it would look trashy as hell, but somehow, she pulls it off. The room also shifts to look exactly like it usually does, white walls and furniture, with lime green and chocolate brown furniture, giving it some color. It's classy and reminds me a lot of Shaylee. Speaking of Shaylee...

My gaze finds her and I groan at the shell shocked look on her face. Her eyes are bouncing around the room over to Fate, and back around the room, never quite settling. So far, Shaylee has only been exposed to the more subtle and realistic magic of the Fae. Fate, for whatever reason, has the kind of magic you read about in corny novels. Nobody understands it, we just speculate on it and as far as we can figure, it must be a magical boost from God that comes with being Fate.

Shaylee's widened eyes are now staring at Fate's face, enraptured. Oh right, she's seeing another of Fate's idiosyncrasies. Despite almost every other feature matching the rest of the Fae, the big difference is that her eyes are purple. Not blue or green like all other Fae, but a deep amethyst. It's weird. And when she studies you with those piercing jewel-like orbs, it can be creepy as shit. Fate is always in crazy mode with her loud and flamboyant personality, but somehow, her eyes can look serious and right through you, all the while she's heartily laughing and cracking jokes. Then, there is the fact that she has a perpetual glow. Similar to the way the rest of us look when we are accessing our magic, but hers never goes away. Creeps me the fuck out.

She turns to Shaylee, who has risen from the floor, and practically flounces over to her and embracing her in a big hug. "Welcome, girl! I've been waiting *ages* to meet you!" She stresses the word ages as though Shaylee had been here for years without meeting her as opposed to weeks. *Insert eye roll here.*

She grabs her hands and drags her over to a long, white couch and flops down, pulling Shaylee with her. "So, tell me," she whispers conspiratorially, "What's Aden like in bed? I've been trying to tap that for years, but he's a stubborn ass. I don't know what his problem was, I mean, *come on*, I'm hot, right?"

Shaylee's shock seems to be wearing off because she giggles and glances at me, her eyes dancing with merriment. I glower in response.

"So?" Fate encourages again. "Is he an animal? Or does he just put on a macho show and he's really a pussycat in bed? Oh! Is he hung? Seriously, it's crazy how many mouthwatering alpha guys that are out there who disappoint you in the bedroom with their tiny packages."

"Can we move on from this discussion, please?" I plead loudly, to drown out her words.

Shaylee gives me a sympathetic look that is completely

ruined by the naughty smile on her face. She turns back to Fate. "Yes, no, and definitely," she answers in a stage whisper.

Fate's eyes light up with delight at Shaylee's willingness to play along. She turns and gives me a thorough inspection from head to toe and on the way back up, pauses to consider my... package. "Interesting." I'm not sure if she is referring to my dick or to Shaylee's response but either way, I am, yet again, squirming uncomfortably.

"Well," she sighs melodramatically. "That's a sad opportunity wasted. But..." she trails off for effect. Her theatrics are getting ridiculous. "If you're ever entertaining the mood for a ménage or to swing, just let me know!" *Kill me now.* Why are there so many women in my life determined to fuck with me? *Ok, not the best term, considering the topic of conversation.*

"I don't suppose we could get to why we're here?" I grumble.

Fate rolls her eyes at me, "Don't get your panties in a fucking wad, Aden." She perks up, having just thought of something. She turns back to Shaylee. "Please tell me it's not that, right? He's not hiding a fetish for women's underwear?"

At this point, Shaylee loses it completely and almost falls off of the couch from laughing so hard. *Where is that hole in the ground when you really need it?*

Nineteen

SHAYLEE

My stomach is aching from laughing so hard. This woman is a breed all her own and I love her. I know I shouldn't take pleasure in it, but the way she needles Aden, and gets him so creeped out, is pretty damn entertaining. He gives me a dirty look that is clearly indicating his branding of me as a traitor. I just manage to squelch more giggling and keep my face straight.

Fate gets up and takes a seat behind her desk. We each move to one of the two chairs positioned in front of it. She sits back and considers me a moment before turning to Aden with an amused smile.

"I wasn't sure which way this was going to go, especially considering that your decisions were not premeditated, but made in the moment. I guess I haven't been paying that close of attention to you two lately." She cocks her head and studies me for another moment, then smirks at Aden. "She doesn't know, does she?"

Oh. "No, he finally told me last night," I interject.

Fate smiles at me in delight. "No, no. I'm not talking about that. I'm talking about you being pregnant."

Ever cell in my body goes haywire and I jump to me feet screeching, "WHAT????"

It can't be, he wouldn't—I'm not... I start wringing my hands together, the stress of the moment causing my grip to be almost painful. "You must be wrong. There's no way. I mean we've got years before." My words are stuttering from the scattered thoughts bouncing around in my head. It suddenly breaks through, the way that Fate was talking about it. As if Aden knew...

I whip around and am slightly mollified to see the shock on his face. He shakes his head for a moment, mostly likely in denial, because that's certainly what I'm feeling. But, there is something in his expression that is suspect.

Could Fate be wrong? She must be. But, my thoughts are coming together and I start to remember little things. Being so tired yesterday, how hungry I was this morning, getting sick yesterday and this morning. But, all of that happened in the last day. Those could be symptoms of the flu.

Fate's gaze is bouncing back and forth between the two of us, vastly amused by our reactions. I start pacing in a little two foot by two foot spot, and I can only imagine that I look like a wind-up toy in a box, that turns around abruptly every time it hits a wall.

I know I'm freaking out, I just hope Aden isn't; I'm not sure we could handle the situation if we are both about to crack. The next time I turn and I'm facing him, I look to see his face has shifted. His shock has morphed into a mixture or excited wonder and...pride?

Oh, give me a break.

"Seriously, Aden? You think you could put away your extremely inflated man card and instead of focusing on the fact that you successfully knocked up your girlfriend, how about we figure out what the fuck we are going to do now that you've KNOCKED UP YOUR GIRLFRIEND!!!" My voice has gotten progressively higher and now, I'm practically screaming.

Aden doesn't say anything and I growl and return to pacing. After a few quick rotations, I turn around and bump right into Aden's strong chest. I need his strength and I melt right into him. He smooths my hair back and kisses the top of my head. "We can do this, baby. Everything will work out the way it's supposed to."

Fate snorts and I whip my head in her direction. When she notices my face, which I'm sure conveys every emotion related to fear and shock, she waves her hand lightly, "Sorry. That's just a funny phrase." She accompanies the words with a killer smile. I'm starting to wonder what it was I liked about her. "No, I mean, because people say that as if I can tell them exactly what is supposed to happen in their life, like their destiny is 'pre-ordained'." She uses sarcastic bunny ears to put quotations around the last word.

Aden sits down in my vacated seat and drags me onto his lap, before wrapping me up in his arms again. He gives Fate an exasperated sigh, then asks, "Would you get to the point of why we are here, already?"

Fate sticks her tongue out at him peevishly and I almost laugh. Almost. She gives him a slightly evil grin and then meets my gaze. "It wasn't on purpose. I'll give him that. But that doesn't mean he was careful about it."

I stiffen at her words and Aden lets out an aggravated groan. "What the fuck, Fate? Did you really have to go and make things worse?"

It hits me then, all of the times we didn't use protection. We used it more often than not but when I say 'we' didn't use protection, I mean it. As much as I'd like someone to blame, it doesn't change the fact that I didn't insist on it every time, and it definitely doesn't change the fact that apparently, I am now pregnant. *Holy shit, I'm fucking pregnant.*

I sit up and grasp Aden's chin, bring his face around to mine. The daggers he was throwing at Fate, swiftly change to a slightly embarrassed and wary look. I've calmed down enough now to give him a tremulous smile. "It's as much my fault as yours, Aden. It takes two and I wasn't exactly insisting that you use protection every time." A look of relief washes over his face and is immediately followed by one of adoration.

He gives me a sweet, lingering kiss. "I love you, baby." Before I can respond, we are interrupted by a gagging sound.

"Ugh, this soul mate business is going to kill me one of these days. Seriously, I'm going to choke on the sickeningly sweet scent of love in the air."

Aden's back to glaring daggers and I'm back to stifling my laughter.

"Sexual tension? That I can do. You want to throw down right here? No problem, I can sell tickets, join in, film it for posterity, whatever you want. But this gooey crap," she motions to the two of us, "I think I need a good hard fuck to get it off of me."

I can't keep the snort in and I erupt into hysterics, while Aden just looks up at the ceiling and shakes his head. I'm pretty sure he's asking God what he was thinking when he chose this chick to be Fate.

"Ok. Ok. Back on topic." Fate seems to rein herself in a little and leans back in her chair again, watching us. "So, here's the skinny, as far as I can see it right now. Things are going to get darker out there. I'm not sure when, but someone's made a decision already that has set this course for the worse and it's very unlikely that it will change. I know you've been wondering if Shaylee's power is the result of genetics or something, but in reality, you've been given your enhanced gifts for a specific purpose and it definitely requires you to work together."

I want to ask her questions, but Aden gives me a little

squeeze and a miniscule shake of his head. So, I keep my mouth shut and listen.

"I'd tell you more about your purpose, but I can't right now because the motions are not set in stone. Until they are, you just need to keep preparing, keep training, do...whatever it is you guards do." She scoots her chair in and rests her elbows on the desk, her hands in fists under her chin. "Shaylee, the baby complicates things a little bit, but not as much as you might think. Keep training until it's physically necessary for you to stop. Once the baby is born, get back to it quickly. Yours' and Aden's fate has not changed, it's just been tweaked and I know you'll be able to handle it."

I'm a little confused, but Aden seems to be following her, so I guess I'll get the "skinny" from him later.

Fate's eyes cloud with despair for a moment, before they clear up, returning to the bright intensity they've been the rest of our time here.

"Aden, there was one thing you were right about; Shaylee was discovered before she was marked. I'm pretty sure they turned a Fate reader." Aden stiffens again, and leans forward, his face a mask of fury.

"Are you fucking with me?" I'm taken aback by the ferocity of his tone and peek at Fate to see if she's offended by it. But, she seems to equal his sentiment, because she doesn't take the bait laid out right there in front of her with that statement. I'm also a little rattled because that is a question that I wouldn't normally ask someone in Rien. But, things are just different for Fate; she plays by a whole other set of rules.

"No. I'm not one hundred percent sure. This particular Fate reader's destiny has been flitting around so much with indecision that I can't get a good handle on where he'll land." She pauses for a moment, seemingly considering her next words. "It seems as though they turned him before he was marked. I'm even more baffled as to how he was found out.

But, because he wasn't marked yet, his fate is murky. He doesn't stand solidly on our side or theirs."

Fate looks to the ceiling, and for the first time, I see a slight sadness enter her features, but she closes her eyes, and like last time, it is gone almost before it was there.

"I can't know everything. You understand that, right?" her question is filled with intensity, brittle with stress. Aden nods but waits for her to get it all out. "Sometimes, it's almost impossible to know whether sharing something will change your destiny, rather than giving you a nudge in the right direction, so that you can make your own choices that will lead you to the right future."

She closes her eyes again and rubs her temples. This entire conversation is playing out in front of me and I feel a little like a spectator at a play. I see and hear everything, but I'm not really a part of it. And yet, so much of the play seems to be about me.

"Look, I can't tell you what will happen, as I said, it's changing too rapidly right now. But, I can't get a handle on whether I should share this information, so I'm just going to take the leap." She looks straight at Aden now, and I am startled when I see the reproach in her gaze. "You've forgotten that there are still shadows in Rien. At night, the shadows are more alive than we want to think. He's been in the shadows, Aden. He continues to stalk her."

Aden gapes at her in disbelief, then something seems to dawn on him and it quickly turns to rage, he's almost shaking with it. "Are you telling me he's been in our home at night? That he's been the evil in my dreams?"

I gasp at his words. *No.* Fate's head swivels toward me and she nods.

"He—he tried to suffocate me, didn't he?" The words get clogged on their way out and I have to control the need to gag.

Fate doesn't respond, just continues to contemplate me.

Aden, however, has all kinds of responses. He lets out a string of curse words and phrases that have my ears turning a little pink.

"Why the fuck didn't you tell me, Shaylee?" he roars.

I bristle at his accusatory tone and snap right back. "Because I thought it was a dream, jackass. Why didn't *you* tell me that you'd been having dreams like that?"

My reasoning deflates his argument and he hangs his head for a moment before laying it on my shoulder and whispering an apology. His hand is softly rubbing my belly and I feel a warm little glow under his administrations. "I won't let anything happen to you." He nuzzles my neck and murmurs, "Either of you."

"Are we back to this again?" Apparently, Fate is done with this meeting because she stands up and begins to walk toward the door. "Take it to your bedroom, would you? I'm off to find someone to take me to mine." Her words don't carry the humor that they did before.

I SNUGGLE up tight to Aden and revel in the safety I find in his arms. The car ride home had been silent, and when we arrived, Aden rushed us up to our apartment, intent on avoiding everyone. He silently undressed me, and then stripped off his own clothes, before crawling onto the bed and pulling me down with him, wrapping his body around me. We've been in this position for over two hours, silent and safe in each other's embrace. But, I'm getting a little worried at where he's disappeared to in his head. Something has been on my mind, so I decide it's as good a place as any to ease into conversation.

"Aden?"

"Hmmm?" I almost miss it, because his face is buried in

my neck. He nuzzles it lightly and a sweet shiver tingling starts up at my center. I try to keep my focus on the conversation I want to have, but he's not making it easy.

"Are you happy about the baby?"

He stills, and then raises his head so that his emerald eyes are gazing steadily into mine. "I'm over the fucking moon, baby."

I can feel the light glowing inside me at his words. I've spent the last couple of hours thinking about being pregnant and every moment, I got just a little bit more excited about it. Sure, it would probably have been better to have waited, but now that this little life is growing inside me, I can't imagine it any other way.

"Me too," I say softly. He smiles widely at me, his dimple popping out and making that tingle get a little stronger. He makes me feel loved, worshiped, and adored. I don't care if those are technically all the same thing; I feel each one of them.

"I'm excited to see our baby grow here." His hand, that had been resting on my belly and rubbing light circles, slowly starts to move up until he's cupping my breast. The tingles are igniting into a burn and it's spreading to each nerve throughout my whole body.

He squeezes it lightly, and then begins toying with my nipple. Everything seems to have changed in a day because they are over sensitive and I gasp at the rush of lust traveling from the hardened peak straight to my pussy. "I love your tits, baby. But, I certainly have no problem with them getting bigger." I giggle then moan when he lifts my breast up and slowly licks around the dark pink area before sucking the nipple into his mouth. I moan again and fidget just a little, bringing my legs together to try and relieve some of the pressure. Aden growls low in reply, and comes up over me, using his knee to part my legs before settling in between my thighs. When the hot, hard pressure of his cock pushes against me, I cry out and grip him with my legs around his hips.

"Fuck, baby, are you more sensitive?" He tests his theory by pressing a little harder against me, causing me to whimper and lock my legs even tighter. He's looking down into my eyes, watching my reaction to his movements and he gets a satisfied little grin that turns sly in an instant. "You're already so wet down there, baby. I can feel it coating my cock, making it slick and hot." His words ignite me, just like he knew they would and I'm about three filthy words from coming.

He rocks into me a little harder this time, and then seals his mouth over mine, his tongue thrusting into my mouth in the same rhythm. It only takes another minute before I'm shaking with tremors of release. Aden moves down from my mouth laying hot, wet kisses all the way down to my breasts. He suckles, licks, kneads, all the while still rolling his hips, causing shockwaves to course through my body.

"I want to take you in my mouth and feel you come around my tongue, baby. But, I don't think I can wait. You're so fucking sexy and your responses have my cock ready to explode."

I squeeze him between my legs with all of my strength. "I need you, Aden. I need you, now."

Without any preamble he rears back and sinks deep, deep inside me. His mouth crashes down on mine and his kiss consumes me. I feel as though every part of me is fused with every part of him. Our souls, our hearts, and our bodies are one. The pace is frantic, both of us anxious to take that leap together.

"Are you ready?" His breath is coming out in pants and I can feel his body contracting.

"Yes!"

"Let go, baby. Let go."

With his next thrust, I scream and shoot off like a rocket,

splintering apart, shattering into an oblivion like no other. His shout registers through my haze as he joins me in the stars and the feel of his orgasm rushing through him, heightens the sensation on every inch of my skin.

We ride each other through to the very last pulse and then collapse in a languid heap. He rolls to the side, slipping out and chuckles at my whimper of protest. Moving some wayward hair out of my face, he kisses me tenderly and whispers that he loves me, then turns me onto my side and pulls me in to his protective cocoon.

"Aden, when you said Saliysuli to my grandparents, you were telling them we were forever, right? That we are fated?"

"Yes. I wanted to make sure they understood that you belong with me. You'll always belong with me." He's placing little kisses along the shell of my ear and I sigh in contentment. "Did you see the carving on the headboard?"

I nod, I hadn't thought about it since I first saw it. "Did you have it done after you found out we were fated?"

"No. It was on the original design when I had it built. No one has ever slept in this bed with me but you. This bed was always intended to be where I would sleep with my soulmate." I can feel him grinning into my hair, "The mother of my children." He pauses and I think he's done. "My wife," he adds in a whisper.

I turn my head, my face beaming, and give him a kiss. Then settle back down into his embrace. At this moment, the world beyond us ceases to exist and we are just the three of us. Safe, warm, loved, and completely happy.

Blissful moments are often a precursor to its opposite. But, I don't want to think about that.

ADEN

SHAYLEE WAS UP sick again in the early morning, so I decided not to wake her when I got up. I can't bring myself to leave her right now, so I call Ean and ask him to come over so we can talk.

Once he arrives, I motion for him to have a seat on the couch and I grab us each a mug of coffee before joining him in the living room. The sun has been up for a few hours and it's streaming through all of the open windows, warming me and giving me strength. I don't know what the hell is going on, but this motherfucker who is stalking Shaylee has his days numbered.

I fill Ean in on our conversation with Fate, about the dreams, and the time Shaylee was almost suffocated. Since Ean also lives here, I need his help figuring out how this Fallen slipped in and out of my home without my notice.

"I slept with the fucking light on last night, Ean. I should have felt him, especially when I'm with Shaylee. Everything is magnified between the two of us, so how the hell did this guy get away with this?"

Ean is leaning back against the couch with his arms crossed

over his broad chest, a deep frown on his face. "There's nothing special about the locks on our doors and this person could be as capable as anyone at picking it. It's not like we have some kind of magic protective spells that we cast." He rolls his eyes. The ridiculous notions that humans have about our magic usually make us laugh, but all I can work up, at this moment, is a sarcastic grunt of agreement.

Ean leans forward and rests his elbows on his knees, his arms hanging loosely between them. "As for why you didn't notice, I honestly don't know, Aden. I met with her a while ago to talk about the increased amount of Fallen I've been running into on assignment." His face twists into what I assume in annoyance. "She kept changing the fucking subject to—" He breaks off and shakes his head, as though to get back on track. "Anyway, she wasn't very forthcoming. There's something going on, Aden, and it pisses me off that Fate is leaving us hanging in the wind about it."

I've crossed one leg and have the ankle resting on top of the opposite leg, and as my agitation grows, it begins to bounce. I still the action, but then run my hands over my hair, needing to move something to expel the anxious energy I feel. "She said it wasn't solid enough to share right now. I get that, I really do. And if it doesn't have any effect on solving my current problem, I really don't give a shit right now."

Ean gives me a dark look. His mind is completely focused on the job, these days, and he is running himself into the ground trying to be a protector for all of the Fae. He only ever sees the many, not the one.

I shake my head and lean forward, mirroring his position and look him dead in the eye. "She is what matters *most* right now, Ean. One day, when you've met your fate, you'll understand. Until then, you have to trust me and help me get this guy."

Ean snorts in derision. "Yeah, I need to be tied to a soulmate like I need a vow of celibacy. I don't need that kind of distraction."

"Aden, I—Oh, hi, Ean." Shaylee walks into the room and gives a little wave when she sees him. She's wearing small, silky robe that doesn't cover nearly enough of her and when she moves toward the kitchen, the back lifts to where she is almost showing off her delectable ass; the one that belongs only to me.

I jump up out of my chair and hastily make my way to the kitchen. She's pulling down a mug and I snatch it from her hand, giving her a quick hard kiss when she frowns up at me.

"Let me get that for you, baby. You go and get dressed and I'll make you some toast too."

"Aden, please don't tell me that you're going to treat me like an invalid for the next nine months," She says, "Because if that's the case, you'll be getting to know that couch really well."

I slip two fingers into her belt loop and bring her close to me, then grasp her hips while I dip my head to whisper in her ear. "First of all, let's be clear about one thing. Under no circumstances will we ever spend a night in our home not in the same bed." I lean back a little, making sure she understands that I am completely serious. Her eyes widen just a little, but a corner of her mouth ticks up when she nods in agreement.

"Second," I say quietly, "I'm not trying to treat you like an invalid, I would simply like to you to put on a little more clothing before Ean gets a view of what is only mine to see." I run one of my hands around and down, bringing it up underneath her robe. When my hand meets nothing but smooth, naked skin, I groan, realizing that she didn't put on any panties. Her eyes go impossibly wide and she gasps, having obviously forgotten her state of undress. I swivel her around to face the hallway and give her ass a little pat to get her going.

She scampers down the hallway without protest and I heave a sigh of relief knowing that she'll be covered up in front of Ean. I'd hate to have to beat the shit out of him for leering at my girl.

After I'm seated again, with toast and coffee ready on the end table next to me, Ean and I dive into conversation about what our next steps should be. Shaylee comes back from the bedroom, walks over to grab her breakfast, and moves toward the other arm chair. Before she can get a step, I place my hand on her arm and pat my lap. She blushes and glances at Ean, who is smiling broadly at her, and the red flush deepens. I throw Ean a dirty look before returning my gaze to Shaylee, and tug lightly until she gives in and sits on my lap. I'm not going to deny it. I need her near me right now. I settle her comfortably and turn my attention back to the topic at hand, while she munches on her breakfast.

"I don't think moving to another apartment will make a difference." I feel a burst of anger and slam my hand down on the armrest of the chair. "How the fuck did this get past me?"

Ean blows out a breath and looks at me warily. "Don't get defensive, ok? Just let me get this thought out before you shut it down."

"Just spit it out, Ean," I snap. My patience is getting thin, but I don't have it in me to feel the least bit remorseful about it right now. Shaylee slips an arm around my shoulders and softly strokes her fingers through the hair on the back of my head. Immediately, I feel myself calming.

"When you've found your other half, it calms your soul. You're able to relax into a peaceful state, having comfort and safety in each other's arms." I'm taken aback by Ean's words, he sounds as though he's speaking from experience. But, he's never said anything about finding the one he's fated with. I file that talk away for another day and listen as he goes on.

"Is it possible that being together caused you to settle into a more vulnerable state? Less aware of what's around you because you're wrapped up in each other?"

I want to scoff and tell him that he's crazy, but there is some value to what he is saying. "I suppose that could contribute. But seriously, Ean, do you really think *that* alone would cause me to be entirely oblivious to that kind of evil being so close to me?"

He sighs in frustration, scrubbing his face with his hands, and flopping back against the couch. "No. I think it may be a part of it, but I also agree that you would never let your guard down so completely."

"Aden," Shaylee says, her voice speculative. "I'm still learning about all of this, so help me understand something." She is still pondering so I don't bother to encourage her; I just wait for her to form her thoughts.

"Fate readers. They help find the children who are half, right?" I nod in agreement, while Ean just cocks his head to the side and listens.

"How do they do that?"

"I'm not one hundred percent sure how it works. I don't think it is something that could really be described. But, I know it's something like seeing them in their mind. Fate is how the whole "fortune teller" garbage caught on as a trend in the human realm. She sees and feels the fate of others. But, she sees them individually, so she has to piece it all together," I explain what I know. Shaylee's face is scrunched and she's tapping her chin with one finger. Seemingly, contemplating what I'm telling her.

"It's too much for one person to handle, so the fate readers are there to help catch some of the things that she might miss from being overwhelmed. Everything is run by her eventually, and she always has the final word." I'm not sure what she is looking for in my explanation, so I finish and wait for her to share what's on her mind.

"You're always telling me about different legends, folklore, and such, which have been twisted and skewed by humans." She pauses, "We've—well, humans; I guess that doesn't include me anymore. Anyway, they often believe that they are guided to their fate through dreams." She looks at me expectantly, "Is there any truth behind that belief?"

It begins to dawn on me and I start to see what she's getting at. "Yes. Fate uses dreams to help push people in the right direction. Even with fate readers; she can't meet with everyone."

Her face lights up a little as her thoughts come together. "Didn't Fate say that she thought this Fallen was a fate reader?"

Ean's been quietly listening but, at this, he sits up straight, anger emanating from him. "This Fallen is a fucking fate reader?" Ean's voice is deadly and, if I had the time right now, I would worry about what this knowledge will do to his already obsessive need to work. But I wave him off, gesturing for him to back off and let me think.

"I think you might be on to something, baby." My mind is running now, forming conclusions and possible plans. "If he's a fate reader, he may have been affecting our dreams, causing us to dream about what we were feeling in reality so that, when we woke up, we were convinced that it hadn't been real." *Fuck.* This is going to really complicate things. But, Fate had warned us that things were about to get darker.

Ok. One thing at a time. First, we take care of the fucker threatening Shaylee.

"So, let's take him down."

Ean's head snaps to me and his eyes narrow, like he's trying to figure out if I'm serious. *Oh yeah. I'm going to send him straight to his master's arms.* "Are you sure you're up for that?" Ean's voice holds a slight note of disbelief and, as much as it annoys me, he has a point. I don't shy away from the fight, but neither do I go out looking for it the way that Ean does. Sometimes, I'm convinced that he has taken it upon himself to rid both realms of every single Fallen.

"Without a second thought," I vow, my voice brokering no argument.

I glance at Shaylee to see how she's handling all of this, and am slightly taken aback to see that she isn't fazed by this. In fact, she's tapping that finger again and looks lost in thought.

"What's going on in there, baby?" I tap my finger lightly against her temple. This seems to break her out of her reverie and she turns her whole body to face me more fully.

"I have an idea." The look in her eyes reminds me of Dr. Evil. Clearly, she's concocted some kind of devious plan. I'm not sure I like where this is headed, and I don't even know the plan yet.

"We need to draw him out. Bring him to us, so that we are in control of the situation and have covered every contingency plan."

I feel my eyes narrow in suspicion; she had better not be thinking what I think she is.

"So, let's give him what he wants. I can lure him to me and lead him to where we've designated."

I was already shaking my head halfway through the first sentence. "No way. Abso-fucking-lutely not."

"But—"

"No."

"But, I just—"

"No, Shaylee." I manage not to raise my voice to her, but the finality in my tone puts a mulish look on her face.

"Why the hell not, Aden?!" Shaylee on the other hand, is shouting. "You can't treat me like I'm breakable. Why have I been training this hard, if not to put my skills to use?"

She rants on for another minute or so about chauvinistic men and my asinine need to keep her in a bubble, and who knows what else. I stop listening to the words and simply wait for her to calm down before I play my trump card. Her tirade begins to run out of steam and when she notices my lack of reaction, she regards me with suspicion.

"Shaylee, you know me better than that. I may not like you being in danger, but I would never keep you from your fate to be a Mie'Lorvor. Especially considering the power-house we are as a team." I place my finger over her lips to keep her objections to herself for the moment. "I think you've forgotten about something. Or, should I say, someone?"

Comprehension comes over her and she slumps a little, her indignation deflated.

"Who?" I'd forgotten Ean was even there and his question startles me. *Cat's out of the bag now.*

"Shaylee's pregnant," I can't suppress the pride that rings in my tone and out of the corner of my eye, I see Shaylee roll her eyes and sigh.

Ean doesn't comment at first, his gaze bouncing back and forth between us, probably trying to decide if we think this is good or bad before he reacts. Apparently satisfied with the smiles on our faces, he stands and walks over to us, pulling Shaylee up into a hug. I reluctantly let her go and try not to be annoyed that another man has his arms around her.

"Congratulations, beautiful. I don't know why you chose this asshole over me, but I guess, if he makes you happy, I'll just have to let you go."

Shaylee giggles and kisses him on the cheek, while I grind my teeth together. "Thanks. We didn't plan it, but we are incredibly happy about it." Her words soothe my irritation a little, but I still stand up and pull her away from Ean, back against me.

Ean gives me a look of pity, "No offense to Shaylee, but I pray that I'll never be as pussy-whipped as you, brother."

Just thinking about that day puts an evil smile on my face.

It's only a matter of time. I just hope he gets his head out of his ass long enough to recognize her when he finally meets her.

He backs away from us as though he doesn't want to catch our fated germs. "I'm going to go meet up with Brannon and Kendrix and fill them in. We'll meet back here, down in the den at around nine. That work for you?" He doesn't wait for an answer before walking to the door and opening it. With one foot out the door, he pops his head back in to send Shaylee a smile and me a chin lift. Then, he's gone.

Shaylee turns around and wraps her arms around me, holding me tight and running her hand soothingly up and down my back. I let out a sigh as my mind settles under her administrations. She looks up at me and props her chin on my chest, "Are you sure there isn't a way for me to bait him without endangering the pregnancy?"

Just the thought has my blood pressure spiking with fear. "I'm not going to take that chance."

"You're right, I'm sorry. I'd never put our baby's life at risk."

I kiss the top of her head and hug her close. "Let's get some training in. I think we could both use the tension relief."

Her arms go slack and she leans back to frown at me in concern. "How much training can I do?"

"You can be as active as you were before you were pregnant until the third trimester, when you'll have to start pulling back. However, you'll need to stop all the ab work and watch out for things like twisting too hard when you're sparring. We'll probably lay off the fighting and focus more on your magic."

Shaylee's brow furrows and she glares at me. "How do you know this stuff? From all the other women you've gotten pregnant?"

I can't help the bark of laughter, causing her scowl to deepen. "I've been training for a long time, baby. You think I haven't come across a trainee who was pregnant in the last fifty years?"

Her expression morphs into a sheepish smile. "Oh," she sighs, which is quickly followed by a look of shock. "Fifty years?" her voice has become a little shrill and its then I remember, I've never mentioned how old I am.

"Baby, you had to know I'm at least twenty-one years older than you; I've been watching you your whole life."

"So, exactly how old are you?"

"Seventy-six."

"Damn, Aden, robbing the cradle much?" Her sarcasm is laced with amusement and the little bit of worry, I'd felt at the subject, flees.

Her smile is drawing my attention to those sweet, pink lips, begging to be kissed. Who am I to turn down a beggar? I put a hand at the back of her head and guide her mouth up to meet mine. My tongue licks across the seam of her lips and, when she opens, I slide it in slowly, savoring her taste. I suck on her plump, bottom lip and give it a little nip, before soothing the spot again with my tongue. Shaylee whimpers lightly and desire for her slams into me, running full speed ahead. Without breaking our connection, I sweep her up into my arms and head back to the bedroom. There will be time for training later.

Twenty-One

SHAYLEE

I CAN'T KEEP my eyes off the familiar steps of home. I love Rien, but I miss the home where I grew up, my mother, my aunt, and the city. I'm vibrating with energy, ready to bolt, the second that Aden finds a parking spot. When the car comes to a final stop, I leap out and dash up the steps to my house, fling open the door, and call out for my mother. We had no way of letting her know that we were coming, so I'm overjoyed to see her come rushing around the corner from the kitchen, shock and elation on her face.

I keep moving toward her until I can throw myself into her embrace, reveling in the comfort that can only be found in the arms of your mother. The scent of cinnamon fills my nose and I breathe deeply, letting the smell remind me of my childhood and my parents.

It feels as though I've been gone years instead of months, and I don't want to waste a second of it, especially considering the convincing it took to get Aden to bring me here.

. . .

IN THE DAYS that had followed our talk with Ean, the boys exhausted every resource they had, attempting to locate the man hunting me—without bait. It was incredibly frustrating to sit on the sidelines and watch them fight my battle without my help. But, Aden was right; you never know what could happen. And, I wasn't about to take a chance and risk my pregnancy.

I continued to train, but with Aden so focused on this Fallen, I was spending a lot of time alone and it made me more homesick than usual. I missed my mom. After training one day, I decided to broach the subject of a visit to my mom. I hedged my bets by softening him up in the shower (Ok, so I hardened him, and then softened him, if you want to be picky about it.)

Lying in bed that night, I told him I wanted to go visit my mom. He felt it was a terrible time to go, especially with the Fallen after me, and things looking darker in general. But, since he would be with me, I argued that I would be plenty safe. Finally, he played the "it's too dangerous because you're pregnant" card, but I was ready and waiting for it. I wanted to tell my mom that I'm pregnant. I couldn't imagine what it would be like for her, or for me, to not know until I was several months along or worse—had already had the baby.

We might as well go now, before things get any more dangerous. I'm pretty sure that he continued to argue with me so that I would try to coax an agreement out of him with my body. I was very convincing.

MY MOM, aunt, and uncle have come over for a welcome home dinner. It seems surreal, after all those years, to be here with Aden, now that we are together. I think Aden knows I'm nervous about it because he's had his arm slung over the back of my chair, gently rubbing my back since we finished eating.

After my mom serves some cake (I get two slices because, hey, I'm eating for two. Oh...this is going to be great!), Aden gives my hand a squeeze and I just blurt it out. *Way to have finesse, Shaylee.*

Mom blinks at me a few times and the lack of reaction starts to freak me out a little bit, but Aden's hand begins rubbing again and my muscles relax. Then my mom jumps up from the table, the quick movement surprising me and causing my heart to jump right out of my chest. The next thing I know, I'm being pulled from my chair and having the stuffing squeezed out of me. My mom is practically bouncing on her toes, and I laugh with relief and pleasure that she is so excited. My aunt trots around the table and convinces my mother to let me go so that she can congratulate me, as well. So, my mother moves on to Aden, but he's a great sport and lets her gush all over him about her grandchildren. *Children?*

Rhosyln steps back and her husband, Uncle Michael, gives me a warm hug, as well. "Congratulations, sweet pea." *I really do miss my family.*

He steps back and meanders over to Aden, patiently waiting for my mother and aunt to stop smothering him. After a minute, he clears his throat to draw their attention and whatever they see on his face, has them moving out of his way and coming back to me. They are tittering on about baby stuff, but I'm listening intently to the conversation being had between Uncle Michael and Aden.

My uncle is standing in front of him, legs braced apart, and arms crossed over his chest. He's closer to my height than Aden's and his shaggy, brown hair, and even shaggier mustache, take away from the imposing figure he is trying to be. To Aden's credit and, my everlasting love, he stands across from Uncle Michael, his arms clasped behind his back, subdued and respectful.

"You got my sweet, innocent niece pregnant?"

I can see that Aden wants to smile at my uncle's description of me, and I hope he doesn't look my way because I'm sure he wouldn't be able to keep it in if he saw the fire-engine-red (At least, that's what it feels like.) blush covering my face. Sweet and innocent are not words I would use to describe what Aden and I do in the bedroom, or bathroom, or couch, kitchen, car...basically wherever we are when we are about to combust.

"Yes, sir."

"I don't see a ring on her finger."

Aden leans forward and somewhat whispers his response, "Not yet, sir."

His words light that glow within me, the one that is reserved for him, warming me from the inside out.

Apparently, that was all my uncle needed to hear, because he gives a curt nod and shakes Aden's hand. "Well, congratulations, then."

At some point, my mom and aunt must have noticed my lack of attention because when I turn back to them, blinking away the moisture in my eyes, they are both smiling broadly at the exchange. Everybody's approval means so much to me and I have to fight the tears off even harder. *When the hell did I get so emotional?*

We visited and celebrated for another couple of hours until my aunt and uncle left for home. Aden excused himself to go unpack and get our room ready, but was waylaid by an argument with my mom over where he and I would be sleeping. It was the best entertainment I'd had all night. In the end though, Aden won out because my mom couldn't dispute with his logic of wanting to be near me, since I'm still in danger. He left us alone after that and I know he was simply giving me some time with my mom. *How do I shut off these damn water works?!*

I sat on the couch, snuggled up next to my mom and told

her about everything that has happened, since I left. However, I downplayed the danger over the fact that I'm being hunted by a Fallen. By the time we called it quits and decided to go to bed, it was pretty late and we hugged goodnight. I found myself surrounded by her cinnamon scent and some of my worries melted a little farther away.

I wander around the kitchen now, looking for a late night snack. I'm so freaking hungry *all* of the time. I'm seriously going to be a whale before I hit my last month. My head is buried in the refrigerator when Aden's hand snakes around my waist and yanks me back into him. Then the big caveman drags me back to the pantry, where he proceeds to give me dejavu. Only this time, it finishes in my bedroom the way I expected it to last time. Ok, not exactly like I expected—it's so much better.

THIS EATING FOR TWO THING?—IT'S really working for me. I sit back and groan, rubbing my stomach to alleviate some of the fullness stretching it. *You're eating for two, not five, Shamu.*

Hayleigh drops what's left of her Shack Burger in the basket and does the same thing. "Damn, Shaylee. You were right, best fucking burger and cheese fries, I've ever had." She blows out some air as if to make room. I nod smugly, with an amused chuckle. I've really missed her and Laila.

Hayleigh showed up unexpectedly at my mom's house a week ago. We've been here three weeks and Aden wanted to take the opportunity to check in with his charges while we are in the human realm. But one of them is in Montana and another in Spain. He can use his magic to get there, but it's a little tricky when you're not just crossing realms. I was feeling a little homesick for Rien (I know, I know. I was homesick for

New York, and now Rien.), so when Hayleigh arrived and told me she would be staying with me while Aden was gone, I was beyond excited (I definitely noticed that it wasn't Ean, Brannon, or Kendrix, and he was subjected to, no end of, teasing about it from me and Hayleigh until he left).

It's been a long time since I've been able to show off my home city and unfortunately, when you live here, you tend to overlook all the fun, touristy stuff. I only do it when someone is visiting. I'd dragged her all over the city, to a bunch of my favorite spots. But—let's face it—it's New York. You'd need a year of doing nothing, but being a tourist, to see everything here. It helped to keep me from missing Aden quite so much.

I was worried she wouldn't have much fun because she is so quiet and serious a lot of the time. However, she opens up and relaxes a little more around Laila and me, so I shouldn't have been surprised that she seemed to really enjoy herself. I haven't gotten the full story from Laila. I don't even know if Laila knows the full extent of it, but Hayleigh ostensibly comes from a pretty broken family and it's made her rather jaded. I've made it one of my goals to bring her out of her shell. So far, it's worked fairly well, when it's just us girls.

"It gets dark here so early; it's screwing up my internal clock," Hayleigh comments thoughtfully. "We should probably be getting back."

I manage not to sigh at the timetable that is always set for me; our nights out are always done when the sun goes down. Sadly, in New York, during the winter, that's around five thirty in the evening. I sneak a look at my watch and see that it's just after six. Oops, we stayed out a little late tonight. *Ugh, how pathetic it is to say that at six o'clock. Are we little old ladies now?* Either way, I respect Aden's wishes, so we clean up our garbage and head for home.

When we step outside the restaurant, I feel an unnatural rush of cool blow through my body. It's as cold as only a northeast winter can be, but this seems different somehow. Not as biting, but just a cool breeze, flowing through my body, oddly from the inside out. It makes me slightly wary, but I push it aside and walk hastily beside Hayleigh in the direction of home. We turn down 67th to walk from 1st Ave to 2nd Ave before moving up the block to 86th. It takes us a moment to notice that something is off. That's when we realize that all of the streetlamps are out. *The whole block?* However, there are no lights on in the apartments and town homes that line the block, either. I can feel the same unease rolling off of Hayleigh that is pulsing in my veins. I've been in the sun all day, hallelujah for that, so I bring the heat of my magic closer to the surface, making my skin slightly radiant, matching Hayleigh's countenance.

She grabs my arm and pulls me to a stop in front of a single family brownstone that is obviously under construction, then grabs my hand and heads for the door.

I tug her hand back and force her to stop before we are on the first step. "Um, Hayleigh. I'm not a huge fan of horror flicks, but even I know that when the heroine enters an abandoned building at night, she usually ends up in little pieces, buried in the basement," I say somberly.

She rolls her eyes, and moves up the steps, firmly towing me behind her. "First of all, those movies are ridiculous. Second, I doubt any of those women were Fae. And third, we are only passing through to get to the backyard," she chides.

Backyard? It's extremely rare to find a building with a yard in New York City, but there are a few in the area, such as the house where I grew up. I'm about to ask how the hell she knew there was a yard but then I realize that standing just the right of the stairs, we are in front of an alley between the two buildings. The light on the buildings behind give off just enough glow to see a gate on either side at the end. Both of these buildings have an outdoor space, but the home she wants to enter is clearly vacant.

I follow her without persuasion now, understanding where her mind has gone to. I knew we were probably being trailed by a Fallen, possibly more than one. I just didn't want to admit it. But, knowing that Hayleigh is headed for a back-yard, where we have direct access to all of the elements, I really can't ignore that instinct any more.

The house is quiet and dark, but we hurry through without incident, reaching the door to the back and wrenching it open, all the while she's muttering about how Aden is going to kill her for letting his pregnant girlfriend be in danger. Now is not the time, but one of these days I'm going to have a "come to Jesus" meeting with everybody about their irrational assumptions that I cannot take care of myself.

I'm close behind Hayleigh, so when she stops suddenly, I ram right into her, although she barely moves an inch.

"Hayleigh, what the hell?" I gasp. I'm met with silence until the sound of the slamming door shatters it. Shuffling to the left of her, I look for whatever it is that has her avid attention.

A man is casually leaning on a twisted and gnarled tree that has grown by the back fence. His face is somewhat hidden in the shadows, but there is something familiar about him.

He casually pushes off of the tree and comes forward. "I'm disappointed in you, Shaylee," he scolds. His voice is kicking up the instinct that I know him. "I could forgive you for being with another man, but now you're pregnant? This just won't do," his tone indicates disappointment. *Who the hell is this guy?*

He continues to close the gap between us, and at that moment, his face is highlighted by the glow of the moon.

Recognition hits me and I gasp, taking an automatic step backwards in revulsion.

Killian. Fucking Killian.

I'm completely stunned at his appearance. His features had begun to darken as he got older, his hair becoming dirty-blond and his green eyes becoming hazel. However, a lot of children start off with features that become the complete opposite as they grow. Generally, it happens in their child-hood, but I just assumed it wasn't that way for everyone. By the time he turned twenty-one, he had become a brunette with muddy-brown eyes and a more olive complexion.

Now, his hair is inky-black, cut slightly long so that it spilling over his collar and forehead. You would think that in the dark, I wouldn't be able to see his eyes all that well, but they slice right through the distance between us and their color is so dark that I can barely see where the pupils end and the irises begin.

The cold rush I'd felt earlier is intensified in his presence, and I can feel it trying to cloak my magic, putting out the fire by denying it oxygen. Fear is clutching me, trying to figure out how to protect myself and get out of this.

Hayleigh has been watching our exchange in silence, her only movement . . . a small shift towards the right side of the steps that lead down into the garden. She is leaning against the wall, her hands behind her back, observing the sight in front of her with very little reaction. Her lack of emotion and the completely neutral expression of her face are confusing me—I suddenly feel very alone.

He gives me what, I think, is supposed to be an indulgent look, but it just comes off as a sickly smile. A small, but strong, wind whips behind me and gives me a push, knocking me down the stairs. I stumble, but manage to stay upright without having to reach out and steady myself on the nearest solid thing, which right now is Killian. The cold evil, emanating from him, makes my skin crawl and I am immensely grateful that I'm able to avoid touching him.

"So, what shall I do about our current situation?" he asks rhetorically. I keep silent and wait cautiously to see where this is headed.

He takes a wide stance and crosses his arms over his chest. It reminds me of how Aden stands sometimes, but while it makes him look strong and opposing, Killian seems small, like a little boy, trying to appear as a man. The wind pushes lightly on my back again and Killian advances to meet me. I power through the cold seeping into my body and pull the earth up to form a small bump on the ground. I find the tiniest measure of relief when my plan works and he trips over the hump, giving me time to step aside and nudge him with the wind so that he isn't able to find his balance and crashes to the ground.

He grunts out a string of curse words and slams his fist in the grass. "You're going to piss me the fuck off, Shaylee." He climbs back to his feet and calmly brushes the dirt and grass from his shirt and pants. However, the façade is broken by the fury in his gaze. Killian's back is to the house now, so he doesn't notice the movement on the porch and I see Hayleigh has retreated back to the door of the house. Her betrayal knifes me, but I don't have time to focus on that, right now. At least she isn't joining his ranks.

"What exactly do you want, Killian? Why are we here?" my voice is heavy with irritation. I don't want to provoke him, but it helps to mask the fear. I'm ready to face these situations; it's what I've been training for. But, not while I'm pregnant. It was why Aden insisted someone always be with me here, so that I would never end up in this situation, facing a Fallen alone.

"You're not as special as they think you are, you know," he sneers. I don't know, so I raise an eyebrow, requesting an explanation. "Oh, you don't know, do you?" He laughs manically and now I'm convinced that someone is about to jump out of the darkness and yell, "Cut!" An idea filters into my mind and I almost dismiss it but... So far, this situation is right out of a bad movie. So, maybe I can do that thing where they play on the bad guy's ego to give me enough time to form a plan. I want to roll my eyes at the stupidity of this plan, but hey, what have I got to lose, right?

"Why don't you tell me, Killian?" I do my best to adopt a bored expression.

"Did you know they were looking for Aden?" Killian watches me for a reaction and he's got my full attention now, but I keep my features schooled not giving away my interest. "When they killed your father." The coolness of my demeanor cracks when he brings up my dad's murder. Killian catches the minute slip and his thin lips spread into a creepy smile. *How did I ever think this guy was attractive?* I know somewhere in my subconscious that I should be concocting plans, but I'm completely focused on his story.

"Yup." His lips smack together and I hold back a cringe. "I don't know all the ins and outs of the grapevine, but someone found out about the power that Aden and the one he is fated with, would develop. I guess their goal was to turn him or kill him, but the asshole always managed to shake them. Like I said, I don't know all the particulars; I don't really care." He shrugs, but there is something in his expression, a gleam of that ego, shining through.

"But, you know more than they think, don't you, Killian?" I state, pandering to his cocky attitude.

"Of course I do!" he snaps. "I'm the one who led them to you in the first place. They should be grateful to me, not shutting me out. After all, I'm the one who found you again, aren't I?" His smug expression and sinister smile return. "They found your aunt, since she doesn't have any children that would shield her magic. Watching her, led them to your dad, who they then cornered in the alley. His magic was pretty weak from being in the human realm for so long. Anyway, he was being obstinate and no help at all." He rolls his eyes. "Stupid man," he adds. My fists and jaw clench with anger, both aching from the strain, but by some miracle, I'm able to keep the emotion from bleeding into any other visible signs.

"Anyway, I guess he pissed off the wrong guy because one of them stabbed him." He shrugs nonchalantly, like the death of another person is just no big deal.

"Funny thing is; they had no idea that you were Aden's fate. I was raised by a dark Fae and dating you was just a happy coincidence." *For you.* "Then I turned twenty-one and we realized I was a fate reader. For a half Fae to be a fate reader is spectacularly rare." His conceit is brimming now and I realize that he's so sure I'm enthralled with him, that he isn't paying me much attention. I start searching the exits as discreetly as possible, while still making the requisite noncommittal sounds as though I'm listening intently.

He starts droning on about our "courtship" and how I'd callously thrown it away. That we could have had a perfect life together and he was always watching me, caring for me, and a whole bunch of other bullshit. *This guy lives in fantasy land, doesn't he?* If I can get him to back up to the railing to the porch, maybe I can keep him plastered against it with a stiff wind, long enough to run. I'm contemplating just how to get him to back up when my attention is caught by his next words.

"Well, you've gone and ruined the future I had planned for us. I decided not to suffocate you that night; give you another chance." He sighs melodramatically. "I thought maybe we could just cut out that thing growing inside you. But, no; you're beyond tainted now. I'm just going to have to kill you."

ADEN

HAYLEIGH SILENTLY SWINGS the door open and I slip through onto the porch. She'd managed to keep her phone hidden behind her back and send me a text to let me know what had happened. Thank God I'd already arrived back in New York and was at Shaylee's house, waiting for her. Hayleigh had succeeded in melting into the background so that, with his full attention on Shaylee, he would forget all about her. If he noticed her movement at the door, he would most likely assume that she was leaving to save herself.

Shaylee had wisely kept him talking, not too hard since its clear this guy is an arrogant bastard. She hadn't seen me yet, and I tried to keep it that way for as long as possible. I have no doubt that she would be able to keep from giving off any indication that she'd seen me. But, it will just be easier if she is as surprised as Killian.

I creep down the steps, just to his right, along the outer wall that juts out just beyond the porch. Hayleigh follows silently, but she moves to his right, ready to protect Shaylee when I've got Killian's attention.

I'm forming a strategy when I hear his threat to Shaylee. I

flip my shit and pull a sudden burst of wind from behind him, shoving him right into the wall next to me. I spin him around and slam him up against it, my hand pressing tightly into his neck.

"You know, Killian, when you started dating Shaylee, I know there was something off about you." I can feel him trying to blow me away but the thing is, in this little fairy tale, I'm the big fucking bad wolf and I'm going to crush his motherfucking house. I press his throat even harder and he begins to sputter, his skin turning the color of eggplant.

"Then you went and started treating her like shit and I had to have a little talk with you. That's when I knew you were Fae. But, being the sniveling little rat that you are, I didn't see you as being any further of a threat to her." I've kept my tone light as though we were just having a conversation, but now I drop it down and it becomes menacing when I bring our faces only inches apart. "I won't make that mistake again."

"Well, well, well. What do we have here?" A new voice slithers into the darkness, bringing a surge of cool power into the air. He's a Fallen but I know better than to take my attention off of Killian, so I trust Hayleigh to take care of the newcomer. I take note however, that Killian's eyes are now full of terror and his attempts to remove me have ceased.

Who the fuck are you and what do *you* want?" Shaylee spits. I can't help but smile at how feisty she is.

"No need to be crass, my dear. I'm Aodhagan."

I don't like having my back to this guy, so I cause the roots from the tree, a few feet away, to grow in our direction. Once they reach the wall, they begin to climb up, twisting and winding all around Killian, keeping him immobile and fixed to the wall. Being in this close of proximity to Shaylee boosts my abilities; Killian won't be able to do much from his little perch. I might have made the roots a little tight; it's possible he is struggling to breathe right now. I mentally shrug and turn to face the Fallen, standing much too close to Shaylee.

He reminds me of someone, with his lengthy, straight, black hair, falling down well below his shoulders, with a deep widow's peak on his forehead. His face is long, with a patrician nose, narrow, dark eyes, and a small, thin-lipped mouth. Suddenly, Shaylee's Harry Potter references don't seem so far off.

I reach out my hand and motion her over to me. "Baby, come over here."

She makes a wide berth around Aodhagan and walks to my side. Hayleigh is hanging back again, blending, forgotten until she's needed. "You haven't answered the whole question. What do you want?" I bite out.

"Well, I was looking for Killian. It seems you found him first." He examines Killian and raises his eyebrows slightly. "It looks as though you're not very fond of each other."

Shaylee snorts in contempt. "Actually, he found me and well, yeah. You could say I'm not *fond* of him."

Aodhagan's inspection shifts to Shaylee, curiosity sparking in his eyes. "I have introduced myself, would you be so kind as to return the favor?"

His speech pattern is niggling at me, trying to ferret out a memory. He is obviously much older and hasn't lost the refined speech and posture of his day. Curious, I decide to give an inch. "I'm Aden Foster." There is a flash of recognition in his eyes; visible, despite the bland expression on his face.

"Hmmm. Aden Foster. It's nice to finally make your acquaintance. I do believe the others of my council have been searching for you." This information brings the memory closer to the surface, but I still can't quite grasp it. He's a member of the Fallen council and yet he has come personally searching for Killian?

"What is it you want, Aodhagan?" I don't even try to hide my impatience.

He studies us for a moment. "You are Shaylee? You're fated with Aden?" His voice holds mild curiosity, but there is something dark hidden behind it. There seems no reason to hide it, so I answer, "She is."

The darkness emerges as his gaze whips back to Killian, and for a moment he is unable to hide his disapproval and rage. "Killian was instructed to bring the whereabouts of certain Fae directly to us," he quickly morphs his countenance back to one of only mild interest. His eyes shift just the tiniest bit, but enough to know that Killian was not supposed to approach Shaylee on his own.

"He has chosen to go against the council one too many times and I was tasked with bringing him in to be...chastised." His hesitation explains some of the terror I'd seen from Killian. I don't think it's a stretch to believe their version of chastisement involves a great deal of pain. "If you would remand him to my custody now, we'll be on our way."

I have no sympathy for what Killian would endure under the thumb of the Fallen council. However, he is a fate reader so they won't kill him and that's not acceptable to me. Not only did this son of a bitch try to kill Shaylee, but she'll never be safe from him if we don't end him.

The Fae are not ones to seek violence, we are not malicious, but our role as protectors becomes even fiercer when it is our family. I would not choose to kill someone if there were any other way, but I know, deep down, that Shaylee will always be in danger.

"I'm afraid I can't let you have him." Again, I see the slightest crack in his pleasant demeanor and his angry disapproval becomes faintly visible before it vanishes.

His probing gaze is steady on Shaylee and me, seeming to contemplate his options. He even turns to glance at Hayleigh, having not forgotten her as we'd thought. She steps forward, not in a threatening way, but simply in a statement that she is there to aid the situation. There is a miniscule change in him like he's decided that going against us is a lost cause. "Very well, I would be a fool to pit myself alone against three other Fae, and even more of a fool, considering the power between you two." He dips his head in farewell and glides toward the back gate, tapping the tree as he steps past it, eliciting a gasp from Killian. Just as he steps one foot through the exit, he pauses. "Tell your friend, Ean, I look forward to making his acquaintance," he calls without even turning around. Then, he is gone.

His cryptic words have the three of us wearing matching frowns. There is something about that man...

I shake off the encounter and move on to my next task, wanting to get Shaylee home and safe. I pivot on my heel and step back in front of Killian, but before I finish him, I decide to take the advantage he provides us. I loosen the hold of the roots and wait, while he gasps for air and some of the bluish tint on his skin begins to recede.

"Killian, I'm going to ask you once and you're going to give me an honest answer, because, if you don't, I'm going to let this tree slowly squeeze the life out of you. Suffocation seems fitting for you, doesn't it? But, if you give me what I want, I'll make it quick. Mostly." The last word is mumbled under my breath but Shaylee must have heard it because she frowns darkly at me. I can see the indecision in her eyes, that she doesn't want me to kill him, but she has come to the same conclusion that I have. She takes one of my hands with both of hers and the warmth that we share in each other's presence spreads. She's seeking comfort in our connection and to calm her discordant thoughts. She nods, and even though I know I'm doing the right thing, being of one mind on this makes it easier to swallow.

Killian nods, his face resigned.

"Were you the only one hunting Shaylee? Or do we have to worry about the Fallen council coming after her?"

His voice is rough and raw when he answers, "No, they know the only value in either of you is if they have you together and are able to turn you both. They don't believe you are a true threat to their plans and so their focus is elsewhere. However, should the opportunity arise to separate you two forever, they might take it." He stops and coughs a few times, the speech, seemingly, having exhausted his throat muscles. "I was only supposed to mention your location, if I came across you," he gives me a little more, his voice wheezing. He coughs again. "They don't," cough, "want to make the effort."

I don't feel dishonesty radiating from him and from the corner of my eye, I see Shaylee's quick nod, signifying that she agrees. I hesitate longer than I would have thought. I don't relish the thought of destroying another of God's creatures. But, he has made that choice and he'll have to die for it.

It's difficult to do, but with Shaylee near, I'm able to manipulate the water and air above to shift charged clouds together at just the right spot and a bolt of lightning strikes Killian, killing him instantly.

I drop my head in fatigue. Without the sun, that kind of power drains you. To be honest, my head is also hung in sorrow. I don't regret my actions, but it still hurts my soul to take another life. Shaylee steps to face me and wraps her arms around to hold me tight. Her warmth seeps into my bones where I feel a chill that has nothing to do with the outside temperature. Hayleigh comes to stand beside us and she places a hand on my arms and gives a soft squeeze.

She is ready to head home and I give her a nod of acknowledgement and a smile of thanks. She returns the gestures, squeezes Shaylee's shoulder before stepping back and with a light radiance, she is gone.

Shaylee and I burn the remnants of the tree and body, and then bury them in the ground. After we are finished, we make our way to her mother's house. The lights are burning bright and I'm sure Violet is worried sick because Shaylee is always home by this time of night. We walk inside, prepared for her tears and questions and once she's settled down, we explain the night's events. Shaylee has fallen asleep on the couch, her head resting on my chest, her feet curled up under her. I bid her mother goodnight and carry her down to our room. She wakes as I begin to undress her and takes over the task. Naked, we fall into bed, our bodies each seeking the other, and we finally succumb to sleep.

Two weeks later

Excitement is coursing through me as I pace the living room floor waiting for Shaylee to come upstairs. Her mother, aunt, and uncle are all seated in the room, waiting as well. I want to walk over to the stairs and yell for her to get her sexy ass up here immediately, but I manage to restrain myself.

Finally.

Her soft footsteps are coming down the hall and then I see her beautiful face. It lights up when she sees me. Her gorgeous smile, making me shift as I feel more than my heart tightening at the sight of her. *I can't fucking believe she's mine.*

Time to make sure the rest of the world knows it too. I go to her side and grasp her hand, bringing it to my lips for just a moment. Then I guide her to one of the elegant chairs in front of the fireplace. She knew we were all having dinner together tonight, as we are leaving to go home tomorrow. So, there is no surprise in seeing her family here. However, she gives me an odd look when I seat her instead of all of us moving to the dining room for dinner.

I lower myself onto one knee (even the Fae follow some human traditions) and watch her eyes widen, staring at my hand, which now holds a small, blue box. The box is vintage and the exact color of her eyes, so I thought it a fitting home for it until it's placed on her finger.

"Baby," I start. She slowly raises her eyes to meet mine, tears brimming in her eyes, making the blue look so much more like the ocean. "We both know I'm better at demanding than asking, and I don't think I could get through a flowery speech without gagging." There are titters of laughter from everyone, but I barely hear it, my only care for the woman who is destined to be mine for eternity. "I love you, for eternity."

"Forever," her soft whisper adds another string to the bands that bind us together.

"Will you marry me?" I'm actually pretty proud of myself for asking, instead of just dragging her to a justice of the peace.

She leans forward and lays her warm lips over mine, and I wish away all the other people here so that I could sink myself into her and get lost there.

She sits back and swipes the box from my hand. "Hey!" I protest.

She ignores me and whips open the box to find a platinum ring with a round diamond on the top. The band is a series of twists, creating linked infinity signs and, in each little opening, it alternates being set with a sapphire or emerald.

She sucks in a breath at it, pulls it out, and examines it, then gives me a sly smile. "Ok. This is worth marrying you," she says with a shrug, but she isn't able to keep the act up and she bursts into laughter before planting a solid kiss on my lips. "Hell yes, I'll marry you!"

I pull her in for another deep kiss, but we're interrupted by well wishes from the family. Shaylee's mother decided she doesn't want to return with us to Rien, she's comfortable with her life and wants to eventually be with her husband. Shaylee was understandably disappointed, but she also understood and we promised to be here as often as possible. It was because of this that I chose to propose here, without my family. However, the wedding will be interesting, when my family descends on New York for a week. God help us all.

Epilogue

ADEN

"ADEN! You are never touching me again!

Shaylee's voice rings down the hospital walls where I'm standing outside our room on the phone. Apparently, she was loud enough that Ean could hear her because he starts laughing uncontrollably.

"Ean, just get your ass down here. And do you know where the fuck Laila is? I can't get ahold of her to tell her Shaylee is in labor."

Ean's laughter stops abruptly and he sucks in a breath. "Why would you think I'd know where Laila is?"

"I don't know, Ean. I just can't find her. You both live there, what the fuck ever! Just tell her if you see her." I hang up before I hear Ean's response and run back into the room where my wife is holding out her hand to me and when I reach her side, she gives me a sweet kiss.

Shaylee's sudden mood swings are giving me whiplash, she's a sweaty mess, and she's the most beautiful thing I've ever seen in my life. She grips my hand tightly as another contraction hits, then again, less than a minute later. "Where the hell is the doctor?" I rear my head back slightly at her yell, to avoid a busted eardrum. Lucky for me and everyone else in the world, the nurse arrives to take us to surgery.

～

SHAYLEE

I hear a light knock on my hospital room door and tear my eyes away from my husband, rocking our daughters in his arms. That's right—daughters. As in plural. As in two for the price of one. I love them so much already, but the day we found out I was having twins was the day I sent Aden to the store for a case of condoms. Just so we're prepared after the babies are born.

Laila pops her head in and smiles brightly, "Hey! Can I meet my sweet nieces?"

I wave her in, grimacing at the pain in my stomach from the C-section. When Ean follows her through the door, I'm surprised to see them together; Laila's been icing him out for months. They both look a little rumpled and I narrow my eyes as I study them. I'm exhausted and about ready to drop, but I'm not stupid. They are both glowing—just faintly—sporting what can only be described as "bed head", and completely avoiding each other's gaze.

Holy shit! They were in fucking when Aden called Ean!

Ean notices my perusal of him and gives me a smile before his eyes slide away and he ignores me. Well, that's an interesting development...

～

ADEN

Kendrix kicks my ass for the third round in a row and I decide to give up. He helps me up off the ground with his eyebrows raised into his hairline. "What's up with you, man? Are the twins keeping you up?"

Lost in thought, *again*, I almost miss the question. "What? Oh, no the twins are actually sleeping most of the night and they are pretty good at going right back to sleep after Shaylee feeds them."

An image of Shaylee feeding the twins invades my mind, but it's not the act that has my attention. The image has now shifted to Shaylee laid out on the bed for me, those plump naked tits just begging to be licked and bit—

"Aden!" My head jerks up. "What the fuck is going on with you, man?"

Don't use that word... I shift; my pants uncomfortably tight.

I try to keep my mind out of the gutter, but it's no use. "I've got to go." I start stripping off my gear and heading toward my bag.

"What?" Kendrix looks at me, bewildered.

I sigh. *Oh screw it.* "Shaylee told me last night that she feels ready." He still looks confused. "I get to fuck my wife tonight, dude."

Kendrix looks completely taken aback for a minute. Then he laughs and shakes his head. "Well, at least some of us are getting laid."

"Damn straight."

I get everything together and sprint out of the gym up to my apartment and burst through the front door. Shaylee is washing bottles at the sink and jumps half a foot in surprise.

"Are the girls napping?" I ask, rounding the bar to where she's standing.

"Well, hello to you, too."

"Hello. Are the girls napping, baby?"

"Yes. Why are you—" I don't wait for her to finish, I throw her over my shoulder, grab the monitor, and go directly to our bathroom.

"Strip." I start the shower and begin pulling my clothes off at record speed. I glance up and see Shaylee still standing there fully clothed with an indignant expression. I start pulling her clothes off for her.

"Aden! Wait. What is going—would you stop?"

"Baby," I manage to speak as I bare every inch of her stunning body. "I can't wait anymore. I need to fuck you." Again, I don't wait for her. She's finally naked, so I grab her and crush my mouth down on hers. I've been at half-mast all damn day. *You've been as half-mast since the day she gave birth.* The moment I reached the apartment and saw her, my hard on was up in record time. Now, feeling her naked body plastered to mine, I get impossibly harder. I don't know how the fuck it's possible, but I do.

She kisses me back with equal fervor, our tongues dancing and exploring every crevice. I nip her bottom lip lightly, then kiss and lick my way down to her throat and above those fucking awesome tits. "Fuck, I've missed you too, Aden." Her words light a fire that blazes through every inch of me as I grasp her ass and roughly lift her up, so her legs wrap tightly high around my waist. *That's more like it.* Her tits are at the perfect height and I pull a nipple into my mouth, licking, sucking, biting. They are still overly sensitive and she is almost coming apart at the seams.

I lower her body just enough to rest her wet—oh, so fucking wet—pussy up against my cock. I suck her nipple into my mouth and rock against her at the same time. Holy fucking shit. Shaylee bites my shoulder to muffle her scream as an orgasm tears through her. It takes everything thing I have not to come at that moment.

I stride into the shower, stepping under the hot spray and holding her as she continues to shudder lightly. Our mouths are sealed together, my tongue sweeping around her mouth to get every bit of her taste. I tug on her hair to give me better access and slant my mouth over hers, changing the angle and upping the intensity.

I want to give her everything, to make this about her, but I don't seem to have any control over my body right now. I move to press her back against the wall, lift her just slightly and line my cock up with her pussy; I can feel the heat pulsing from it, and I can't hold back any longer. I slam inside, burying myself as deep as I can go, then pull back a little and repeat it, each time going a little further until I'm bottoming out on each thrust.

Shaylee is trying desperately to keep her voice down but I'm lost to all reality and I want to hear her screaming my name. "You're so fucking tight, baby. I could fuck you for hours and never get deep enough." Her whimpers are escalating to moans and it just spurs me on.

"Am I going hard enough for you? Is my cock pounding your pussy the way you like it?" I'm about to lose it, so I still for just a moment trying to gain control, until Shaylee sinks her teeth into my bottom lip and pulls, before letting it pop out of her mouth.

"Fuck me, Aden. I want it all. I want you to stretch me with your dick and fuck me so hard I won't be able to move one damn muscle tomorrow without knowing you've been inside me."

There's nothing left to say. I fuse our mouths together and set a fast but rhythmic pace, pounding into her hard and wild. When she starts chanting my name, I let her mouth loose and latch onto a nipple.

"Aden! Yes!"

I'm so close I can't do anything but rest my forehead between her tits and drive my hips just a little bit faster. "Oh fuck!"

Now it's me chanting. "Fuck! Shaylee, oh fuck! Yes, baby!"

I know I'm going to come, so I slide a wet hand down between us and press my thumb down firmly on her clit. She screams my name and it breaks down my last vestiges of control, shooting off inside her, coating her with me, branding her over and over as mine.

My body is shaking from the force of my orgasm, so I drop her legs to the ground, but hold her tight against me and lick her mouth, dipping my tongue in, sucking on her lips, and letting the shockwaves settle. After an eternity of kissing her, I step back just an inch and pull out.

After all that, I'm still hard as a fucking baseball bat. Shaylee lazily looks down at my swollen cock and gives me a coy smile. "That looks like it hurts." I give her a jerky nod, unable to respond because her hand is wrapped around me.

She drops to her knees and takes excellent care of my problem. Her mouth is almost as hot and wet as her pussy and after she swallows a few times, I come in her mouth with a shout and she takes every last drop. I married the perfect fucking woman.

Sated, we take our time washing in the shower and then step out to dress, stealing kisses and touches the whole time. I grab the monitor (My kids are the best. Stayed asleep so Daddy could have some Mommy time), and pad out to the kitchen to make dinner. Shaylee lays down for a short nap before Alysia and Felicitae wake her up, ready to eat. We spend the evening relaxing, playing with our girls, and snuggling on the couch with a movie. When they are down for the night, I take Shaylee back to bed and do what I couldn't earlier; I take my time, learn every inch of her delectable body all over again, and make love to her. Right as I'm about to slip in to her, she stops me. "Damn it, Aden. Grab a condom." I frown at her, I hate those things.

"Baby, I need to feel you," I pout.

She looks uncertain but I slide in just the littlest bit, reminding her what it feels like bare. She moans and I slide just a little more, then she nods. *Hell yes.*

"But, you have to pull out." *Fuck.*

When all is screamed and done, I waited too long.

SHAYLEE

No. no. no. I stare at the little stick and watch the two lines turn pink.

"Aden! I'm going to fucking kill you!"

He pops his head into the bathroom and sees what I'm holding. He puffs up with pride and I somehow refrain from damaging the body part that did this to me.

He winks. "Oops."

Ean & Laila's story is available now!

Books by Author Elle Christensen

The Fae Guard Series

Protecting Shaylee (Book 1) – Available Now!

Loving Ean (Book 2) – Available Now!

Chasing Hayleigh (Book 3) – Available Now!

A Very Faerie Christmas (Book 4) – Available Now!

Saving Kendrix (Book 5) – Available Now!

Forever Fate: (Book 6) – Available Now!

The Fae Legacy (A Fae Guard Spin-off)

Finding Ayva (Book 1) – Coming 2022

Silver Lake Shifters

An Unexpected Claim: Nathan & Peyton (Book 1) – Available Now!

An Uncertain Claim: Nathan & Peyton (Book 2) – Available Now!

An Unending Claim: Nathan & Peyton (Book 3) - Available Now!

A Promised Claim: Asher & Savannah (Book 4) - TBD

A Forbidden Claim (Book 4) – TBD

A Vengeful Claim (Book 5) – TBD

The Slayer Witch Trilogy

The Slayer Witch (Book 1) - Summer 2022

The Wolf, the Witch, and the Amulet (Book 2) – Summer 2022

Stone Butterfly Rockstars

Another Postcard (Book 1) – Available Now!

Rewrite the Stars (Book 2) – Coming 2022

Daylight (Book 3) – TBD

Just Give Me a Reason (book 4) – TBD

All of Me (Book 5) – TBD

Miami Flings

Spring Fling – Available Now!

All I Want (Miami Flings & Yeah, Baby Crossover) – Available Now!

Untitled – TBD

Ranchers Only Series

Ranchers Only – Available Now!

The Ranchers Rose – Available Now!

Ride a Rancher – Available Now!

When You Love a Rancher – Available Now!

Untitled – TBD

Happily Ever Alpha

Until Rayne – Available Now!

Until the Lighting Strikes – Available Now!

Until the Thunder Rolls – Coming 2022

Standalone Books

Love in Fantasy – Available Now!

Say Yes (A military Romance) – Available Now!

Bunny Vibes – Available Now!

Fairytale Wishes (Mermaid Kisses Collaboration) - Available Now!

Books Co-authored with Lexi C. Foss

Crossed Fates (Kingdom of Wolves) – Available Now!

First Kiss of Revenge (Vampire Dynasty Trilogy Book 1) - 2022

First Bite of Pleasure (Vampire Dynasty Trilogy Book 2) – TBD

First Taste of Blood (Vampire Dynasty Trilogy Book 3) – TBD

Books Co-authored with K. Webster

Erased Webster (Standalone Novel) – Available Now!

Give Me Yesterday (Standalone Novel) – Available Now!

If you enjoy quick and dirty and SAFE, check out Elle Christensen and Rochelle Paige's co-written books under the pen name Fiona Davenport!

Website

Acknowledgments

Thank you seems like such small words for the amount of gratitude I have for those who support and love me. But, I'll say it anyway and hope that you know it doesn't scratch the surface.

To my eternal one and only, thank you for putting up with me, for never making me feel guilty when I have to take time away from you to write, for loving my ideas and believing in their success. You never doubt me, and only ever encourage me to believe in myself. Thank you for always being willing to do "research" for my books, they wouldn't be steamy or romantic without you. Your support in what it takes, through time and money, to be a new author is priceless and I can't imagine what I would do without you. I love you and I will love you for forever.

To K. Webster, thank you for always being such an amazing mentor. My books would never become finished works without you. You've taught me so much, always take the time to chat, brainstorm, and help me without ever making me feel as though I'm bugging you! You are truly brilliant and I'm so grateful to have you as a friend. I would hate to see what my life would be if you took the other half of our shared brain and left! Besides, who else would I ask all of my penis questions?!

To my editor, Jacquelyn. What would I do without you? Our twisted senses of humor are a special kind of crazy, so I know you'll appreciate my jokes! You've always been a friend and a support, so it made it all the sweeter to have you as an editor. I appreciate the snort laughing I do through all of your notes. Thank you be for pushing me to reach my potential. You've Got It (The Right Stuff).

A big thanks to Stacey Blake from Champaign Formatting. You always make my pages so beautiful!! You're such a gem and I'm so happy I was sent in your direction.

To Danielle, what can I say? I would not have survived writing this book without you being a sounding board. Our inappropriate jokes and stories made me laugh on the crappiest of days. It was such a pleasure to brainstorm with you on my novel as well as yours. Our unique experiences with love and sex made for some interesting conversations, and some weirded out looks from my husband! Thank you for supporting me, for letting me give back to you what other authors have given to me, and for becoming a cherished friend. I look forward to the day we finally meet in person, although we might need to have warning labels attached to us!

To all of the authors who have inspired me, taught me, and supported me. I am honored to call you friends and colleagues. Rochelle Paige (and son), K. Webster, Aurora Rose Reynolds, Ella Fox, Anne Jolin, Zoe Norman, Jacquelyn Ayres, Danielle Ione, Autumn Grey, Leighton Riley, and so many others, I wish I could name you all! To the C.O.P.A girls, having a safe and positive environment to connect and support each other means the world to me. I still get a little intimidated by the amount of awesome in this group, thank you for letting me be a part of it.

To Heather and Melanie, I don't how the hell I would survive the craziness that is my life without you. It's hard to keep up a blog once you make the transition to author, so I am immensely grateful that, because of you both, I haven't had to quit blogging. Your beta feedback, your support, enthusiasm, and friendship mean everything to me. Don't ever leave me or I'll be flapping in the wind with nothing to hold on to!

To my favorite friend, my oldest friend, my best friend. There is no filter between us, I am just me. You are a safe place, a place where I can lay all of my troubles, share my joys, and be all kinds of little girl silly with. When you tell me that you are proud of me, there are no words for how that makes me feel. I am forever grateful that our friendship has only become stronger through the years. You and hubs know ME. All of me. And without you, I would be a little less steady and a whole lot less confident in who I am. Thank you for always being there for me. I will always be here for you. I love you like the 80's love Stevie Nicks.

To my Cupcakes, you are all so sweet (pun intended because I'm a nerd that way). Thank you for laughing at my jokes, being excited about my books, and sharing it with others. You brighten my day and, so often, make me feel like a rock star! I'll keep baking, you keep licking the frosting (wow, that sounds way dirtier than I meant it).

To all of the amazing bloggers out there who make an author's dreams become reality. It would be impossible to be a successful author without you. A special thanks to Escape N' Books for all that you do to support and pimp me and my books.

To Bare Naked Words, IndieSage PR, and Tasty Book Tours, the world knows about Protecting Shaylee because you work so hard. You rock my socks off!

And to all of the book lovers, writing would just be a hobby if we didn't have you to share our passion with. Thank you for taking chances on new authors and supporting the ones you love.

I'm sure I've forgotten people, but that doesn't mean I don't recognize all that you do for me. Know that you all shape me into the writer that I am. Thank you for everything.

To the one who blessed me with my talent, thank you for giving me something that filled the gaping hole, left in my soul, when I stepped away from my last career. For giving me a talent that brings me such joy.

About the Author

About Elle Christensen

I'm a lover of all things books, a hopeless romantic, and have always had a passion for writing. Between being a sappy romantic, my love of an HEA, my crazy imagination, and ok, let's be real, my dirty mind, I fell easily into writing romance.

I'm a huge baseball fan and yet, a complete girly, girl. I'm an obsessive reader and have a slight (hahaha! Slight? Yeah, right) addiction to signed books.

I'm married to my very own book boyfriend, an alpha male with a sexy, sweet side. He is the best inspiration, my biggest supporter, and the love of my life. He is also incredibly patient and understanding about the fact that he has to fight the voices in my head for my attention.

I hope you enjoy reading my books as much as I enjoyed writing them!

Stalk Me
Website
Newsletter Verve Romance

Printed in Great Britain
by Amazon

80138078R00142